350

Praise for *The Wild Sight*

"Smashing romantic suspense… McGary never shortchanges the sizzling romance between Rylie and Donovan as she weaves in ancient legend and recent murders, building to a dramatic, memorable conclusion."

—*Publishers Weekly*

"Northern Ireland's violent past combined with supernatural elements add an intriguing twist to this modern love story."

—*Booklist*

"Enchanting and always engrossing… Thrillingly innovative with an unforgettable storyline, and the emotion will keep you devouring every word."

—Single Titles

"Intriguing… the romance is bursting with passion."

—Darque Reviews

"A masterful blend of mystery, magic, and romance… had me up 'til all hours of the night because I literally could not put it down."

—Long and Short of It Reviews

"A highly atmospheric and intriguing mystery… McGary keeps the sexual tension at a sizzling high."

—BookLoons

"A fascinating  romantic suspense. The ce Junkies

Praise for *The Treasures of Venice*

"Lost jewels hidden hundreds of years ago, a sexy Irish hero and an exotic locale make for a wonderful escape. Don't miss this charming story."

—Brenda Novak, *New York Times* bestselling author of *The Perfect Liar*

"A brilliant novel that looks to the past, entwines it in the present and makes you wonder at every twist and turn if the hero and heroine will get out alive. Snap this one up, it's a keeper!"

—Jeanne Adams, bestselling author of *Dark and Deadly*

"McGary's satisfying, fast-paced romance is filled with passion and deception that resonate through the centuries."

—*Booklist*

"Samantha and Kiernan's romance is the stuff dreams are made of, and their adventures... will keep you on the edge of your seat."

—*Romantic Times* Book Review, 4 Stars

"A captivating story of romance, suspense, and historical legend... painted against a beautiful backdrop of romantic Venice. I was entranced from page one."

—Armchair Interviews

"Enthralling romantic suspense... Loucinda McGary weaves extraordinary stories with her incomparable writing abilities."

—Single Titles

THE WILD IRISH SEA

A windswept tale of love and magic

LOUCINDA McGARY

sourcebooks
casablanca

Published by Sourcebooks Casablanca, an imprint of Sourcebooks,
Inc.
P.O. Box 4410, Naperville, Illinois 60567-4410
(630) 961-3900
FAX: (630) 961-2168
www.sourcebooks.com

Printed and bound in Canada
WC 10 9 8 7 6 5 4 3 2 1

I dedicate this book with much love and many smiles to my rosebuds: Shawna, Jennie, Laura, and Emily.

Prologue

THE LOURING SKY OPENED AND DRENCHED PARKER O'Neill before he could turn his high-prowed rowboat for shore. His afternoon adventure of observing marine wildlife abruptly halted, he squinted through the growing darkness at the rocky bluffs of Malin Head. Surprised at how far distant they appeared, he cursed himself for not throwing in the extra bucks for an outboard motor, while he wrestled to keep a grip on the wooden oars with his wet hands.

Rain ran from the backs of his clenched fists down his wrists, inside the sleeves of his mackintosh raincoat, and soaked the cuffs of his shirt. A sudden gust of wind threw rain into his face, plastering the front of his hair to his forehead and sending rivulets down the sides of his neck, once again inside the coat.

The phrase from the guidebook that had convinced him to buy the heavy coat leaped back to mind. *Summer squalls can hit unexpectedly on the Donegal coast.*

No shit, Sherlock!

Well, he was the genius who had wanted to visit the auld sod and get back to his roots. Only this was a bit closer than he really wanted to be. *Thank you very much.*

He should have stuck with a pint of Guinness in the local pub and a lesson on playing the bodhran from an Irish lass who thought his Yankee accent cute. Instead, here he was stuck in a rowboat a half mile from land getting soaked in a deluge.

Thinking of a warm pub, a girl, and a brewski, Parker rowed harder. But the same wind blowing rain inside his jacket had also whipped the gently rocking sea into a choppy cauldron that thwarted his forward progress to a standstill. The craggy heights of Malin Head taunted him from the same distance while more raindrops stung his face.

The next gust of wind carried the unmistakable sound of human voices on it. Parker turned his head to track the noise. In the growing gloom, he could make out another vessel, quite a bit larger than his rented curragh. By squinting, he saw it was a sailboat, though its sails were furled. The mast stabbed erratically at the rain as the boat bobbed like an oversized cork on the rough waves.

The stern faced him now, and he could see two figures grappling with each other. One shouted.

Parker started to answer, but before he could utter a sound, a third figure appeared, arms extended. The unmistakable crack of a pistol tore across the waves. Parker flinched and lost his grip on the oars. Momentarily transfixed in horror, he watched one man slump forward. The other caught him and heaved him over the back of the boat. A length of heavy chain trailed after.

A murder!

Holy shit! He'd just witnessed a murder!

A megadose of adrenaline rocketed through him, and Parker grabbed the oars and rowed for all he was worth. Unfortunately the pair in the sailboat must have heard him. Another shout echoed through the downpour, followed swiftly by another pistol report.

Parker put his head down and kept rowing, puffing his cheeks with his rapid breaths.

Two more shots rang out. The second splintered the wood in front of the right oarlock.

Shit! Shit! Shit! Shit! Shit! he chanted, all the while rowing like a maniac.

The next bullet ripped through the wood close to his ankle. Seawater spewed into the opening. Instinctively, he lurched forward and another bullet tore through the side of his mackintosh, grazing a fiery trail across the flesh over his ribs.

He fell from the bench seat into the rising water in the bottom of the boat. The little vessel dipped drunkenly with the sudden shift in weight while yet another bullet lacerated the hull.

More water gushed in.

Oh God, I am seriously screwed!

Parker tried to pull himself back onto the seat, but slipped and banged his forehead against the oarlock. As he slid down to the bottom of the boat, he called out with his mind as he'd done so many times in the past. A mental cry to the other half of his being, the sister with whom he'd shared a womb and everything else.

Amber...

Help me, Amber...

Even though she was half a world away and couldn't possibly hear him, much less help him, he fell back on the long ingrained cry.

Crissakes! He was a thirty-year-old man about to die if he didn't do something quick.

He knew what he had to do. He was a sitting duck in this tub. His only hope was to swim for it.

He crawled to the opposite side of the boat, sloshing up water all around him. His ribs burned like the salt water was a red-hot poker, and he hissed in a sharp breath.

As the curragh dipped toward the sea, Parker risked a quick glance toward the shore, but he couldn't tell if the bluffs were any closer. At least he was a good swimmer, though he didn't really like swimming in the ocean. But he liked being shot a whole lot less.

With that morbid thought to cheer him, he launched himself over the side into the cold, black waves.

As the icy water closed over his head, too late he realized he should have shed the mackintosh. The heavy coat pulled him under as effectively as an anchor. He clawed at the fastenings while he sank deeper and deeper. Finally freeing his right arm, he thrashed his way to the surface just before his lungs burst.

Amber! his brain screamed as he gulped in air.

He went under again before he worked his left arm loose. As he struggled in the weird, muted twilight world beneath the surface of the waves, something brushed against his leg.

Something substantial.

In the moment he wrenched his left arm from the sleeve of the coat, Parker caught a glimpse of a dark, sleek shape gliding under him.

Fuck!

Were sharks this close to land?

Then he remembered he was bleeding…

Chapter 1

KEVIN HENNESSEY HELD OUT HIS HAND TOWARD THE smoldering turf fire and listened to the wind rattling through the eaves and down the chimney. Rain pinged on the tin roof as the third squall in a week, and by far the strongest, buffeted the lone cottage.

So much for his pleasant seaside holiday.

But what did he expect during summer in Donegal, especially in these parts? His old man had lived here nearly ten years when he'd died this spring, and the entire time, he groused to anyone who visited that Malin Head possessed only three kinds of weather—barely tolerable, foul, and more foul.

A rapping noise interrupted Kevin's reverie. Had one of the shutters on the front window blown loose? Jaysus, but he hoped not. He most decidedly did not want to go outside in the dark and the rain to fix the bloody thing.

The noise came again, louder and unmistakable, and thoroughly improbable. Someone was pounding on the front door. Kevin turned in slack-jawed surprise at the realization. The house stood at the end of a perpetually muddy lane, an isolated sentinel on the ragged bluff, more than three kilometers from its nearest neighbor.

No one ventured out here without an express invitation. 'Twas the way Declan Hennessey had liked it, and Kevin preferred it the same.

What feckin' neddy would be out in a storm like this, then?

He snatched the battery-powered lamp off the end table and strode to the front door to find out.

Gripping the light in his left hand, he threw the bolt and eased open the heavy wooden door.

A dripping figure in a yellow rain slicker stumbled forward. Nearly dropping the lamp, he stuck out an arm, and the woman steadied herself. He knew the stranger was a woman the moment her slender fingers gripped him, a Yank judging from her muddy jeans and trainers.

She jerked away from him as if burned, her dark eyes enormous in her pale face, wet hair plastered against her head.

"Are you a policeman?" she asked, her accent confirming his assumption that she was indeed American. "They told me at the pub that a policeman lived at the end of this road."

Where the devil had she come from? Kevin peered around her into the yard but saw no vehicle.

Another gust of wind blew rain into his eyes and made the woman teeter unsteadily on the doorstep. He grabbed her forearm, dragged her over the threshold, and shoved the door closed.

"My father was constable of our village in County Derry," Kevin answered gruffly. "But he's been dead these past three months."

"I'm sorry, but are you Mr. Hennessey's son? They told me you were a policeman too." The woman's voice crackled with tension, and deep shadows purpled the skin beneath her eyes. "I need your help. My brother's in trouble, and I have to find him!"

She swayed against him again, and Kevin recognized that it was exhaustion, not the wind or rain, making her unsteady.

"Let's have a cuppa first, shall we?" He surprised himself with the invitation, but something about her wouldn't let him turn her back out into the rain. "I'll take your coat and then put on the kettle."

Shoving a lock of wet hair off her forehead, she squinted at him in confusion before understanding spread across her face. "Oh, you mean tea."

"Yes." Kevin spoke slowly and carefully as he held out his hand. "But give me your coat first. Miss, uh?"

"Oh, sorry! O'Neill, Amber O'Neill." She pulled one hand out of her wet slicker and started to shake his, splattering drops of water on his shirt and the floor. "Oh no! Sorry…"

"'Tis no matter." He watched her peel the soggy garment off. Underneath, her T-shirt was also damp and clung enticingly to the nicest set of tits he'd seen in many a day.

Bloody hell!

He didn't ogle women's tits. Not since he went off the sauce. But here he was, gawking like a schoolboy. He grabbed the dripping coat and turned quickly away to hang it on one of the pegs beside the door.

"Are you Mr. Hennessey's son?" she persisted.

Taking a deep breath, he composed himself before he turned and answered. "Yes, I'm Kevin Hennessey, but I'm afraid I'm not a policeman. Not anymore."

A stricken look clouded her eyes, which he now noticed were the same golden brown as her name, Amber. A strangled sound gurgled in the back of her throat as her knees buckled under her. Kevin grabbed with both his hands on her forearms. The lamp clanked onto the tiles in the process, and the noise made her flinch.

"My brother…" she murmured and flailed one hand toward the doorknob.

"Come inside and sit down," Kevin urged, still rather stunned by his sudden, unreasoning need to assist her.

He wrapped one arm around her shoulders and retrieved the fallen lamp with the other, then guided her into the sitting room.

"How long since you've eaten?" he asked when she'd settled onto the sofa in front of the fireplace.

Amber O'Neill gave a slight shake of her head and gnawed at her bottom lip for a moment. "I dunno. I ate a candy bar in the Shannon airport."

Her answer caused him to thump the lamp down onto the end table with surprise. "You drove straight here from the Shannon airport? That must have taken what, eight or nine hours?"

"I dunno," she repeated, staring at the mud and dirty water dripping off her shoes and the bottoms of her soaked jeans. "I'm not even sure what day it is."

"'Tis Thursday night," he replied, but she didn't respond except to give an expansive yawn. "I'll just put on the kettle then. Won't take a moment."

He disappeared into the kitchen, which had been added long after the cottage was first constructed and therefore had gas, electricity, and running water. Quickly filling the electric teakettle, he plugged it in and grabbed the tin of McVitie's Digestives before he hurried back to his unexpected guest. She sat with her head slumped forward in what looked like a meditative state.

"Biscuit?" He pried the lid off the tin and held it out toward her.

Her golden eyes moved, uncomprehending, between the tin and his face.

"Please help me." Her plea sounded soft and tremulous as she removed a broken cookie. "Something terrible has happened to Parker."

"Your brother?"

"My twin."

Kevin tried to picture a man with her delicate features—wide, luminous eyes, full alluring lips—and failed miserably. His gaze strayed again to her chest, and he cursed himself for being such an insensitive lout. He looked away fast.

"If you drove from Shannon, where's your car? I didn't see it in the yard."

"Stuck in the mud a little way down the road."

He was certain he knew where. The lane dipped down into a particularly boggy patch about five hundred meters from the cottage. No wonder she was dripping with rain and mud. He would probably need more than his da's old Range Rover to pull her hired car free of that mess.

When he finally dared look at her again, she hardly seemed able to hold her head up. It lolled against one shoulder, the movement startling her back to momentary alertness.

"What's that weird smell?" she asked, staring at the piece of shortbread in her hand and then popping it into her mouth.

"Turf." Before he could give more of an explanation, the teakettle whistled. The sound made Amber O'Neill jerk in surprise again. "I'll brew up the tea and be right back. Would you like a sandwich?"

Still not looking at him, she nodded dumbly.

Kevin hightailed it back to the kitchen. He filled the teapot with teabags and hot water, and wondered what he was supposed to do with the strange woman in his sitting room. He was rather sure that the petrol station in Carndonagh had a tow truck, but it was almost ten o'clock. Would they answer a call this late? His mobile sat in the charger on the counter, however, when he picked it up, he discovered the storm had interrupted the signal—an unfortunate, but regular occurrence.

Fecking lovely. Now what?

While the tea steeped, he threw together a sandwich from a hunk of soda bread, some leftover chicken, and a tomato. If Amber O'Neill was as hungry as he suspected, she shouldn't be choosy. With everything arranged on a tray, he strode out to the sitting room.

Amber O'Neill slumped sideways against the arm of the sofa, asleep. He sat the tray on the end table, then shook her shoulder.

"So tired," she murmured, her eyelids slipping back down.

"Miss O'Neill? Amber?" He tried again with the same result.

She seemed more unconscious than asleep, and her hands felt clammy cold when he chafed them between his. Considering they couldn't get her car unstuck until morning, and the nearest B&B was also in Carndonagh, might as well let her sleep awhile.

Kevin moved the woven lap robe from the back of the sofa to her shoulders. Then he knelt at her feet, untied the muddy trainers, and slipped them off. Her socks were dripping wet too, so he pulled those off as well. She had pretty, slender feet with bright coppery polish on her toenails. Funny how he'd never found a woman's feet attractive before.

The bottom half of her jeans were as wet and muddy as her shoes. She really should take them off, but she hadn't stirred so much as an eyelash while he'd removed her shoes and socks. Just thinking about how she would look without her clothes made his lad twitch with anticipation.

Sweet Jaysus!

He couldn't do this!

Standing up, he grabbed her by both shoulders and shook vigorously.

"Miss O'Neill! Miss O'Neill, you need to take off these wet clothes."

Her head rolled forward like a broken doll, while her eyes opened in uncomprehending slits.

"Your clothes are wet." Kevin shoved his fingers under the waistband of her jeans and shook her again. "You must take them off."

"Mmmkay," she whispered, reaching for the top snap and zipper.

As soon as he realized what she was about to do, he averted his eyes. She rustled for a moment, but when she went silent, he looked back to see Amber O'Neill passed out again with the jeans crumpled round her knees. Trying to keep his eyes on the floor, he bent down and pulled her pants the rest of the way off. Much as he tried not to look, he couldn't help but get a glimpse of creamy thighs and high-cut white knickers that brought his lad to full alert.

Shite!

He rocked back on his heels and nearly toppled over. She squirmed and shifted her legs under her on the sofa cushion. Cursing under his breath, he jerked the lap robe down to cover her. Then he gathered up her wet things and all but sprinted out of the room.

———

Sudden, sharp pain lanced through Amber's side and radiated over her body while cold, black water closed over her head. Beneath her, sinister, dark shapes swam ever nearer in the murky gloom. She thrashed wildly, her lungs crying out for air.

"Parker!"

Her own cry awakened her. Bolting upright, she gasped for breath while she looked about an unfamiliar room bathed in diffused light. A peculiar, earthy smell filled her nostrils.

Turf...

The word popped into her brain at the same time a strange man burst into the room. Tall and well-built, his white T-shirt was tucked half in and half out of his unbuttoned jeans. His feet were bare.

"Are you all right?" His voice was a deep, lilting brogue as he stopped short at the end of the sofa where she sat.

"Fine! I'm..."

Grappling to sort through the images crowding her sleep-addled brain, Amber reached under the blanket to adjust her own shirt, which was hiked up around her ribs. To her horror, she discovered her jeans were MIA and one bare calf and knee lay exposed.

Oh my god! What had she done?

Sensing her thoughts, his crystalline blue eyes jumped from her leg to her face, and then darted away while he ran his hand through his short, dark hair. She huddled into a tight ball, clutching the blanket under her chin.

"Where are my…"

"I'll just get your things," he exclaimed over the top of her query, turned, and disappeared from the room.

Knuckling the sleep from her eyes, Amber concentrated on the last thing she could remember. But thinking with a bladder at the bursting point was hard to do.

"Hennessey," a ruddy-faced man with white hair had told her. "Two 'n's, two 's'es. Right at the crossroads, to the very last house at the end of the lane."

But it had been raining, a sudden downpour. She winced as just the thought of water made her bladder cramp.

At that moment, Hennessey with the two 'n's and two 's'es reappeared. His T-shirt was completely tucked in, and his pants were fastened. He carried her shoes in one of his hands, her socks in the other, and her jeans were draped over his beefy forearm.

"Here you are, then. Afraid they're still a bit damp."

Amber snatched the jeans and, while he looked discreetly in the other direction, jerked them on.

"I really need—"

"Loo's through there," he interrupted, pointing with her shoes.

She leapt off the sofa and sprinted in the direction he indicated, not bothering to zip or button her own fly.

A few minutes later, after finding much-needed

relief, Amber turned on the faucet to wash her hands and looked in the mirror over the sink.

UGH! Bloodshot eyes with dark circles under them stared back. Her slightly-below-chin-length bob stuck out all over in a tangled mass of spikes and curls.

Worse than she thought! Plus she had no immediate way to fix anything. All she had with her were her passport and plane ticket in a travel pouch around her neck. Everything else, admittedly not much, was stowed in her backpack in the trunk of her rental car.

Splashing water on her face, she straightened her hair as best she could with damp fingers. *Hopeless.* She patted the water off her cheeks with the hand towel that carried a faint earthy odor not unlike the smell of the turf fire.

Kevin…

This time a name popped into her head.

Kevin Hennessey. But he said he wasn't a policeman.

Didn't matter. Amber took a deep breath and squared her shoulders. Somehow she would convince Kevin Hennessey to help her find Parker. She had to. Before it was too late.

She knew her brother was alive. Their connection was too deep, too much a pervasive part of one another. The moment she'd stepped off the plane in Shannon, she felt as if someone had set off a homing beacon in the far recesses in her brain.

The beacon grew stronger the farther north she went. Now here she was at the northernmost point in Ireland, the place Parker said he was headed in a postcard he'd sent nine or ten days ago. The card she'd received just hours after a horrific mental scream awakened her, left her shaking, sweating, and fearing for her brother's life.

She'd had only one other experience remotely similar. The summer they turned ten, Parker fell out of a tree and broke his ankle. Even though Amber had been all the way across town at a piano recital, the sensation hit her like a physical blow, sending her to the floor to writhe in agony. She never forgot that horrible feeling, but this time had been far worse. And this time she had been thousands of miles away.

Stepping out of the bathroom and into the tiny utility porch, Amber found herself facing an ancient wringer washer, which stood between a stainless steel stationary tub and a wooden clothes rack. It might have been an advertisement from the 1940s, except her modern yellow and white tennis shoes, relatively free of mud, sat atop the washer. One white sock protruded from each. Her gallant host must have set them there when she ran for the bathroom.

Claiming her shoes, she stepped through the door into the kitchen. Kevin Hennessey, now wearing a plaid woolen shirt over his white T, stood in front of a huge monstrosity of a cookstove the same approximate vintage as the washer. His short, black hair also stuck out at odd spiky angles, and dark stubble covered the lower half of his face, but somehow he still managed to look good.

Really good.

Hell's bells! Where had that come from?

She pulled a wooden chair out from the kitchen table and sat so that she faced away from him to put on her shoes. After glancing at her watch, which was still on California time, she squinted out the window over the sink.

"What time is it?" she wondered. "And how long was I asleep?"

Amber didn't realize she'd spoken aloud, but she must have for Kevin Hennessey answered, "'Tis almost half past six, and you were asleep for eight hours, give or take a few minutes."

Eight hours?

Didn't feel like half that long. Must be jet lag.

Her shoes still felt squishy inside, but she tried to ignore it as she tied them and stood up. "I need to get my car."

"The garage won't open 'til seven. Might as well have a bite of breakfast."

He pronounced it "gare ahjudge," and he raised his voice over the sizzle of something frying in a cast iron skillet. Something that smelled heavenly.

Her stomach rumbled loudly in anticipation, and she found herself sitting back in the chair, facing toward him.

On the counter near the sink, a teakettle whistled. He turned and poured steaming water into a teapot, his movements spare and obviously practiced.

She watched him for a long moment before she said, "I—uh, I need to get my things out of the car."

"Eat first," he declared, handing her a fistful of silverware before she could get up again.

Obediently, she separated the spoons, forks, and knives into two place settings. She put one set in front of her and the other in front of the chair on the opposite side of the table. She'd no sooner finished than he plopped a steaming plate of food in front of her and another on the end of the table.

"I usually sit here," he said, scooting the silverware over.

"Sorry," Amber murmured, eyeing the mound of fried potatoes topped with half a grilled tomato. A fat banger sausage kept them separated from an equally large pile of scrambled eggs on the other side of the plate. She gave a little start as a smaller plate with two thick hunks of soda bread plunked down in the table's center, followed by a butter dish and cream pitcher.

"Dig in, then." Kevin Hennessey urged, turning to pour two mugs of tea.

He didn't need to tell her twice. In the ten seconds it took him to fill the mugs and set one in front of her, Amber's mouth was too stuffed with eggs to say thank you. She couldn't remember the last time breakfast tasted this good. But that might be because the most she ever ate was a bowl of cold cereal or a carton of yogurt as she ran out the door to work.

For five or six minutes, she shoveled in food like a third-world refugee, not thinking about anything but the next bite. Finally mopping up sausage grease with the last of her bread, she reached for her mug of tea to wash it all down, and looked straight into Kevin Hennessey's icy blue stare.

"So tell me about this brother of yours," he said, slowly spreading butter over his hunk of bread. "What kind of trouble is he in that requires the police?"

His tone made her gulp, causing her last bite to hang up in her throat. She coughed and had to take several swallows of tea before she could reply. "I, uh… I'm not sure. But I think—I'm afraid he… he's hurt."

His gaze never wavering, he took a drink of his own tea before he said, "There's no one in Malin Head can treat a serious injury. Are you sure he's here?"

"Yes. I mean, pretty sure." Amber squirmed under the intensity of his scrutiny. He might not be a policeman now, but he certainly knew about interrogation. "The last I heard from him, he was on his way here."

"Perhaps he changed his mind," Kevin Hennessey said in an oh-so-rational cop voice that set her teeth on edge and made her shake her head a little too emphatically.

"Not without telling me."

"You're very close then," he mused. He stacked the empty plates and piled the dirty silverware on top of them before he added, "Isn't that a bit unusual, given your ages and all?"

If she had a dollar for every time she'd heard a query like that, she'd be a wealthy woman.

"We're twins," she said succinctly, then when one of his black eyebrows quirked she added, "I know my brother very well."

Saying nothing further, he rose and put the pile of dirty dishes in the sink. Amber stood too, glad for the lull in his questioning. Perhaps it wasn't such a good idea to solicit his help after all. In the chilly morning light, trusting a strange man with her secrets, even one as good-looking as Kevin Hennessey, felt like a scary proposition. But what choice did she have?

The things I do for you, Parker. Damn your miserable hide!

"Thank you for the breakfast, but I need to get my things out of the car. And if you could call that tow truck for me, I'd really appreciate it."

But when she turned, his hand shot out and captured her by the wrist. "Just stall the ball."

Heat radiated from his fingertips straight up her arm and suddenly made her remember that she had woken up on his couch half-naked, but with no knowledge of how she got that way. As if he were thinking of the same thing, he hastily let her go.

"The mobile's still out. We'll have to take my car to the village." He started toward the utility porch. "And I'll need my boots first."

Her gaze automatically dropped to his rather large bare feet, which made her think of long ago speculations she and her junior high girlfriends had about boys with big hands and feet. She should thank him for his offer, but the only sound that came from her bone-dry mouth was a wheezing cough.

Kevin Hennessey didn't notice, because he had already disappeared through the connecting door. He reappeared just as she reached for the mug of tepid tea to try to lubricate her parched vocal cords. She sloshed the bitter dregs around her mouth, nearly gagging, while he dropped rubber boots next to his chair. Then he sat down and pulled on heavy wool socks.

Looking away, Amber tried once again to force out words. "Uh... S-sorry Mr. Hen—"

"Kevin," he said abruptly, causing her to stare right into his glacial blue eyes. "My name is Kevin, and you've not changed your mind about needing my help, have you, Amber?"

No matter how cold his eyes, the way he said her name sent a flood of heat roaring through her. Heat that she didn't need or want. That would only get in the way of trying to locate Parker. Not trusting herself to speak, she shook her head.

Kevin shoved his feet into the rubber boots and stood. "Let's go then, and perhaps we can find that brother of yours while we're about it."

Please, God. Let it be so easy! Amber prayed.

Chapter 2

SUNK TO ITS AXLES IN A LAKE OF MUD, THE HIRED CAR looked forlorn and vulnerable, much as Amber O'Neill herself did. Kevin had chanced a few sidelong glances in her direction, but now that they'd reached the stranded vehicle, he could look at her full on. Huddled on the far side of the Rover's worn bench seat, she made him think of some cornered wild thing—skittish and wary, but ready to stand her ground if threatened.

He would apply no pressure then. *At least not at the moment.*

He asked for her keys, and even though he knew it would be nigh on useless, got out and unwound the yellow nylon rope from the Rover's front crossbar. Skirting the mud until absolutely necessary, he waded out and sunk past his ankles before he reached the car's back bumper. Once he secured the rope, he opened the boot and removed the black backpack, which proved not nearly as heavy as its bulging side pockets would indicate.

What kind of woman traveled this light? he wondered as he struggled out of the mire, the deep mud nearly pulling the boots off his feet. Certainly none he'd ever heard tell of.

Back on firmer ground, he tried unsuccessfully to stamp off the excess mud. Quickly giving up the effort for a lost cause, he opened the door of the Range Rover, handed Amber her pack, and pulled an already soiled rag from under the seat. He managed to clean his boots enough so that he could work the pedals and climbed into the driver's seat. But before he could wipe his dirty hands on his pant legs, she shoved a flimsy moist towelette at him.

"I teach eight- and nine-year-olds," she explained at his startled look. "I buy these things by the gross." As soon as he took it, she began brushing her hair and sticking in clips.

Hands clean, Kevin started the engine, stuck it into low gear, and though the rope went taut, the Rover went absolutely nowhere. He tried again with the same result, the motor grinding and groaning. But before he could give it a third go, Amber O'Neill touched his wrist with her long, slender fingers. He jerked away, unsure at first if it was himself or the Rover that choked.

Her lovely golden eyes met his. "It's hopeless, isn't it?"

He cleared his throat. "I'm afraid so."

Turning the key and setting the hand brake, he got out and unfastened the rope from the crossbar. No sense in wading out into that mess again. Then he checked his mobile to be sure there was still no signal and tried not to think about what kind of even bigger mess might lie in store for him if he stayed in close proximity to this pretty but disturbing Yank.

At a quarter past seven Kevin parked on the main street of the village. Anyone who went out fishing, whether for food or sport, was already going or gone, so this end of the street farthest from the water appeared nearly deserted. With the exception of the bakery, the half-dozen shops were still dark and closed.

After trying his mobile one more time, he addressed his quiet passenger. "There's a pay phone inside the pub. I'll find someone to let me in. Back in two shakes."

"I'll go too." She scrambled out the passenger door before he could stop her, the backpack slung over her left shoulder.

Typical American. Brash and impatient.

Still, he couldn't help but notice how the slanting morning sunlight set off fiery red highlights in her dark hair. Plus, whatever she'd brushed over her face during the ride here made her look healthier and not so deathly pale.

Teeth clenched, he strode around to the side entrance of the village's only pub. Luck was with him, for the Guinness truck sat blocking the alleyway, no doubt making a delivery. He recognized the publican, Charlie Donahue, standing in the open doorway.

"Morning, Donahue. Mind if I use the phone?"

"Naw, help yourself, Hennessey," the other man replied, his gaze fastening on Amber O'Neill's chest, though the nasty old bugger was probably twice her age.

Kevin shoved past him to the phone, mounted on the wall between the two WCs. As he looked up the number for the garage, he could hear Amber asking Donahue about her brother.

The delivery driver squeezed by, two silver kegs on his hand truck, and set Kevin's mind on the path it always took when he was in a pub—the thick, rich taste of Guinness as it rolled inside his mouth. Or the pleasant, slow burn of whiskey flowing down his throat, bringing the blessed haze of forgetfulness once it seeped into his brain.

His fourteen months of sobriety hadn't dulled the pleasurable memories even a wee bit. He doubted fourteen years would. The best he could hope for was distraction, and Amber O'Neill was certainly that, missing brother or no.

He finished the call, hung up the phone, and walked back to where Donahue chatted jovially with Amber. The publican's fingers trailed down her arm as he handed back a snapshot. Kevin didn't miss the jerky movement as she pulled away. Deliberately, he stopped and stood between her and Donahue.

"Afraid you're third in the queue. The tow truck won't be here for at least two hours." Seeing her crestfallen look, he continued, "We might as well walk down to the pier. Maybe someone there's seen your brother."

Relief and eagerness washed over her pretty face. "Okay."

"Come back this evening, darlin'," Donahue invited as they turned and walked away.

Kevin noted with satisfaction that Amber rolled her eyes at the invitation. He paused at the main street and grasped the loose strap of her backpack.

"I can carry this, shall I?" Then when she sputtered in protest, he added, "Unlike Charlie Donahue, I'm trying to be a gentleman."

She ducked her head a bit sheepishly. "Oh, okay."

After surrendering her luggage, she followed him the two blocks down to where the pavement curved around a pebbly beach with a short wooden pier. A half-dozen rickety fishmonger stalls and carts crowded near the foot of the pier, and gulls cried out in air that smelled thick with salt water and lingering fishy residue. Two deserted wooden curraghs sat just beyond the lapping waves, and Kevin counted four more bobbing out near the encircling arm of the breakwater. Several people and a pair of mongrel dogs milled about in a scene that could be modern or a hundred years old.

Business as usual in Malin Head.

"Let's have that snap of your brother, and we'll show it 'round."

He tried not to think about her nicely curved arse as she pulled the photo from the back pocket of her jeans. Instead, his perverse subconscious flashed up the memory of her sinuous thighs and white knickers.

Shite!

After all this time how could he suddenly be attracted to a woman? *This* woman? He thought he had put all that behind him after he and Caitlin called it quits.

Shaking his head to clear it, Kevin took the snapshot of a lanky-looking man whose brown hair flopped into one eye. He couldn't see much resemblance to Amber, but in his experience with the Police Service of Northern Ireland, photos were often not terribly accurate.

"Allow me," he said, and approached a matronly woman he knew from the years his father had lived here. "Morning, Mrs. Fitzpatrick."

The woman stopped scrubbing the tiled counter of her stall and nodded, the smell of bleach rising around her.

"We're looking for Miss O'Neill's brother and wonder if you might have seen him?"

Mrs. Fitzpatrick stripped off one of her rubber gloves and moved her reading glasses from the top of her head to the tip of her nose before she took the photo. After peering at it for a long moment, she handed it back to

Kevin with a shake of her head. "Sorry, no. But my mister will be hauling in his catch in another hour or so. You should ask him." Then she gazed at Amber in silent appraisal from top to toe. "Your lady friend's a Yank? Doubt your father'd approve."

"No," Kevin quickly denied. "That is, yes, she's a Yank, but she's not a lady friend. I... she..." He cleared his throat. "I am my father's son after all."

The woman clicked her tongue as she shoved her fingers back into her glove. "Well, your father's dead and buried, God rest him. And it seems to me you've punished yourself long enough for something 'twas never your fault."

She wasn't the first to say so, though Kevin knew better. But he chose not to argue about a matter that was most certainly not Mrs. Fitzpatrick's business. Besides, she'd already gone back to scrubbing. He ignored Amber O'Neill's questioning look and showed the photo to the next passerby.

Five more people replied negatively to Kevin's query, the last, Michael Coyle, scarcely glanced before shaking his head. But a teenaged boy peering over his shoulder piped up, "Ho, Michael! Is that the Yank rented one of your curraghs on Monday? And were ya not complaining on Tuesday how he hadn't returned it then?"

"Mind your tongue, Connor," Coyle replied. "Or you may find the devil's put a red nail in it."

Undaunted, the dark-haired youth continued, "Must have been him since he was the only Yank 'round here all week. Until you now, Miss..." He sketched a nod in Amber's direction. His eyes, Kevin couldn't help but notice, lingered on her chest.

Jaysus! Was this wee gobshite even old enough to shave?

"O'Neill," she answered, extending her hand. "Amber O'Neill, and that's my brother, Parker, who's missing."

"My pleasure!" The teen vigorously shook her hand. "I'm Connor Magee, and I was about to tell me Uncle Michael that I think I saw his rented curragh washed up on the rocks just t'other side of the point."

"I'm not your uncle," Coyle groused, but no one paid him any heed.

"Where?" Amber cried while at the same time Kevin demanded, "Take us there."

Connor Magee looked pleased with himself as he addressed Kevin. "Ya got a jammer then?"

"Parked by Donahue's," Kevin replied.

The annoying little git kept pace with Amber, the two of them being roughly the same height. As they walked, the youth immediately launched into a stream of questions. "Where in the States do you live, Miss O'Neill?"

"California."

Her short answer did nothing to discourage him. "Bleedin' savage! You must be a film star. Or maybe you're on the telly?"

She shook her head. "I'm a teacher."

"You're bloody jokin'! All my teachers were manky old nuns. If I'd had one half so fine as you, I'd 'a become a bleedin' scholar."

Kevin coughed to cover his derisive snort. Amber slanted him a look. When they reached the Rover, Connor Magee crawled into the back, still talking. Kevin actually felt some sympathy for Coyle, who was the brother of the teen's stepfather, and had been saddled with Connor all summer.

If Kevin had hoped the noisy engine would silence the boy, he soon discovered his mistake.

"I'm from Sligo," the youth babbled, leaning close to Amber's ear. "I thought 'twas the most boring spot on God's green earth, 'til I got sent here to Malin Head."

"Fasten your safety belt," Kevin ordered. "And tell me when we're getting close."

He drove off the paved lane onto the rough track that skirted the edge of the bluff, while Connor blathered on.

"Did ya come to find your roots then, Miss O'Neill? Grianan Fort's the ancestral home of the O'Neill clan, don't ya know."

Kevin saw Amber's breath hitch at the mention of the place.

"I know. The last I heard from my brother was a postcard from that fort." She pressed her lips into a thin, worried line. "He was on his way to Malin Head."

"Me Gran was an O'Neill. Perhaps we're relations." Connor paused long enough to poke Kevin on the shoulder. "We can walk down from that ravine yonder."

Kevin pulled to a slightly higher, relatively dry spot and parked the Rover. The wind blew ragged clouds across the horizon, but it didn't smell to him like more rain was coming soon.

Amber shoved her backpack as far under the seat as it would go. "I suppose it'll be fine."

"To be sure," Connor affirmed with a roll of his eyes. "There's no one about in this middle of bloody nowhere."

The three of them picked their way down the side of the shallow gully that slanted to the sea. Though

walking proved tricky, at least they were sheltered from
the wind. In less than fifteen minutes, they reached the
rocky, wave-whipped shore. There was no beach, and
even now at low tide, the waves crashed almost directly
onto the face of the bluff.

Connor took the lead. Turning back in the direction of Malin Head, the youth scrambled over the
rock escarpment sticking scant centimeters above the
foaming water. Kevin stayed close behind Amber, who
wasn't nearly as surefooted as their guide. Neither was
he, thanks mostly to his rubber boots. But he noted with
grim satisfaction that the pounding surf had at long last
squelched Connor's conversation.

After a long ten minutes of slipping and crawling
over and around wet rocks, Connor cried out, his skinny
outstretched arm pointing seaward. Kevin strained his
eyes and finally distinguished the black-tarred prow
wedged between a boulder and a jutting finger of rock.

In her haste, Amber lost her balance and would
have fallen if Kevin hadn't grabbed her upper arm
and jerked her against his chest. Her soft body pressed
against him, and instant attraction sparked like a jolt of
static electricity.

"S-sorry!" She wrenched away, overbalancing
once more.

Careful to grasp only her elbow, he murmured,
"Steady now. 'Twill be no good if you're soaking wet
again." Though in truth, the thought of undressing her a
second time was quite tempting.

"C'mon!" Connor called out, his voice nearly whipped
away by the wind and waves. He practically had to crawl
on hands and knees to reach the small vessel.

Kevin trailed after him, not loosening his hold on Amber. One of his feet slipped on a piece of seaweed and hit the water, luckily not up to the top of his boot. Amber wrapped both her hands around his arm and tottered just behind him, her hair blowing wildly about her head.

"Shite!" He heard Connor swear as the boy reached the boat.

A half-dozen more treacherous meters, and Kevin saw the reason for the teen's exclamation. Seawater came almost up to the plank seat in the center of the curragh, and one splintered rib stuck out of a rip in the tarred canvas near the prow.

"Parker?" Amber questioned, her voice tinged with panic.

"No sign of anybody." Connor stated the obvious as they reached him, but Amber grasped the pointed end of the prow and scanned the waterlogged interior, her eyes darting frantically to and fro.

"Any other damage?" Kevin asked, surprised to see one of the oars had somehow managed to stay in the oarlock.

"Another rip over here near the bottom." Connor stood near the empty oarlock on the other side. "Doubt she's salvageable."

"But what about my brother?" Amber's voice had grown outright shrill as she shoved her hair out of her face. "Where is he?"

"Knacker probably ran her aground, and the storm last night threw her up here on the rocks. Michael says tourists pull that shite all the time."

Amber glared at the boy. "Not my brother. Parker's not like that at all."

A splinter gouged into Kevin's thumb, and he jerked his hand away and stared at the rough hole in the wood. Disbelief raced through him. The perforation couldn't possibly be what it appeared. He rubbed his shirtsleeve across his eyes and looked again just to be certain, but after all those years in the PSNI there was no mistaking what he saw.

Suddenly Amber was next to him, her golden eyes probing his, then following his fingers to where they rested on the oarlock. "What is it?"

"'Tis a bullet hole."

"W-what?" Her beautiful eyes went completely round as she reached for the wood.

"No shite?" Connor exclaimed. "Bleedin' savage!"

Amber's icy fingers collided with Kevin's as she touched the oarlock. Color draining from her face, she made a strangled sound and then doubled over, clutching her side.

"Someone's shot Parker," she managed to gasp.

Then her eyes rolled back, and she sank toward the ground. Fortunately, Kevin only had to take a step to catch her.

"Holy Jaysus! What happened?" Connor scrambled around the boat next to him.

"She fainted." Kevin shifted her limp body so that he had a firm grip under her armpits. "Afraid she does this rather a lot. Can you give her a wee pat on the cheeks?"

The youth's own eyes bulged in alarm, and he swallowed hard. "Sh-she looks dead."

"Trust me, she's not." He glared at the boy until Connor finally reached and timidly laid his grubby fingers on her cheek.

"She feels so cold!" His voice cracked on a high, girlish note as he jerked his hand away.

"For feck's sake! Just look at her chest, and you can see her breathing." Kevin jostled her a bit and spoke close to her ear while Connor stared mesmerized. "Amber. Wake up. C'mon now."

She gave the barest hint of a moan, but didn't stir.

"Do ya think she's had a fit of some sort?"

The thought had only just occurred to Kevin as well, plus they couldn't just stand about waiting for the tide to come in. "I don't know, but you have to help me carry her. Grab her feet and step carefully."

Connor hesitated for another moment, his gaze darting from Amber's unconscious face to Kevin's stern expression. Obviously convinced by the latter, the youth silently obeyed.

Between the pair of them, they maneuvered the unconscious woman off the rocks. But when they reached the ravine, they had to shift their burden so that Kevin had her left arm draped over his shoulder, while Connor had her right. Amber groaned again a little more loudly, but still didn't regain consciousness until Connor tripped over a sprig of gorse and dropped her.

She moaned and flailed her arm, but Kevin managed to pull her around and against him again. With her feet off the ground, they were almost nose to nose, her breasts poking against his chest. Stifling a curse, his grip tightened, and he gave her another small shake.

Her eyelids fluttered, but then her head sank back to rest against his neck. He jostled her again until she faced him once more.

"Amber! Wake up, luv! I need you to help me here."

Her lids lifted halfway, and she murmured, "Wh-wha? Where?" Much to his relief, her eyes must have focused for they popped open wide. But she was still a dead weight in his arms.

"Steady now. I'm going to pick you up." He turned to Connor, who had regained his feet and didn't look worse for his fall. "Give us a hand then."

With a bit of assistance from the youth, he heaved Amber over his shoulder in an emergency carry position. She shrieked in his ear during the process, so obviously her breathing was fine, and he'd certainly carried far heavier burdens. Going uphill out of the ravine proved a bit tricky, however, and her wiggling didn't help.

"Hold still," he ordered, sorely tempted to give her derriere a smack.

"Put me down!"

"Half a minute and I will."

With a grunt of triumph, Kevin reached flat ground. Connor sprinted ahead and had the back door of the Rover open. After a dozen more steps, Kevin shifted his unwilling load and laid her on the bench seat. He'd no sooner let her go than she popped into a sitting position.

"I'm fi... Ooo!" She clutched her head with both hands, and he pressed her shoulder back toward the seat.

"Stay down. I'm taking you to a doctor."

She caught his hand. "No! Please. I'm all right. Just take me to your house and let me lie down. I'll be fine." Her cold hand squeezed his, while her golden eyes implored him. "Please, Kevin?"

The way she said his name did unexpected things to his innards. Not unpleasant exactly, but startling in their intensity. He pulled his fingers out of her grasp and ran them through his hair.

"We need to find out what's wrong with you."

"I know what's wrong," she countered. "And I'll be fine. Really. Besides, we can't miss the tow truck."

"Are ya preggers?" Connor piped up.

While Kevin gave him an outraged look, Amber burst out with a hysterical little giggle. "Definitely not."

"Me mum did all sorts of weird shite last year when she was," Connor muttered.

"Get in," Kevin told the boy. Then to Amber he said, "Stay down. We'll go and wait for the tow truck."

———◦◦◦———

As they bounced along the rutted dirt road, Amber slowly raised herself to a sitting position, all the while concentrating to keep her breaths deep and even. Her head swam a little but not enough to worry that she might pass out again.

Parker had been shot. But he wasn't dead.

She'd learned both those facts from touching the bullet hole in the oarlock. The moment she'd touched the wood, the knowledge blasted into her mind as if it were happening to her. And that strange beacon she'd been experiencing since setting foot on Irish soil indicated that her brother wasn't far from where they'd found the boat.

But she'd lied to Kevin. While she presumed it was her magnified mental connection to Parker that caused her loss of consciousness, she'd never reacted like this before. Weird and scary and with a strength that bordered on violent, their usual shared telepathy felt a hundred times stronger. It had to be because of the dire circumstances.

Tentatively, she reached out with her mind to the place where she and Parker connected, but once again, her brother wasn't there. During their adolescence, they'd learned to put up blocks when they wanted privacy from each other. Except this felt different. Amber probed the edges of the mental wall and could only distinguish the slightest essence of her brother. Almost like he couldn't respond, couldn't breach the gap separating them.

Swamped with anxiety, she withdrew and looked up to meet Kevin's icy blue stare in the rearview mirror. She gave an involuntary gasp.

Connor, who'd been uncharacteristically quiet, broke his silence to ask, "Ya all right, Miss O'Neill?"

"I'm fine," she answered automatically, but she wondered if somehow Kevin knew what she had just tried to do.

Of course he didn't!

The idea was preposterous. She'd never met anyone who possessed the ability she and Parker shared, and she had most certainly looked, though not openly. So had Parker.

They'd learned early on that admitting to their connection turned them into science experiments. But carefully and covertly they'd both reached out mentally to countless people, and neither of them had ever made a connection with anyone else.

Still, she and Parker had never been in a situation like this. The saying about desperate times and desperate measures popped into her brain. Dropping everything to make a trip to Ireland she couldn't afford was desperate all right. But she had a bad feeling she wasn't done, that her next desperate act would be to confess the mental ties with her brother to Kevin Hennessey. The very thought sent icy tentacles of dread clawing at her scalp, like when the neurologists had stuck on those electrodes twenty years ago.

She could see her rental car stuck in the middle of that nasty mudhole, so they must be close to Kevin's cottage. With Parker's life hanging in the balance, she needed to decide pretty darn quick whether or not to trust this Irishman. He had been trustworthy thus far, as near as she could recall. The mouthy teenage boy was another matter.

Amber cleared her throat. "Connor, would you mind waiting with my car for the tow truck? It'll be here soon, won't it?"

"Ten to fifteen minutes, I expect," Kevin affirmed as he pulled the vehicle to a stop. He extracted his cell phone, checked for service, and shoved it back in his pocket with a low curse.

Connor accepted Amber's offered car keys and got out of the Range Rover, though not happily. Kevin drove the remaining short distance in silence, and parked close to the cottage's front door.

"Are you all right to walk?" he asked, opening the vehicle door for her.

"I told you I was fine." Nerves made her tone snippy.

"You were also unconscious for close to twenty minutes." Scowling, he grabbed her elbow and led her the dozen yards to the door.

His touch felt warm and set off an uncomfortable sensual awareness that bounced through her nervous system. Surely if anything had happened between them last night, she would know.

He didn't let go until they were inside and both seated on the couch. Rattled by his closeness, she scooted into the corner as far away as she could get and tried to figure out how to start.

He fixed her with a level, unwavering stare and solved her dilemma. "So then, what do you need to tell me that you don't want Connor to hear?"

Kevin Hennessey certainly didn't beat around the bush.

She pressed her lips together and squirmed, wondering just how much she should tell him. How much would satisfy him? And then the thought of satisfying him took her mind off on a whole unwanted tangent.

"Is it about you or your brother?" he persisted when she hesitated.

"Both. Sort of… I mean…"

One of his black eyebrows inched up a fraction and flustered her even more. Trying to regain her focus, she gazed into the cold grate of the fireplace, and took a deep breath. Traces of the odd, earthy smell of peat lingering in the air teased her nostrils. Though it made no sense, the odor comforted Amber, left a feeling of protectiveness.

"Remember earlier when you asked about my brother and me being close?" She hadn't hesitated last night when she was cold, wet, and exhausted. Or this morning when she was confused and hungry. Taking another fortifying breath, she went for broke. "We're actually connected. Mentally. We have been all our lives. We call it mindspeak."

Kevin made a slight sound in his throat, just loud

enough for her eyes to jump to his face, where she plainly read disbelief. "You mean you talk to your brother in your mind?"

"Yes, with words and images, and I can feel what he feels." No going back now. She clenched her hands together in her lap, determined to make him understand. "Emotionally and physically. Not all the time, but sometimes. That's how I know he's—" The memory of searing pain and the image of the bullet hole momentarily stopped her words.

"Hurt?" Kevin finished, obviously still skeptical.

Amber nodded, squeezing her hands more tightly, willing away the myriad misgivings and unpleasant memories. Parker was all that mattered. All she had. She must find him and soon.

"You felt this clear 'round the world in California?" Kevin's incredulity was plain and totally understandable. If she hadn't suffered it firsthand, Amber wouldn't have believed it either.

"Yes." She answered with complete honesty. "I've never experienced anything from so far away. That's how I know it's bad. Really bad."

Chapter 3

"YOU THINK I'M NUTS, DON'T YOU?" AMBER ALREADY knew the answer by Kevin's expression, and it didn't bode well for locating her brother.

Another reason never to talk about what she and Parker shared. Most people flat out didn't believe it, and those who did… She refused to go down that ugly memory lane right now. Instead she fervently wished she could take back the last few minutes.

"Well, I can see why you'd rather our lad Connor not know." Kevin rose to his feet and paced over to the window. He stared outside for a moment, tapping his fingertips on the sill before he turned back to ask, "So why is it you don't know your brother's exact whereabouts?"

The fact that he wasn't totally dismissing her claim heartened her a little. Perhaps she hadn't completely misjudged him after all. "I seem to be having the same issue as your cell phone. Service is temporarily unavailable."

"You're sure 'tis temporary?" She flinched at his bluntness, and he bobbed his head by way of apology. "Sorry, but I need to ask."

"That's… okay." Amber didn't really want to make light of the situation anyway, the possibilities were too scary. Twisting her hands in her lap to hold back her fears, she continued, "I'd know if Parker… if he wasn't there. He is, but he's not answering me."

Kevin paced from the window to the couch and back

again, apparently weighing options. As he walked, he ran his hands through his short-cropped hair, as if that helped him make a decision.

"I think you'd best contact the authorities," he said at last.

Her shoulders slumped, and she sighed in defeat. "If you don't believe me, neither will they."

"'Tis not about believing in this mental telepathy or whatever 'tis you say you have." His dismissive tone changed, and he stared out the window again. "The facts are your brother is missing and there's a curragh washed up on the rocks with a bullet hole in it."

He made it sound perfectly reasonable and straight-forward. But something in the back of Amber's mind refused to accept such an easy solution. Nothing had been reasonable or straightforward since her brother's agonizing distress signal woke her up on Monday morning. Since then, she'd been in a waking bad dream.

Still, she had been trying to seek help from the authorities when she'd landed on Kevin's doorstep last night. The niggling hesitation she now experienced when he brought up the idea made no sense. Nevertheless, she felt it.

"Ah, I see the tow truck coming down the lane." Kevin turned away from the window to spear her with his probing blue gaze. "Are you all right to go meet him?"

"Sure, I'm fine." Amber got to her feet, glad that her legs didn't wobble and betray her. "And thank you."

"'Tis nothing."

Like a true gentleman, he held the front door, and

then the passenger door of the Range Rover for her. He didn't mention another word about Parker and her abilities. She hoped that was a positive sign.

They arrived on the scene at the same time as the tow truck, and within ten minutes the driver had freed her rental car from the mire. Unfortunately, the car still refused to start. While Amber stood feeling superfluous, Kevin, the driver, and Connor all peered under the hood, tapping various parts and offering up speculations. Finally, they all agreed that the car should be towed to the garage in Carndonagh for the mechanic's ministrations.

"I'll go along and take you to see the authorities," Kevin offered while the driver hooked the car back up to the truck.

When she protested, he insisted, and Connor chimed in, "Are we going to the police about your missing brother, then?"

"We are, but you're not," Kevin informed him. "I'll drop you back at the village. Tell Coyle what we found, but don't move the curragh 'til the constable has a look."

"Aw, bollocks!" the boy complained. "Just when things was getting interesting."

Even though he whined all the way to Malin Head, Kevin gave Connor's objections no more credence than he had hers. Obviously, when Kevin Hennessey made a decision it was final.

Once the youth was out of the car, Amber dared to speak. "I really appreciate your help, especially after I showed up at your door like that."

The tiniest hint of a smile tugged at the corners of his lips, the first suggestion of one she'd seen. "And what red-blooded Irishman would turn down a damsel in distress?" He paused for a beat before adding, "Even if she is, by her own admission, a wee bit nuts."

"Hey!" She poked him in the upper arm, glad for any kind of diversion. "What kind of knight in shining armor are you?"

A flicker of what might have been pain flashed through Kevin's sapphire eyes. "One whose armor is rather more tarnished than shiny, I'm afraid." Then he blinked, and the moment might have never happened as his tone went light again. "But those were your own words. I never said I agreed."

She played along. "You never disagreed either."

The smile increased a fraction and made him look even more appealing as he glanced at her from the corner of his eye. "True enough."

Was he actually flirting with her?

No male over the age of nine had shown any interest in her for such a long time that Amber wasn't sure. One thing she did know, she suddenly felt incredibly out of her depth. Anyone as good-looking as Kevin Hennessey undoubtedly had women lining up for his attention, all of them prettier and younger than she was.

She reached up to smooth the tangled mass of her hair and tried to calculate exactly how long it had been since her last shower. *Ugh!*

No way could he be flirting.

Pulling her backpack from under the seat, she found her hairbrush and tried to fix some of the damage done by the wind.

—∿∿—

Kevin slipped another sidelong glance in her direction as Amber started messing with her hair again. In the sunlight shining through the windscreen, it shone a deep, dark red, like live, smoldering embers. His fingers itched to bury themselves in it and test the warmth.

Gritting his teeth, he willed away the unbidden thought. No woman deserved the likes of him. Referring to himself as a knight with tarnished armor was laughable. More accurately, his armor was rusted. From liquor.

"How long have you lived in Malin Head?" Her question interrupted his self-recriminations.

"I don't live here. I'm on holiday." Forced on him by his sister Sharletta and her husband Harry. But Amber didn't need to know all that. "My father lived here ten years so I'm familiar enough with the place."

She put away the hairbrush and pulled out some sort of cosmetic before she asked, "Where do you live?"

"Armagh. 'Tis in the North, not the Republic."

He cast another quick glance at her and could plainly see that she didn't understand the difference, so he gave her a brief explanation. Better to engage in small talk than listen to his thoughts. She seemed glad for the distraction too, for she asked him a few more innocuous questions and answered some for him until they reached their destination.

After the tow truck left the car with the mechanic at the lone petrol station in the area, they hiked the two blocks to the municipal building. The constable's office was on the second floor of the squat brick building. James Shanley sat behind a computer screen, a mound of papers at his elbow and a scowl on his florid face. When

Kevin rapped on the doorframe, he smiled with what looked like relief. Kevin made brief introductions.

"Ah yes, Hennessey," the constable murmured in mid-handshake. "Sorry about your father's passing."

Kevin muttered appropriate thanks and moved on to outline the story of Amber's missing brother and the rented curragh with a bullet hole. She supplied occasional details but left most of the talking to him. He carefully left out any references to Amber's claims of mental telepathy, and simply said that she became alarmed when her brother didn't contact her.

Shanley scratched his square jaw and studied him for a long moment. "Are you sure 'twas a bullet hole?"

When Kevin nodded, the constable sighed. "I s'pose you're PSNI like your father?"

Kevin nodded again.

"Since I'm nigh onto drowning in this infernal paperwork, I'll take a drive out to Malin Head in another hour. Shall we meet in front of Donahue's, say at noon?" He then made a copy of the photo of Amber's brother and took down a detailed description from her.

Back at the petrol station, the mechanic's news was not so grand. Whatever ailed the car appeared major, and so far, the car hire company had not responded to calls. When the mechanic suggested Amber pay for the repairs and iron out the details with the company later, her pretty face blanched. Then she pulled out a neck pouch, dug in it, and extended a credit card. Kevin noticed that her fingers trembled slightly.

In the Rover, he asked, "Shall we get you squared away at the B&B before we go back to Malin Head?"

She refused to look at him, but stared straight ahead,

hands clasped tightly in her lap. "I uh… I can't really afford the car repair and the B&B. My credit card is maxed out."

She hung her head in what he guessed was embarrassment, though heaven knew he was the one who should feel ashamed of the images crowding his brain. Images of her in only her knickers and T-shirt.

After a long moment of silence, she added in a wistful tone, "I really need that car."

"You can sleep on my sofa then, if need be."

Jaysus! That came out too quick and easy!

What the devil was wrong with him, blurting out the first thing that popped into his head?

Amber turned and met his gaze, something akin to gratitude shining in her golden eyes. Gratitude, unease, and something more.

In the far, deep corner of his soul an urge stirred that he hadn't felt in a very long time, if ever. Protectiveness, possessiveness, a longing akin to the thirst for drink. *Disaster waiting to happen*.

The front tire bounced into a pothole and jerked Kevin's attention back to the road. Not a moment too soon, for he'd driven half off the pavement.

"Thank you," Amber murmured. "That armor of yours is getting shinier by the moment."

He gave a small audible snort, but didn't move his eyes from the road. After another long, uncomfortable silence, he said, "We'll find your brother."

"I know."

Neither of them spoke again until they were in sight of Malin Head village.

"Do we have time for me to get cleaned up at your

place?" Amber asked. "I've been wearing these same clothes for what feels like a week."

His mind immediately jumped to her out of her clothes. *Bloody fecking hell!*

He coughed to keep from cursing aloud. "Sure, we've time."

Making the turn at the crossroads, he drove as fast as he dared so that the bouncing of the Rover kept his thoughts occupied with the road.

Kevin carried her backpack into the cottage and placed it on the end of the sofa before he excused himself to clean up the kitchen. Maybe keeping her out of his sight would also keep her out of his thoughts. When he was up to his elbows in soapy water, she walked in with a bundle of clean clothes, a plastic bag of cosmetics, and a hair dryer.

"Towels are in the cupboard under the sink," he told her, refusing to let himself take a second glance.

Apparently he needed to be out of hearing range too, for the moment he heard the water start to run, images of Amber wet and naked leaped into his mind. Erasing them proved an exercise in futility, so he finished the dishes as fast as he could and hurried outside.

The mass of clouds on the horizon meant another rainstorm was on its way. He went into the shed and filled a bucket with chunks of peat for the fire he would inevitably need once the storm did hit.

When he walked back inside the cottage, the shower had blessedly stopped. Instead, the hair dryer hummed. Banishing the memory of sunlight sparking fire in her thick hair proved a wee bit easier, though not so easy as he'd have liked. Cleaning the grate and laying out the fixing for a new fire only went so far toward occupying his mind.

Unbidden doubts about how he would be able to sleep with her bedded down in the next room intruded into Kevin's mind. He would do it just as he had stayed sober these past fourteen months and eleven days. By sheer force of will. Nothing more, and nothing less.

Just as he managed to convince himself that he could indeed ignore his baser instincts, Amber O'Neill strolled into the room and gobsmacked all his reason right out the window.

Even disheveled he'd thought her attractive, but now in fresh clothes with her hair shining sleekly almost to her shoulders, he knew stunning was a more apt description. His mouth went dry and dusty as the peat clinging to his hands.

"Hope I didn't take too long." She shoved her bundle of dirty clothes inside the backpack while he gaped like a fecking neddy. "I'm ready. Are you?"

"Half a minute." Kevin brushed passed her and went into the loo to wash his hands and splash cold water on his face.

Unfortunately, her scent, sweet flowers with a hint of tart citrus, permeated the little room and aroused him beyond reason. Just like staying sober, this would be no easy task. Gathering the few remaining shreds of his willpower, he stalked out to the Rover, silently berating himself the whole way.

She followed him to the vehicle. "Is something wrong?"

"Another storm's coming."

After fastening her seat belt, she looked at the bank of dark clouds. "Crap! We've got to find Parker before that."

He said nothing, just concentrated on the rutted lane. But after a few moments of silence, he dared a quick glance at her. She sat with her elbows propped on her knees, and the fingertips of both her hands pressed against her forehead.

So that's how she did her so-called mind-talking then?

For the next five minutes, he sneaked more looks her way, but she didn't move. When he turned at the cross-roads to the village, she finally straightened with an audible groan, her expression a mixture of worry and frustration.

"Dammit! Why won't he let me in?"

Having no answer, Kevin parked in front of Donahue's, just behind the constable's car. They found Shanley inside the pub, a corned beef sandwich on the bar in front of him.

"Hope you don't mind if I have a wee bite first," the constable said, flicking an appraising eye over Amber.

"As a matter of fact, there's a storm brewing." She looked to Kevin for confirmation, so he gave a sketchy nod. "So if you don't mind, Constable Shanley, I'd really like to go now." She gave one of those stern schoolteacher looks that Kevin felt sure struck terror in the hearts of her students.

Shanley huffed in aggrieved dismay, but didn't argue. Instead he signaled the publican. "Wrap this up for me, will you Charlie? I'll eat it on me way."

"Hello, darlin'." Donahue greeted Amber with a lecherous smile. "Shall I fix you a sandwich as well? On the house."

"No, thank you." Amber's tone had all the warmth of an arctic ice floe as she pivoted and walked toward the door.

Biting back a grin, Kevin followed.

They reached the entrance just in time to collide with Connor Magee, who was rushing inside. "Are we off to show the constable the curragh, then?" he asked by way of greeting. "You aren't gonna faint on us again, are ya, Miss O'Neill?"

Amber assured him she would not. Then much to Kevin's chagrin, the youth bounded into the front seat of the police car with Shanley. He and Amber were obliged to sit in the cramped and uncomfortable backseat.

"Funny thing, Miss O'Neill," Shanley said around bites of his sandwich. "Nobody in Donahue's could recall ever seeing anyone who looked like that brother of yours."

"What a bunch of skangers!" Connor cried. "Didn't me Uncle Michael rent that curragh to him just last Monday?"

"That's not what Michael Coyle told me," the constable contradicted. "He said he couldn't recall any Yank."

"He's daft! Or else his partner rented it to Mr. O'Neill, though I've not seen Silas about all week."

Praying Amber didn't notice the effect being in such close proximity to her had on him, Kevin leaned forward and strained to see around Connor's head. "Isn't that the ravine just up there?"

"'Tis!" Connor confirmed.

Shanley parked on the same spot Kevin had earlier, and the four of them hiked down the side of the narrow gully while the constable finished off the last bite of his sandwich.

Connor kept up his steady stream of chatter. "There's where I tripped and Kevin had to heave you over his shoulder, Miss O'Neill. That's when you finally woke up and yelled at him."

The last thing Kevin needed was a reminder of Amber's shapely derriere resting close to his face. He was plenty aroused already, and he hoped to high heaven it wasn't as obvious as he feared. In front of him, Amber coughed and ducked her head. He couldn't be sure, but she appeared to be blushing. One thing he did know, her khaki slacks and gauzy shirt were not well suited for crawling about on the rocks.

Perhaps she thought the same, for she paused at the mouth of the ravine while Shanley and Connor forged ahead onto the slippery stone shelf. Having reached its zenith a short while ago, the sea had only drawn back a little, and the way was even more treacherous than it had been this morning. Concern for her safety rose in his chest.

"Do you want to wait back at the car?" Kevin had to yell over the crashing waves.

She shook her head, hair rippling in a bright cascade over one side of her face. As she leaned in close to him, her sweet scent momentarily blocked the tangy salt air.

"He's close. I can feel him."

Then she slipped her hand into his.

A scalding heat washed through him, along with an overpowering desire to pull her to him and kiss her until they were both senseless.

"Can you go first so I don't fall on my face?"

Protectiveness obliterated by her touch, Kevin could scarcely hear her question as he battled against his urge. Somehow, he managed to nod, even to take a couple of steps, though heat continued to pulse where their palms rubbed together.

Up ahead, he saw Connor bounding nimble as a

billy goat among the rocks. The middle-aged Shanley wasn't that far behind, picking his way more carefully. Summoning his inner strength, Kevin followed, keeping close to the cliff face, while the waves foamed up a scant meter away. He soon regretted changing out of his rubber boots when he stepped in a hole and water soaked his ankle and the bottom of his jeans.

They muscled on for ten more torturous minutes. The wind whipped a fine spray of salt water over them twice and caused Amber to gasp in protest. At least the chilly mist cooled his ardor, some small favor.

Thinking they must be close, Kevin strained his eyes for any sign of the curragh. He saw Connor pause and then hold out his shoes in one hand as he teetered onto the narrow rock ledge. Then the wind carried the boy's cry of dismay.

"What is it?" Amber yelled in order to be heard. "Where's the boat?"

The curragh was nowhere to be seen.

They came abreast of Shanley a moment later, the constable's expression as thunderous as the rapidly approaching clouds. "This better not be anyone's idea of a joke!"

Letting go of Kevin's hand, Amber struggled toward Connor, who was still carrying his shoes, pants rolled halfway up his shins.

"So help me, Connor," Kevin shouted. "I told you to leave the bloody thing where 'twas!"

"I never touched it! Honest to God! I was helping Mrs. Fitzpatrick clean fish the whole time you were gone, and Uncle Michael was there too."

Shanley bellowed over the top of him. "First a missing

Yank nobody's seen, and now a wrecked curragh that's not here. You been hitting the bottle again, Hennessey? Surely your old man's rolling in his grave with shame."

Seemingly oblivious of the waves washing over her shoes and soaking the bottoms of her slacks, Amber entered the shouting match. "No! My brother is here! I know he is, and we all saw that boat."

"Where is it then?" Shanley demanded.

"If nobody moved it, then the tide must have washed it free." Kevin tried to sound reasonable, but he seriously doubted the latter.

Not with the vessel so full of water and two holes in the hull.

Somebody must have moved it. *But who? And why?*

"Not me and not Uncle Michael," Connor staunchly insisted, obviously guessing the direction of Kevin's thoughts.

"Get on with the lot of you," Shanley declared. "If I'd tuppence, I'd leave you here to walk back."

"Wait!" Amber's tone bordered on a shriek as she waved frantically in the direction of the open sea. "Someone's out there! I just saw a head with brown hair."

"Crazy Yank," Shanley muttered and turned to leave.

"There it is again!"

Kevin grabbed her by the upper arm as she teetered unsteadily. "Amber, stop! You'll fall on those rocks."

"Look! Now there's two of them."

As he looked in the direction she indicated, Connor scoffed, "'Tis seals. The sea is full of 'em this time of year."

"No!"

Looking dangerously close to overwrought, she tried to

pull her arm away. Kevin was obliged to tighten his grip, but at the same time he tried to make his voice soothing. "Connor's right, luv. 'Tis only a pair of seals."

Shanley had paused when Amber cried out, but his expression was openly hostile. "And is your girlfriend a drunken sot, too? I s'pose next you'll be claiming those are selkies."

Kevin glared at the constable, but coaxed Amber gently. "C'mon, luv. We need to go."

"No, not until I find my brother!" She wrenched her arm away and stumbled in the direction the seals had gone.

"Amber, wait!" But she ignored him, of course, and hurried heedlessly over the wet rocks like the crazy woman the constable had pronounced her to be.

As he turned to go after her, Kevin saw Shanley throw up his hands in disgust and head back toward the ravine and the waiting car. For once, Connor wisely followed the constable.

After yelling her name one more time, Kevin concentrated on catching up with her. Crazy or not, he felt responsible for her, especially with the impending storm about to hit.

Much to his chagrin, though Amber moved haphazardly, she maintained a three- to four-meter distance from him for several long moments. Muttering a curse, he put his head down and redoubled his efforts.

In the five minutes he took, it started to rain. A few large drops fell slowly at first, but he knew what was coming. Looking about for some kind of shelter, he grabbed her round the waist and jerked her against the cliff face under a slight overhang. Before the cry of protest could erupt from her mouth, the storm opened up and rain pelted against them like a swarm of angry insects.

"Shite!" Kevin swore. "We need to find shelter fast. These waves will be hitting this cliff in another minute or two."

As if to punctuate the urgency of his words, the next wave foamed around their feet. He looked anxiously in the direction they'd just come, but the downpour obliterated everything more than a dozen meters away.

"No time to go back!" He gazed upward, but the climb looked nigh on impossible.

Perhaps if they tried going over a cluster of boulders blocking their path in the other direction...

"Is that barking?" Amber asked, head tilted, her hair glistening wetly scant millimeters from his chest.

"'Tis the seals. I think they're headed for shelter." He put a bit more space between them as another wave washed up onto their feet. They had to move now!

"C'mon!" He grabbed her hand and pulled her toward the boulders.

Being in the open proved much worse. The rain sluiced down like someone was emptying buckets on them. Going round the grouping of rocks would mean wading into knee-deep water, so they would have to go up. He had to let go of Amber's hand in order to steady himself as he climbed. She followed gamely, right on his heels.

Kevin could plainly hear the barking now, and it sounded like more than just a pair of seals. When he reached a gap in the rocks, he saw why.

The waves rushed into a narrow inlet gouged into the cliff face. Several brown heads bobbed and barked, while the animals waited for the next wave to wash them over the lip of a fissure in the rocks.

Amber's head popped up close to his shoulder. "Is that a sea cave?"

"Yes, and I hope there's room enough for us all."

They'd climbed a good five or six meters above the water. Far enough for a very nasty fall. Kevin inched sideways and down just a wee bit, then he paused to watch the seals ride a wave inside.

A flat top on the next boulder got them almost to the entrance as well. Amber had room to stand beside him.

"Eww!" She gasped. "What is that smell?"

"Seal dung, and rather a lot of it, I'd say." Kevin strained his eyes to see the interior, which appeared to be a large cavern. He hoped to high heaven that seals were the only things inside, because they had no other options. "'Tis a small price to pay for a dry place to wait out the storm. Follow me, carefully now!"

Chapter 4

NEARLY OVERCOME BY THE STENCH, AMBER FOLLOWED Kevin inside the cave without further protest. After climbing down and around a pointy sentinel of rock, they were out of the rain. She heaved a sigh of relief and almost choked on the overpowering odor.

They scrambled over a few more jutting rocks onto a stone ledge. A large pool of water spread below, and on the sandy shore opposite their perch lolled several dozen seals. Most were sleek, dark brown with mottled gray spots on their flanks, though a few were a pale off-white and resembled fat slugs. More than half seemed to be furry speckled babies, and the cave echoed with their cries.

Trying not to breathe too deeply, she leaned an elbow against an upright boulder and surveyed the interior. The shelf where they stood appeared to be the only flat spot on their side of the rocky cavern, and it looked too high for the seals in the pool to climb up.

She turned and saw Kevin had sat down, his back braced against another large rock. "Did you know about this place?"

He gave an impassive shrug. "The north coast is riddled with caves. They've been used by the seals and smugglers for centuries. Don't worry, if that lot could get up here, they'd already be lying about."

His explanation confirmed what she'd already guessed, but something else bothered her about this place…

About the seals...

She shook her head in an effort to clear it. The dim light and the bad smell must be getting to her. "How long do you think the storm will last?"

Kevin shrugged again. "If we're lucky, we'll be back in Malin Head for tea. If not, we could be here all night."

The thought sent a shiver through her.

All right, maybe it wasn't just the thought, because once she started shivering, she couldn't seem to stop. Water dripped from the edges of her hair down the back of her thin, already soaked blouse.

She didn't realize Kevin had moved until his fingertips glided over her bare arm. "You're chilled to the bone."

Unable to protest over the chattering of her teeth, Amber watched him unbutton his wool shirt. Once he had it off, he pressed it into her hand, then in one fluid motion, pulled his T-shirt over his head.

"Take off your wet top and put on this then," he said swapping the T for the plaid wool in her hand.

Mouth agape, she stood momentarily mesmerized by the sculpted muscles of his bare chest. Then he shoved his arms into the sleeves of the wool shirt and turned discreetly away.

Heat crawled up her neck to her face and abated her shivering. Nevertheless, her fingers fumbled with the buttons on her blouse, and she wound up jerking it over her head. Since it was wet anyway, she used the bottom to blot water off her hair before she pulled Kevin's T-shirt over her head.

The soft cotton knit felt slightly damp and still warm from the heat of his body. His scent clung to the material along with traces of the earthy smell of peat—a huge improvement over seal manure!

"All right, then?" Kevin asked.

Amber nodded then realized he wasn't looking at her. "Yes, thanks."

She turned to spread her wet blouse over the protruding rock she'd been leaning against. Maybe that would help the material dry out.

The skin on the back of her neck prickled with the unmistakable feeling of eyes following her movements. But when she sneaked a glance in Kevin's direction, he stood facing away from her, staring out the entrance into the storm.

The feeling persisted, and she looked down into the pool. A lone seal bobbed close to the rocky wall, looking up at the shelf where she stood. A magnetic pull drew Amber close to the edge of the rock, her gaze riveted on the animal. The seal stared back, sorrow and wisdom shining in its large, dark eyes. The pale bristles around its mouth twitched, as if it wanted to tell her something.

Amber knelt in an effort to get closer to the animal and stared down into its eyes. She felt as if she could lose herself in the liquid brown depths of the seal's compelling gaze.

Time and place fell away. Sensations swamped Amber that were not her own, but not totally foreign either.

The ceaseless movement of water.

The grit of sand.

Feelings of safety overlaid infinite sadness and loss.

Separating and recognizing the flood of images and feelings overwhelmed her, until she saw a figure huddled above on a rock and realized she was seeing herself.

Somehow, she had tapped into the seal's mind. The knowledge almost broke the connection, but Amber quickly reached out as she'd done so many times with her brother. Mentally striving to maintain the slender thread between herself and the animal, she sent back her own feelings of anxiety, distress over the missing part of her. An image of Parker shimmered from her mind and a moment later came back, but strangely altered.

She saw her brother struggling underwater, a roiling brown mass of limbs and flippers. She felt the frantic clutching of his fingers, the weight of his body being towed through seething waves, while harsh noises crescendoed and receded. Then he lay prone on the sand, his flesh clammy cold until warm, wet bodies huddled around him, and his slow breaths fell into rhythm with theirs.

"Amber, don't!"

The sharp command jolted through her head and broke the connection. To her surprise, she found herself on her stomach, leaning over the edge of the rock, arm extended toward the pool.

She jerked her hand back just as Kevin said, "They may look tame, but they're wild animals and fiercely protective when they have young."

At his words, the seal dove underwater and resurfaced at the sandy shore. When she hauled out of the water with awkward, labored movements, Amber saw several jagged scars marring her sleek brown hide along with a couple of bald patches.

"She's too old for young ones anymore," she murmured too low for Kevin to hear. *But her maternal instincts had saved Parker's life.*

"Are you sure you're all right?" Kevin towered over her like a colossus, undisputed master of this domain.

"I'm fine. I just…" She blinked before she reached for his offered hand. "I'm fine."

Skepticism shone plainly on his handsome face as she rose to her feet. He backed up a couple of paces, tugging on her hand. "Let's sit over here, shall we?"

A nice safe distance from the edge.

She knew his thoughts as plainly as if he'd spoken.

Their hands still clasped, he folded his legs under him to settle with his back against the rock wall. Amber followed suit and sat next to him, tucking her legs under her. Though Kevin let go of her hand, their arms still touched from shoulder to elbow.

With her senses heightened, the wool of his shirt-sleeve prickled uncomfortably on her strip of bare skin where the T-shirt sleeve ended. Unease crawled like a column of ants down her spine, while the pungent air seemed to thicken into a miasma of desire, uncertainty, and angst that wasn't all hers.

Not hers?

Amber jerked her head at the realization, and Kevin's lips skidded across hers as their noses collided. He huffed out a surprised breath, crystal blue eyes filling her own field of vision. And in that instant, she got a fast, frightening glimpse into his soul.

Guilt, self-recrimination, sorrow, need, and a healthy dose of pure lust slammed into her mind in the split second before she squeezed her eyes shut and severed the connection.

But one of Kevin's hands was at the back of her head, his fingers tunneling into her damp hair, and his other hand was around her waist, pulling her against him. When his mouth settled atop hers, Amber's own yearning and sexual attraction surged to the forefront.

She met his hot, probing tongue with her own, eagerly giving herself over to the sensual heat she hadn't felt in a very long time. His kiss was urgent and a little rough, the stubble of his beard rasping against her chin. That same edge of wildness appealed to her too and drove her to press hard with not just her lips, but her breasts. After such a long absence, the feelings of desire and being desired were more than a little intoxicating, and she succumbed, quickly becoming a willing participant.

A tiny flicker of golden light shone through the red haze of pain enveloping Parker. What felt like fifty-pound weights dragged at his eyelids and made blinking a chore akin to the labors of Hercules. But somehow he managed to do it.

The little yellow light still hovered on the edge of his vision.

Not an illusion after all?

Parker tried to take a deep breath to help focus his eyes. But the task of breathing felt every bit as arduous as blinking and the weight on his chest ten times heavier.

He must be alive because being dead couldn't possibly hurt this much. His knees, hips, and shoulders all ached in sharp protest when he tried to move, and the throbbing pain in his head felt as if his skull had split apart.

But the light taunted him. Made him center his attention. Try to think.

Where was he?

What had happened?

Gradually, he became aware of the scratchy scrape of a woven blanket on his bare skin and a smoother fabric under him. Even with his shallow breaths, he could smell an odd scent of smoke mixed with earth. Overhead came the unmistakable patter of rain.

Rain…

He remembered being in a downpour. Water everywhere, not just rain.

Sea water.

The memory of a cracking retort of a pistol and the sharp sear of pain as the bullet grazed his flesh made Parker flinch and then groan aloud with the effort. He tried to lift his hand and touch his side, explore the trail of the bullet. But moving hurt too damn much, and all he could manage was to twitch his fingers and groan again, the sound raspy and hoarse as it rattled from his dry throat.

A vague rustling sound mingled with the drumming of the rain. Parker thought he might have imagined it, but then a muted voice hissed, "Meri, he's awake! The selkie prince is awake!"

Someone was here!

Parker slammed his eyes shut and held his breath, praying it wasn't the goons with guns.

Light footsteps tapped on a hard floor, and a low voice spoke. Though too quiet for Parker to distinguish the words, the singsong Irish cadence was unmistakable.

"His eyes were open, and he made some moaning sounds." The first voice spoke again with the squeaky excitement of a child.

Slowly, Parker exhaled in relief while the second voice murmured in an admonishing tone, "…eyes open but not awake…"

"'Twas different this time," the child insisted, then impatiently interrupted the second speaker. "I'll just slip in and have a look then."

"No, Ronan!" The order was loud and definitely female. Parker cringed a little in spite of himself.

The mother perhaps?

"Awww! Why not?" the child, Ronan, whined.

"Because!" She hissed in a tone that practically shouted sister. "I'll do it. 'Tis time to give him some tea anyway."

"Shall I get…" Ronan's voice faded as did both their footsteps.

Parker opened his eyes to the yellow candle glow and strained to make out his surroundings. The mattress under him appeared to be lying directly on the floor. His head, shoulders, and torso were propped at almost a forty-five degree angle with multiple pillows and cushions. A blanket was tucked around him from toes to chin.

The candle sat in a dish on top of a wooden crate just beyond his reach, not that he had the strength or the energy to reach for it.

How long had he been here?

Before he could tax his poor aching brain for answers, he heard the footsteps coming back. As he moved his eyes over the roughly whitewashed walls in what he guessed must be the direction of the door, his rescuer walked in.

In faded jeans and an oversized striped T-shirt, she could have easily been one of his junior high students. She didn't look more than thirteen with a childish face and gangly arms and legs she hadn't quite grown into. One hand gripped a mug with the handle of a spoon sticking out of it.

Her eyes met his in cool appraisal. Then she dipped awkwardly in what almost looked like a curtsey.

"Your highness, you're awake."

Behind her and out of his line of vision, Parker heard the child whisper, "Told ya!"

"Shush!" the girl ordered over her shoulder, dark blonde ponytail trailing across her cheek. Then she addressed him again. "I'm Meriol Lafferty, and I've brought you some tea."

As she moved to kneel at his bedside, a smaller, younger child bounced into the room and executed a stiff bow. "And I'm Ronan Lafferty, Prince Highness. I was named for you since Da says Ronan means seal."

"Shhh!" The girl hissed with a severe glance at her brother. "I told you to wait outside!"

Parker struggled to push words out of his parched throat. "Um Par-her," he slurred, unable to enunciate the hard "k" sound. "Where um…"

The boy gave another bow. "You're in our cottage, of course, your highness Prince Par-her. We found you in the selkie cave three days ago. You were hurt so we brought you here in the sled. We couldn't lift you into the main part of the house so—"

"Shut your mouth, Ronan, before I shut it for you!" the girl interrupted.

The child snapped his mouth closed and backed away. The girl leaned toward Parker, offering a steaming spoonful of liquid from the cup. "A wee bit of tea will help your throat, Prince Par-her."

Obediently, Parker opened his mouth, but when he

swallowed, the strong burn of alcohol caused him to give a wheezing cough.

"I added a drop of Da's whiskey," the girl, Meriol, explained, offering another spoonful. "To ease your pain."

Crissakes! The shit tasted like 100 proof!

Maybe that was his problem, a massive hangover.

He swallowed another spoonful anyway. And a third. Then felt noticeably better for it.

After the fourth, he tried his voice again. "Where are your parents?"

Meriol's pale eyes widened in surprise as if he'd asked her to walk on water or something. She blinked twice before she said, "Our mum died almost three years ago, and our da's a fisherman so he's gone a lot. He'll be home soon, I expect."

"So he doesn't know I'm here," Parker hadn't meant to speak aloud. Their father could be one of the guys with guns.

As Meriol nodded slowly, Ronan piped up, "Prince Par-her! Are you a Yankee selkie?"

"Par-*Ker*," he corrected the boy. "My name's Parker, and yes, I'm a Yankee."

The pain throbbing in his head and throughout his body increased a notch. None of this made sense.

Had their father shot him?

Why did they think he was a prince?

And what the hell was a selkie?

He squeezed his eyes shut and cast about in his mind, trying to form coherent thoughts. A tumble of confusing images bombarded him: water, dark shapes, pain…

Then in the midst of the chaos he felt it. The connection that had comforted him for as long as he could remember. The twin who completed his being as much as an arm or a leg. He reached mentally and discovered Amber was close.

Shock made his eyes fly open, severed the fragile link. Not only was his sister nearby, she was engaged in a serious lip-lock with someone!

———※———

The taste and feel of a warm, willing woman stirred feelings in Kevin that he'd believed—fervently hoped—long dead and buried. Feelings that would lead to terrible pain, for if he could awaken these, then far darker and more dreadful memories could come back too.

But the sweet taste of Amber O'Neill's tongue, the insistent press of her lovely soft breasts, ignited a firestorm that incinerated everything but his need to lose himself inside her. His fingers worked their way under the T-shirt and traced a path along her lower back.

She was the one who broke away with a gasp. "Parker! He's alive! He's here!"

Kevin gaped, his mind still in a lust-induced stupor. Though having Amber cry out another man's name, even her brother's, effectively squelched his raging libido.

While she scrambled to her feet, he looked around the confines of their rocky ledge as if he expected her missing brother to materialize from the air. Amber, too, twisted this way and that, searching frantically, both hands at her temples. Her cries seemed to disturb the seals, for a harsh chorus of barking echoed below them.

Finally back in his right mind, Kevin gained his feet and put a restraining hand on her arm.

"I felt him just now, in my mind," she insisted, panting as if she'd run a footrace. "He's here with the seals, or at least he was."

In truth, he was breathing heavy too, same as her. He let go of her and dropped his gaze to his feet.

"I'm sorry, I…" But he wasn't sorry he'd done it. "I mean, I apologize for…"

"I'm not sorry," she said in that flip way Americans all seemed to have. "And I didn't think it was bad enough that you need to apologize."

Completely gobsmacked, he backed away. "I promise you it won't happen again."

But even as the words passed his lips, the long dormant but now fully engaged and desperate part of him doubted he could keep such a promise. Just like all those promises he'd made to Caitlin. And to himself.

Amber, however, didn't appear to have heard him at all. She nervously paced the length of the rock ledge and back. "Isn't there a way we can go down there with the seals?"

A wave of protectiveness such as he hadn't felt in years washed over Kevin, and he spoke without thinking. "'Tis not safe. They're wild creatures, and they could easily hurt you."

"But they didn't hurt Parker, and he was right down there with them. In fact, they saved him." With her arms crossed and in the obviously too large T-shirt, she looked and sounded like an argumentative child.

He answered her like she was a child, a sure way to distance himself from the sensual responses she stirred

within him. "Well, he's not down there now. And
precisely how is it that you know what happened then?"

"The old one in the pool?" She closed her eyes and
took a deep breath. "She told me."

"The seal talked to you?"

*Heaven only knew what crazy thing she would say
next. How could one so lovely and tempting one moment
be so totally 'round the bend the next?*

Without being aware of his action, Kevin backed away.

"Not in so many words, but I saw and felt what
took place with my brother. I guess I tapped into
her mind." Pain flashed in her golden eyes as they
measured the growing distance between them. "I
know it sounds crazy, and nothing like this has ever
happened to me before."

And nothing like her had ever happened to him
before. Did that make them even then?

"I'm sorry, I just..." She threw up her hands in frustration. "I'm so confused!"

They were even on that count as well. His back
touched the wall of rocks, and he slid down to a sitting
position, scooting to an angle. If he put more distance
between them so that she couldn't sit next to him perhaps
he could make sense of what was going on.

"The seals should leave once the storm lets up,"
he said in an effort to placate her. "Then we'll have a
look 'round."

She said nothing, but started pacing again. As
Kevin silently watched her movements, they became
hypnotic. Or perhaps just lack of sleep made his
eyelids droop.

Before he knew it, he'd dozed off, and images of

Caitlin invaded his unconscious mind. Except fair-haired, blue-eyed Caitlin morphed into Amber, who in turn, changed into a selkie. Dark, beautiful, and dangerous.

As the sleek creature tried to lure him into the waves, a rough shake jerked Kevin from the disturbing confines of his dream. His eyes flew open and he looked straight into Amber's golden gaze.

"The rain's nearly stopped," she said. "And the seals are leaving."

Ignoring her offered hand, he struggled upright and saw that the sheets of water at the cave entrance were now reduced to rivulets. Late afternoon sunlight glittered off the drops and the waves beyond them, making him shield his eyes as he stumbled a few steps in his still squelchy shoes.

The tide had pulled back the crashing waves and cut off the pool. Amid intermittent barks, the seals hauled themselves across the sand and into the sea.

"Can we go now?"

Amber's question drew Kevin's attention back to her. She'd pulled her damp blouse over his T-shirt, but hadn't buttoned it. Her hair, though not completely dry, no longer clung in wet, ropy tendrils. Her pretty face looked strained with fatigue and worry.

"Yes, but we need to take care."

Silently she followed him to the cave entrance. Through the drizzle, they picked their way down to the rocky lip that separated the pool and the sea. Since everything was soaked and slippery, their progress proved slow. Plus Kevin kept a watchful eye on the remaining seals. Only a half-dozen adults, all with calves, lay on the sand well away from the cave entrance.

One lone straggler limped toward the waves. Kevin stopped and waited for the creature to pass. Amber bumped into him from behind, and when he reached out a hand to steady her—

The seal turned.

He could have sworn that electricity crackled through the air, but such a thing wasn't possible. Only a crazy man would have said that the seal looked first at Amber, then deliberately turned to gaze back across the sand. Finally it swiveled its head toward a clump of short boulders near the opposite entrance to the cave before it crawled into the surf.

Beneath his fingers, Amber's shoulder quivered. He couldn't tell if rain or tears glittered on the edges of her eyelashes, but she dashed them away with the back of her hand. Then she scrambled around him and rushed the remaining distance to the sand.

"Careful!" he called after her.

Luckily, the seal had disappeared before Amber got off the rocks, and the others didn't seem the least bit interested in her. Kevin caught up to her as she stood beside the edge of the pool staring at the cave floor. All about, the dry sand had indentations and gouges from the comings and goings of the animals.

"Parker was here!" Amber insisted, her pretty face determined, shadows haunting her golden eyes. "But then someone came and…" Her voice trailed away, and her gaze skittered over the churned up sand before settling on the clump of boulders. "I'm not crazy, Kevin! Swear to God, I'm not."

Heaven knew he wanted to believe her, but he couldn't squeeze the lie out of his throat.

"We need to get back to the village," he said instead. "Get some hot food and dry clothes."

Shying away from his outstretched hand, she tramped across the sand toward the boulders. With a heavy sigh, he followed. The direction she was headed was closer to Malin Head anyway, and another path undoubtedly led up to the road between the village and here.

The rain and the waves had swept smooth the sand around the half-buried boulders just as Kevin suspected. A few pieces of driftwood, hunks of seaweed, and other debris lay tangled in the crevices around the rocks. If anyone had been through here, even as recently as this morning, no trace of their passing remained.

While he breathed in a large draught of fresh, clean air, Amber sunk to her knees in the wet sand at the base of the closest rock. She clapped both palms flat against the sides of her head and squeezed her eyes shut.

Still trying to contact her brother.

It was on the tip of his tongue to suggest they try kissing again. Just to taunt her, of course. But then he heard the familiar spluttering sound of an outboard motor. Shading his eyes, he took two steps toward the breaking waves and scanned the sea for the noise's source.

Through the remaining mist of rain, he spied the jutting black prow of the curragh at the same moment a shrill cry rang out. "Hallo! Kevin! Hallo! Amber!"

For the first time in the ten hours since they'd met, Kevin was genuinely glad to see Connor Magee. The boy stood and waved his cap in the air, while someone else, undoubtedly Michael Coyle, sat in the stern of the boat steering it.

Connor shouted again, and Kevin waved back.

"We're about to be rescued," he called over his shoulder to Amber while the curragh angled toward shore.

A note of hysteria tinged her voice. "I can't leave until I find Parker."

Turning his back on the waves, Kevin walked over and lightly touched her damp curling hair. "You're wet, tired, and you've eaten nothing since breakfast. Besides, 'twill be dark soon, and you won't be able to find anything."

Her shoulders slumped and her head drooped in defeat. Behind him, Kevin heard the hull of the curragh scraping on sand. A moment later, Connor raced up to them.

"Kevin! Amber! I told Uncle Michael we'd find you," the boy breathlessly exclaimed. As Amber rose slowly to her feet, Connor cocked his head, regarded her a moment, then looked at Kevin. "Is that your shirt?"

A rosy glow colored Amber's cheeks as she nodded. "Mine was soaked before we found the cave."

Raising his eyebrow at Kevin, Connor thrust his broad-brimmed canvas hat at her. "Here. Would ya like my slicker too?"

"C'mon!" Michael Coyle called out from the beached curragh. "You can talk later."

"Stall the ball half a minute," Connor yelled back. He plunked the hat on Amber's head and grasped her by the elbow. "'Tis only a short ride back to Malin Head."

While Connor towed Amber toward the curragh, Kevin took one more quick glance up the small crescent of sand.

Empty.

But then his gaze moved over the rocks. Sticking up in the midst of the greenish-brown kelp, he spotted an object that didn't belong: a shoe.

A large shoe. The red and gray treads on the sole were unmistakably those of a trainer.

An American trainer.

Chapter 5

KEVIN WASN'T ABOUT TO TELL AMBER ABOUT THE SHOE. He knew it must be her brother's; nobody in these parts wore American shoes. But in his experience, a shoe washed up on a deserted stretch of beach did not bode well for the owner.

Not that Amber would believe him if he did tell her. She would start ranting on about this psychic connection and talking to seals, and Michael Coyle and the rest of the villagers would be ready to lock her up as a nut job. And perhaps they were right.

Heaven knew it shouldn't matter to him. It was none of his concern. But she'd come to him lost, alone, and pleading for his help. Him, of all people.

Somehow, she'd managed to stir feelings in his dead and blackened soul.

His.

And God help him, he intended to protect her.

At least the presence of the shoe proved that a Yank with quite large feet had recently been in the vicinity of Malin Head. Even if he was now sleeping with the fishes, he had been here and wasn't just some figment of a woman's overwrought imagination.

Her thin blouse flapping in the breeze created by their movement, Amber huddled silently in the bow of the curragh, looking wet, bedraggled, and exhausted. Connor asked a string of questions about the cave, the seals… and did she know anything about selkies? But she seemed too weary to muster up any answers.

Undaunted, the youth started recounting the old tales of selkies who shed their seal skins in the moonlight and walked among people, passing for human until they donned their magical coats once more.

"Leave off already!" Michael Coyle groused. "The lady ain't interested, and neither are we."

Connor shot him a withering look.

Kevin pretty much shared the boy's opinion. Something about Coyle bothered him, but he did owe the man for coming out to look for Amber and him.

"Thanks for the ride back to Malin Head." He tried not to let his distaste for the other man color his tone.

Coyle snorted. "Yon wee gobshite wouldn't stop yammering 'til I did. Never gives me a moment's peace, that one. 'Tis no wonder my brother and his missus dumped him on me."

"Like I wanted to spend my summer holiday in this Godforsaken end of nowhere with a bogger like you," Connor muttered too low for Coyle to hear.

"Shanley wasn't too pleased that you dragged him out here for nothing," Coyle informed Kevin.

He bristled at the other man's words. "'Twasn't for nothing." He glared at Coyle. "You're the one with a missing curragh."

"Bloody tourists lose 'em all the time. I expect it'll turn up one of these days."

"And the man who rented it?"

"Ain't none o' my concern. Yours neither." He cast a narrow-eyed look at Amber before he made a dismissive sound in the back of his throat.

Kevin's fingers clenched against his palms, but the curragh was within the breakwater, almost to the Malin Head pier. No point in letting Coyle aggravate him any further, so he said nothing.

Coyle cut the motor just as they came abreast of the wooden ladder used for loading and unloading passengers. Connor secured the prow and scampered up the ladder, offering his hand to help a still silent Amber.

Kevin followed, actually feeling a sliver of sympathy for Connor. Nevertheless, Kevin was glad the boy didn't follow them up the street. The Rover was parked just where he'd left it at noon, but rather than going directly home, he steered Amber inside Donahue's to the promise of hot food.

Since the Friday night crowd, if the group of locals could be called that, hadn't arrived yet, Kevin settled Amber into a snug booth in the far corner. After getting into the curragh, she'd scarcely spoken a dozen words. He hoped a hot meal and dry clothes would help cure up her gloomy dejection. As he headed to the bar to ask Charlie Donahue for the former, doubt nagged at him.

In spite of her rather outlandish claims of mental telepathy, Amber was a bright woman. Perhaps she'd begun to suspect the same thing he did, that her brother had drowned.

The squish of Kevin's soggy shoes brought the image of the American trainer back to the forefront of his mind. Maybe Parker O'Neill's body would wash up on the beach too. Or more likely, it was hung up on the rocks somewhere along the jagged shoreline, and might never be found. Either way, he and Amber were both too done in to go searching tonight. Tomorrow would be plenty soon enough.

Donahue was happy to be rid of the lamb stew left over from lunch. Besides the two heaping bowls to eat now, he dished the rest into a plastic container for them to take for later. Paying for only two meals, Kevin expressed his surprised thanks at the publican's generosity.

As he approached the table, Kevin saw Amber quickly drop her hands from her head to her lap. Obviously, she had tried to contact her brother again, and the look of despair in her golden eyes told him the results.

Kevin emptied his bowl with the finesse and timing of a stray dog, then sipped a second mug of tea while he waited for her to finish her meal. Though her demeanor remained dispirited, Amber ate steadily, if somewhat mechanically.

By the time they left the pub, the sun dipped toward the choppy, windswept sea, and streamers of dark clouds raced overhead.

"I guess you were right about not being able to find anything tonight," she said with a depressed sigh.

"We'll go out again at first light." He tried to sound more positive than he felt. Heaven knew why he should be responsible for her well-being, but the weight of that obligation sat firmly between his shoulder blades.

In spite of the rough road, Amber's chin drooped against her chest before they reached the cottage. Sending her in to have a hot shower, he got the peat fire going, and then helped himself to another bowl of stew. He'd just scraped up the last bite when she eased into the kitchen, a towel wrapped round her hair and wearing his ratty old bathrobe.

She looked damn fine in it, too.

"More stew?" he asked, trying not to see if she wore anything under the tightly cinched robe.

Amber shook her head. "But is it all right if I wash my clothes? I didn't bring a lot with me."

"I'll do it," he replied. "You're practically asleep on your feet. Besides, the washer's a wee bit temperamental."

Though she didn't look happy about it, she reluctantly agreed. He had a lot harder time convincing her to sleep in the bedroom. She finally acquiesced when he flat out lied and said he would wake her up when he'd finished with the wash and other chores. Knowing she was in the next room was not going to be conducive to sleep, but Kevin couldn't tell her that. And another kiss like the one they'd shared in the cave would end in disaster, he was certain.

He'd proved an utter failure at being a husband, father, or even a decent man, and had spent almost four years generally avoiding all relationships. The first two and a half, he hid in an alcoholic stupor like a sniveling coward. But though he'd managed to remain sober these long fourteen months, he knew he wasn't fit for human companionship and might never be. No matter how much parts of him might argue differently.

Amber's eyes flew open, and she sat up in bed, wide awake. In the ten seconds it took her to remember where she was, she found the switch on the battery-powered lamp and stared at her digital wristwatch in the harsh glare of light.

3:28 a.m. Kevin had not woken her up. *Damn him!*

Her bare feet hit the cold stone floor, and she pulled his flannel robe on over her thin cotton nightshirt. She carried the light with her rather than risk tripping over anything on her way to the bathroom. She'd noticed earlier that only the back rooms of the cottage had electricity.

As she tiptoed through the living room, she could see his tall frame sprawled across the sofa in front of the fireplace. One arm hung down so that his fingers trailed across the braided rug next to the hearth, and air huffed gently through his mouth with each breath. The smell of the spent peat fire still lingered in the air.

When she reached the bathroom, Amber left the lamp on top of the washer. He'd spread her clean clothes and a few of his across the wooden rack to dry in a quaint little domestic scene that made her squirm with discomfort.

How many generations of her O'Neill ancestors had lived exactly this way? And why did seeing such a simplistic lifestyle bother her?

After relieving herself, she washed her hands and splashed cold water on her face in an effort to banish the dull ache that throbbed behind her eyeballs. But the pain persisted, along with the frustration of being unable to make the mind connection with her brother.

She'd been dreaming of Parker just before she awakened. Disquieting dreams of him thrashing in the water while loud noises and dark shapes pursued him... Parker lying with the seals, unresponsive, then being dragged away by murky shapes with shrill voices.

The dreams had been spawned by her link with the old seal, she was certain. But she couldn't understand how she'd managed to make that weird connection and not be able to make the familiar one with her brother. The more she thought about it, the more her head throbbed. And the more insistent grew her fear that Parker might not be all right.

Refusing to acknowledge that fear, Amber rushed out of the bathroom, grabbed the light, and stumbled into the kitchen. A glance out the window confirmed that it was still too dark to leave the cottage. Thanks to jet lag and an eight-hour time difference, she'd already slept for nine hours.

Now what?

She set the lamp on the kitchen counter and listened for the faraway sound of the crashing waves. After a long, silent moment, she felt rather than heard Kevin behind her. She turned.

"Are you all right?" he asked in a sleep-fogged voice.

Amber's libido gave a lusty surge. With his dark hair mussed and his T-shirt half in and half out of his unbuttoned jeans, he looked more like a dream than a man. Every woman's wet dream. Her treacherous mind leapfrogged back to the seals' cave to replay the hot thrust of Kevin's tongue and the solid warmth of his chest pressed against her.

"I'm fine," she said, brushing past him. "Sorry I woke you up."

The light cast bouncy, erratic shadows as she tramped into the living room. She set it on the table next to the sofa before she plopped down. Her feet were cold, so she drew them under her, and pulled the blanket Kevin had used across her lap.

He came in, rubbing sleep from his eyes, and sat on the opposite end of the sofa. Her fingers strayed inadvertently across her chin as she remembered the prickly rub of his beard when they'd kissed.

She'd been an idiot to stop.

"Go on back to bed then," he said, tilting his head in the direction of the bedroom.

"That's your bed. You're the one who needs to be sleeping in it." She stretched out her legs so that her toes touched his jean-clad thigh. *Or maybe not sleeping.* "You were supposed to wake me up."

His eyes smoldered dark indigo as they traveled slowly from her feet up to her face. "Guess I forgot."

Amber made a tsking sound. "You're lying to me, Kevin." Her gaze dropped to his beautifully shaped mouth while she leaned toward him. He'd promised not to kiss her again. He couldn't be serious. "What else have you lied about?"

His lips compressed into a tight, flat line, and when she lifted her eyes to his a sudden flash cut across her mind. An object half-buried in the sand? Could it be a sneaker? It passed too quickly for her to be sure. Besides, she didn't really care because her mind was occupied elsewhere.

He blinked twice. "I… What…"

"This?" she breathed, her fingers clutching his T-shirt and her lips finding his.

Her tongue touched his and the same image flashed again. But this time, it was long enough for her to recognize both the shoe and the beach. They jerked apart and stared at each other.

"M-my brother's shoe?" she sputtered.

"What the bloody hell was that?" Kevin demanded at the same time.

"Did you see Parker's shoe on the beach?"

"Did you just read my mind?"

She suddenly realized her hands were fisted in his shirt. Letting go, she stared dumbfounded at her curled fingers, the full impact of what had just happened slamming into her. Mouth agape, she swayed against him, and he gripped her shoulders to steady her.

"You did, didn't you?" Kevin's look of horror made her feel like a sideshow freak. "You read me just like you did that poor bloody seal."

"I-I didn't mean to." Oh God, maybe she was a freak, or a bigger one than she knew. "I've never been able to… Except with Parker. Only him, I swear."

Kevin's voice was deadly calm, but his fingers dug into her flesh. "Stay out of my head, Amber. You won't like what you find in there."

A sob clogged her throat, and she covered her face with her hands to force it back down. She hated to cry, because once she started, she couldn't stop.

"I don't…" she whispered brokenly between her fingers, "…don't know why… this is happening…"

He let go of her, then after a long, silent moment he tentatively touched the hair curling at her temple. "Perhaps because your brother is dead?"

Amber shook her head, tried to speak, but instead of words, that pesky sob burst out. Then to her utter humiliation, a whole string of them followed, along with tears. *Oh hell!* The one thing she did not want to happen.

Kevin put both hands on her forearms, forced them down, and then pulled her across the sofa. She sprawled into his lap, wrapped her arms around his torso, and laid her head against his chest. He felt warm, solid, and safe, and so she gave herself up to the crying jag and let it run its course.

Eventually, the steady beating of his heart in her ear soothed her into intermittent hiccuping sobs. Her cheek and his T-shirt under it were sticky and moist, but Kevin's chin rested on the top of her head, and she didn't want to break the comfortable intimacy of their embrace. She needed human contact, to know that she was still alive, to not feel so desolate and alone.

It had been so very long since she'd let herself touch and be touched. So very long since she'd wanted to…

"'Tis a very long time for me too," Kevin murmured.

Amber's breath hitched, and she stiffened with surprise. Had she actually spoken aloud? Had he?

She pulled away and stared into the smoldering blue depths of his eyes. And she saw right through to his heart and mind. Not since she and Parker had been young children had another person been so open and vulnerable to her scrutiny. Her brother's was the only soul she'd seen laid so bare, back in the days before life became complicated with secrets.

Now Kevin's every thought and memory were exposed. He knew how to withdraw into himself physically and verbally, but he knew nothing of shielding his mind. He'd been right, there were dark places inside him, just as ugly shadows lurked within her. It seemed only right to allow him equal access, to trust him with her innermost secrets in the same way she intended to keep his.

She could see both of them standing on the edge of their own personal darkness. Reaching out, she filled Kevin's thoughts with the same images.

Pain, death, and guilt swirled through his. The emotions seemed to center on a petite blonde woman and a tiny baby in a glass case filled with tubes and wires. Hurt and betrayal filled Amber's own blackness along with the father who had rejected her, the psychiatrists who treated her like a lab animal, and her ex-husband, Josh, who'd used and discarded her.

Writhing with discomfort, she struggled to pull open her long-held barriers and keep herself as exposed to Kevin's scrutiny as he remained to her. The chasm filled with their worst agonies yawned between them.

He didn't retreat. Not on any level.

With a burst of hope, longing, and need, she leapt. And kissed him.

After one brief instant of shock, Kevin kissed her back, his own desire and yearning spilling into her mind in a torrent. She answered with her own rush of passion and the sweet assurance of acceptance. Momentarily startled again, his tongue stopped its erotic probing, and he jerked back, breaking the kiss.

You deserve better than me. His guilt-laced thought echoed between them.

What I deserve might not be what I want, Amber answered, filled with exhilaration at their sudden and potent connection.

Impulsively, she dropped her lips to his jaw and sprinkled a line of moist kisses back toward his ear. Then she reached into his mind once more, and at the same time she whispered, "The past is gone. I want you now. No past. No future. Now."

With a groan of surrender, Kevin rose to his feet. As he scooped her into his arms, a blast of raw sexual need burned away any lingering thoughts she might have had. A moment later, they were in the bedroom where he deposited her in the middle of the disheveled bed.

The only light came from the faint glow of the lamp in the living room. She fumbled with the tie on the robe she wore. He'd divested himself of everything but his boxers by the time she finally got the knot undone. She stopped to stare, one arm still inside the sleeve of the robe.

Even in the near darkness, she could see the gorgeously defined muscles of his chest and the sprinkling of dark hair across his pecs that tapered to a thin line down his flat stomach. A small white scar stood in testament to a long ago appendectomy, the lone blemish on his otherwise perfect form. The jut of his erection against the thin material of his boxers made her hot and wet with anticipation.

One swipe of his hand sent the dangling robe to the floor. His other hand caught the hem of her nightshirt and lifted. Panting, she wiggled and pulled the garment over her head, her breasts bouncing free. But only for a moment, before Kevin quickly captured one in each hand.

"So beautiful..." he whispered as he swirled his tongue around first one nipple and then the other.

The touch sent a jolt of desire racing through Amber that ignited every nerve ending in her body and leapt straight from her mind to his.

"Sweet saints!" He groaned as the shared pleasure struck him.

Then she shoved her hand inside his elastic waistband and gripped his shaft in a firm stroke that nearly overwhelmed both of them with the doubly magnified intensity.

"God in heaven," Kevin panted. "How are you—" He broke off as she stroked him again while nibbling her way across his abdomen.

The feelings seared from his mind into hers and brought her to a gasping halt.

"I don't know," she admitted when she found enough breath to speak. "Do you want me to stop?"

"God, no! But can we slow down so I don't finish before we've scarcely started?"

She couldn't suppress a small bubble of laughter. "I'm almost there myself." Then she guided his hand to show him.

When he stripped away her panties and touched the hot core of her, Amber shuddered. The caress of his fingers inside brought her to the moaning brink of orgasm.

He rolled away, leaving her teetering on the edge. She whimpered in protest, too overcome to do anything else.

Impatient little Yank. His thought was a gentle touch in her mind as he rummaged in the drawer of the nightstand.

She ran her finger halfway down the length of his back. *Yes! I want you now!* She didn't try to hide her urgency.

When he crawled back to the center of the bed, he'd shed his boxers and put on a condom. With a languid smile, he kissed the sensitive skin behind her ear.

Slowly, luv. Another teasing admonishment, while Kevin feathered his lips and tongue down her neck and across her collarbone. His fingers made lazy circles on her thighs.

Lust and need coiled tight and throbbed within her. She fed every sensation back to him, so that by the time he reached her breast, he'd abandoned all pretense of leisure. Panting, she wrapped her legs around his waist.

With a low growl of possession, Kevin lifted his head to claim her mouth, thrusting his tongue between her lips at the same time he pushed his hard length inside her.

Pleasure exploded like a hundred bursting skyrockets. She could no longer tell which feelings were hers and which were his. She only knew she'd never experienced an orgasm quite like the one beckoning just beyond the edge of her consciousness. Their fierce, frantic rhythm sent them into a wild spiral of passion.

Mind and body melding perfectly with Kevin's, Amber let herself burst into a million tiny fragments and found in the release that she felt more complete than she could ever remember feeling.

The sudden, chilly emptiness next to him brought Kevin to instant awareness. In the aftermath of their love-making, Amber had managed to sever the mind connection between them. The resulting vacant abyss inside left him shaken and weaker than a newborn lamb. He'd drifted off with Amber's satiny, naked body cuddled against him, but now she wasn't there.

He sat up and cast about in the diffused light shining through the curtains. Snagging his T-shirt off the floor, he replayed a bit of the intense pleasure that had surged between them, and just the fleeting thought made him hard.

Heaven help him, he'd never had an experience quite like that! But he knew all about craving something so badly that you would surely die without it, and didn't care if you did. That kind of obsession led to madness. If being connected to her brother was anything like what had passed between the two of them, then no wonder she acted strange.

Amber said she'd never made a mental link with anyone else either. Did that mean her brother was dead, and somehow her telepathic powers had transferred to him?

As he pulled on first his boxers, and then his jeans, Kevin considered the ramifications of such a thing. Though having himself so exposed and vulnerable to another person scared him, in truth, all he could think was that there were far worse fates than having his mind, and likewise, his body bonded with Amber's, if only for a short while.

Sleepwalking his way through the nightmare his life had become wasn't pleasant, but he'd convinced himself he had no other option. At first he'd grown dependent on the alcohol to keep him numb to any feelings, but after a while, he'd learned to do without it. Perhaps it was time to trust another person.

Even one who had dropped into his life seemingly out of the blue?

Rattling sounds drew him toward the kitchen. Barefoot, he padded through the sitting room and paused in the doorway. Dressed in the jeans and shirt he'd washed and hung on the rack to dry last night, Amber stood at the counter, stirring something in a plastic bowl. His heart gave a sudden strong thump at the sight of her.

As if she'd heard, she paused and jerked her head in his direction.

"Oh, good!" A slight smile curled the corners of her mouth. "I hope you like omelets."

Her voice seemed to echo through the empty spot inside his mind. The place she'd left barren when she severed their mental connection. A too familiar ache to taste that strong shared intimacy again gripped him.

He shoved it down. "Do I have time enough for a shower?"

"Ten minutes," she said, and went back to stirring.

Though Kevin hurried, he still took fifteen. Besides, the water had been mostly cold, which he needed. Then he'd run his razor haphazardly over his chin and cheeks, which he needed even more. By the time he emerged, dressed in his clean clothes from the drying rack, a plate with a steaming omelet and two slices of buttered toast sat waiting for him.

"Sorry I didn't wait," Amber apologized, a forkful of eggs halfway to her mouth.

"'Tis no matter." He sat down and reached for the teapot.

Their hands collided.

A flash blazed across his mind—desire, trepidation, embarrassment, and a few other things not so easy to recognize. Two quick heartbeats later, he stretched his consciousness toward hers and met a blank wall. His eyes met hers, and she looked away, flustered. So she was purposely keeping herself shielded from him. He poured milk into his tea and analyzed her possible reasons for wanting to keep him out.

"I don't know how you people function without coffee," she said, lifting her own mug to her lips.

Kevin didn't like the sound of "you people" any better than he liked the mental block she'd suddenly erected. All this was moving too fast for him to fully comprehend.

"We manage," he replied, wondering if she could still read him, even if she wouldn't let him read her.

Jaysus, he hoped not.

Over the rim of her cup, her golden eyes sought his. He looked down and rapidly shoveled in several bites without tasting anything.

Bloody unsporting of you, don't you think? He threw the mental challenge without looking up.

Amber set her cup on the table and cleared her throat. "Do you want to talk about your wife and child?"

Kevin nearly choked on the piece of toast he'd just swallowed.

"Ex-wife," he corrected after a moment. "No. Do you want to talk about your ex-husband?"

"N-no." She quickly finished off the last of her omelet, then took her dirty dishes to the sink and began washing them, her back to him.

He concentrated on polishing off the food on his plate rather than watch her. A little while ago, she'd looked far too comfortable standing at the counter stirring up the bowl of eggs. Almost like she belonged there. He cut off that wayward thought with a fast swig of tea.

"I'm sorry," she said without turning round. "I don't mean to read you. It's just that you're so…"

Fecking stupid?

"Different—overwhelming," she finished, whirling to face him at last. "I've never read anyone but Parker before. I'll try not to do it without telling you."

Kevin wanted to stop her words. Cover her mouth with his. Kiss her until they were again both incapable of rational thoughts and actions. Most of all, he wanted to carry her back into the bedroom and feel the sweet, intoxicating pleasure of being inside her mind as well as her body.

Instead, he rose and took his dirty dishes to the sink, being careful not to touch her in the process. Until one of them gained a little perspective on this mental hocus-pocus, they'd best avoid it. He kept his mind a total blank by repeating Hail Marys while he rinsed the plate and utensils, and then dried his hands on the tea towel. Draining his tea with one final gulp, he ran water into the mug and set it on the drainboard.

"Let's go find your brother then."

Chapter 6

AMBER STARED IN SURPRISE. EVEN AT A QUARTER TO seven, half the inhabitants of the little village of Malin Head seemed to be milling around the pier. Kevin, who hadn't spoken a word since they'd left the cottage, wove his way around a dozen or more people, and she found herself hard-pressed to keep up. Her leg muscles ached from all the hiking they'd done yesterday and from their bedroom exercises too. But she would be damned before she asked him to slow down.

Their sudden and unexpected mental link had undoubtedly scared him. Or worse, might have disgusted him. He certainly didn't act like he wanted a repeat performance of their mind-blowing physical and mental joining, so she wouldn't go there either. No matter how much she wanted to.

Parker was out there somewhere, and with Kevin's help, she would find him. She didn't need to think about anything else.

She could see Kevin's goal was the line of small black boats sitting on the sand just above the waves. He'd darn well better get one with a motor, because she certainly didn't feel like rowing. Just as she finished that thought, someone shouted her name, and a hand waved in the air.

Connor Magee rushed up. "Morning Amber, Kevin—"

"Where's Coyle?" Kevin interrupted before the boy could get any more words out. "I need a curragh."

"Ya just missed him, but he left me here in case any tourists want to rent one."

Kevin didn't pause to listen, but kept right on walking the remaining few yards to the boats. Connor trailed after him like an eager puppy. Amber hoped her own feelings weren't quite so transparent. Their shared intimacies had left her thoroughly smitten with Kevin Hennessey.

"Are we going back out to look for Amber's brother, then?" the boy asked, almost treading on Kevin's heels.

"You're not going anywhere if your uncle told you to stay here." Releasing all that sexual tension had not improved Kevin's mood. If anything, it seemed to have worsened.

"He's not my uncle," Connor muttered darkly as they reached the four identical black boats.

Amber could feel the teen's hurt and resentment swirling close to the surface when she stood beside him. Tentatively, she reached out with her mind.

"Well, he's a close enough relation that your mother left you in his care," Kevin retorted, pulling out his wallet. "How much to take the one with the outboard?"

"Twenty quid," Connor said, but Amber plainly heard his thought. *Mum's been a feckin' neddy since she had that bleedin' baby!*

"Jaysus!" Kevin swore. "I don't want to buy the bloody thing."

"Ten then, but I'm goin' with ya." Connor's tone was full of attitude, but his desperation flooded Amber's mind. *You're the only two in the whole feckin' town who treat me like a human being.*

Kevin slapped a bill into the teen's hand and then

shoved his wallet into his pocket. "Here's ten, and you're staying. C'mon Amber."

With a stab of pity, she broke the mental link with Connor and leapt into the boat. Arms crossed and chin jutting with defiance, the boy stood and glared while Kevin shoved the boat into the water. Jumping in before they floated away from shore, Kevin scooted to the rear to start the motor. Within moments, they were skimming over the calm surface of the harbor headed for the breakwater.

Amber scarcely noticed the other watercraft all around them. Instead she thought about how easily she'd linked into Connor and his teenaged angst. What had happened to her? First she connected with the seal, then Kevin, and now Connor. She suddenly seemed to be able to read everyone... except Parker.

"Perhaps because your brother is dead?" Kevin's words from last night echoed inside her desolately unfulfilled mind.

No! Parker couldn't be dead without her knowing... feeling...

She squeezed her eyes shut and concentrated fiercely, calling out for her brother with all the frustration and anguish and uncertainty that had driven her for almost a week.

Damn you, Parker, answer me!

I need you, Parker!

If you're not dead, I just might kill you myself!

Only silence and pain answered her, but she kept trying until she panted with the effort. Until the ache throbbing in her temples made her so dizzy she almost fell off the wooden plank seat.

Her eyes flew open and, concentration broken, she grabbed the side of the curragh to keep from sliding onto the bottom. Then she felt Kevin's concern and compassion flow into her mind like a soothing balm. He offered comfort, and she embraced it gratefully, the warmth easing the pain in her head.

Unbidden, her mind flew to earlier, when sharing thoughts and feelings with Kevin had brought her intense sensual pleasure. A smoldering desire that she hadn't experienced in a very long time sparked and glowed deep in her body. She had never been one for casual sex, but what she and Kevin had shared didn't feel the least bit casual.

She twisted around to stare at Kevin, who sat next to the outboard motor, gripping the handle that steered the boat through the water. Her heart gave a strong thump.

He met her eyes for only a moment before he looked away, disrupting their mental link.

He was learning.

Learning how to shut her out.

They reached open water, and the boat bounced roughly across the choppy surface. Amber turned to face forward again, clutching the plank seat so that she wouldn't bounce too. She didn't resume her fruitless efforts to reach her brother, and she didn't try to read Kevin, since he obviously didn't want her to. She needed to focus on the task at hand.

The only other vessel Amber could see was the white triangle of a sailboat in the far distance. A bank of gray clouds hung on the horizon, while a short stretch of sandy beach curved along the shore. Kevin kept them fairly close to the shoreline or the water would have undoubtedly been even rougher.

Amber squinted at a black object sitting on the sand just beyond the water line. "Is that another curragh?"

He slowed the motor and angled them closer. Within moments, they could plainly see a small black boat identical to the one they sat in, right down to the silver and white outboard motor.

"Must be Coyle," Kevin muttered, steering them in a wide arc that brought them directly facing the beach. "Wonder what the devil he's doing here?"

Obviously, he intended to find out.

After another minute, the boat lifted on the swell of the waves hitting the beach, and he cut the motor entirely. She turned to see him tilting the engine up and out of the water.

"Hang on," he said, as the wave propelled them rapidly toward the shore.

Even though Amber gripped the side with both hands, the jarring lurch when the boat hit sand still almost unseated her. Kevin bounded over the front and pulled the vessel out of the water. Awkwardly, she followed him and tried to help, her sneakers sinking into the muddy sand. With little real assistance from her, their curragh soon sat beyond the reach of the lapping waves, not more than a dozen yards from its twin.

She could see the single trail of footprints leading away from the other boat to a series of small sand dunes that crested the beach. Beyond the dunes and the tall waving grasses behind them, a thin column of smoke rose skyward.

"Is that...?"

"Chimney smoke," Kevin affirmed. "Someone lives here." He strode off in the same direction as the footprints.

Amber had a hard time following because of her wet footwear. Not only did the sand cling, but it quickly flowed over the top and inside her sneakers, making each step grow heavier and heavier.

She finally gave up, stopped, and stripped off both shoes and socks. Dumping out the sand, she shoved her sand-laden socks into her jacket pocket, gripped both sneakers in one hand, and raced after Kevin, who'd already reached the top of the dunes. She lost sight of him completely before she too made it to the crest.

Lucky for her there was only one path through the vegetation. Wide, flat, and not too soggy, she negotiated it easily, even in bare feet. Up ahead, she could see Kevin, his broad back distinctive in his dark blue jacket. Beyond him sat a stone cottage very similar to the one he lived in. She caught up just as they reached the yard.

Michael Coyle stood, hands on hips, close to the front door. On the step above him, wearing an oversized striped pullover, a young girl guarded the door.

Coyle turned and glared at them. "What are you doing here, Hennessey?"

Kevin returned his cold stare. "I might ask you the same question."

In spite of her lingering headache, Amber could feel the strong currents of suspicion and dislike running between the two men. Just for the heck of it, she shifted a little closer to Michael Coyle and tried to read him.

"For all that it's none of your business, my partner, Silas Lafferty, lives here," Coyle said, and though his tone remained hostile, his mind was utterly impenetrable. The same as countless other people she'd tried to connect with, everyone except the seal, then Kevin, and lastly Connor.

Chilly contempt emanated from Kevin as he replied, "We'd like a word with your partner as well. Since you claim not to have rented your missing curragh to Miss O'Neill's brother, then Lafferty must have."

"And I told ya, my da's not here," the girl burst out.

Amber jerked her gaze in the girl's direction and received a mental blast of anxiety. She sent out a tentative tendril toward her.

"Why doesn't he answer his mobile?" Coyle demanded.

The girl's chin jutted up in stubborn defiance in spite of the inner quaking Amber perceived. "I dunno. He took it with him."

Coyle took a step toward her, and she threw out her arms as if to ward him off. "My brother's ill, ya can't come inside." Her pale eyes swept over all three of them. "None of ya."

Amber caught the fleeting image of someone lying in bed swathed in a quilt.

"Shall we fetch the doctor, then?" Kevin asked. And when the girl turned around, frightened eyes on him, he quietly added, "'Tis all right, I won't hurt you. I'm a policeman."

"A bit out of your jurisdiction, I'd say," Coyle muttered under his breath.

"My brother has the croup. He'll be fine by tomorrow," the girl said, and Amber knew even without the mental confirmation that she was lying.

"The minute you see your da, you tell him to call me," Coyle ordered. "You hear me, Meriol?"

"I hear ya." The girl turned and, with a swish of her ponytail, disappeared inside the cottage. The door thudded shut behind her.

"Feckin' wild banshees, her and the wee lad too," Coyle declared as he spun on his heel.

"Where's their mother?" Amber couldn't stop herself from asking.

"Dead these three years come September." Coyle made a dismissive gesture and strode back toward the beach.

Amber watched his disappearing figure for a moment before she turned back to survey the house. Still looking at the tightly shuttered windows, she stood on first one leg, then the other, and slipped on her muddy shoes.

"That girl is hiding something," she told Kevin when she was sure Coyle was out of earshot.

"Perhaps," he acknowledged, though obviously distracted. "But at the moment, we can do nothing about it." He started back toward the beach also, and she hurried after him.

"Did Coyle say the brother was younger?" she persisted. "I don't think he's the one who's sick. The girl thought about someone wrapped in a quilt. Someone who didn't appear to be a child."

Kevin stopped short, and she nearly ran into him. His expression was reproachful and full of suspicion, his tone even more so. "Is there anyone's mind you can't pry into?"

She winced with the sting of his question. "I couldn't read Coyle."

"Well, more's the pity. That might have been useful."

Downcast, she shuffled after him, not trying to keep pace. After the intensity of the connection they'd shared last night, she'd expected—at least hoped—that Kevin wouldn't be... what?

Judgmental?

Scared?

The truth was, this sudden ability to connect with other minds scared her too, and she'd had thirty years of practice with Parker. She knew it was easy to be afraid, not to trust something and someone you didn't know or understand. But she didn't know and didn't pretend to understand Kevin, and yet she trusted him.

He stood waiting at the end of the path.

From the crest of the dunes, she saw Michael Coyle shove his boat into the surf and leap into it. A moment later, his outboard motor whined, and then he and the curragh shot out for open water.

Good riddance!

Amber knew Kevin caught her vehement thought, for the corner of his mouth twitched ever so slightly. But she didn't invade his privacy by linking into his mind. She would wait for him to invite her.

"We're not far from the seals' cave," he said to her unasked question. "I thought we should walk the beach between here and there and see if we find anything."

Like Parker's other shoe.

Or his body.

She didn't need a mental connection to know those thoughts. Pressing her lips tightly together, she drew in a deep breath and nodded.

When they reached the bottom of the dunes, she took

her shoes off again. Even if her feet were cold, it was easier to slog through the sand barefoot.

Kevin shifted his weight restlessly and surveyed the beach in both directions. Staying out of his thoughts was more difficult than she had imagined.

"Go ahead," she said, motioning with the sneakers in her hand. "I'm going to put these in the boat, then I'll catch up with you."

To her surprise, when she reached the curragh he had only walked a short distance, meandering slowly at the edge of the surf. The water lapped at the soles of his rubber boots.

From the corner of her eye, Amber detected movement in the tall grass near the dunes. But when she jerked her head in that direction, she couldn't distinguish anything. She tossed her shoes and socks under the plank seat, then cuffed her jeans above her ankles before hurrying to join Kevin.

They walked silently for a few minutes and stopped to examine a pile of kelp lying in the sand at the high tide mark. Except for the kelp, the beach lay empty, but Amber couldn't shake the tingly feeling of unease on the back of her neck. She looked back at the dunes again, but still saw nothing.

"Something wrong?" Kevin asked.

She shrugged, reluctant to sound paranoid. "I just have this funny feeling, like someone is watching us."

"That's because someone is." His low tone was matter-of-fact. "Up in the dunes. Don't look again, just keep walking toward those rocks." He inclined his head toward a long outcropping that cut through the sand and ran out into the water. "I'll go across and double back.

You act like you've discovered something down close to the water."

They covered the short distance in a matter of moments. The back of Amber's neck still tingled. The girl from the cottage must have followed them, Amber reasoned. But her heart raced a bit anyway.

"All set, then?"

She gave a barely perceptible nod at Kevin's quiet query and turned away from him to skirt the rocks. Spying some dark purple sea urchin spines, she stooped to get a closer look, her pulse still beating too fast. The icy water of the Atlantic washed over her toes and made her suck in a sharp breath, but she didn't retreat.

A reddish-brown starfish had captured her attention when a sharp cry sounded. Whirling around, Amber saw Kevin standing on top of the outcropping, holding a struggling child by the sweater neck.

"Aaaiii!" the child screeched. "Put me down! I didn't do nuthin'."

Definitely not the girl from the cottage, this was a smaller, younger child with brown hair. A boy, most likely, judging from the bowl haircut and grubby canvas pants.

"Anything," Kevin corrected, but not letting go in spite of the boy's struggles. "Who are you, and what are you doing here?"

"I didn't do anything neither!" the child insisted. "I'm Ronan Lafferty, and I live right over yonder."

He flapped one scrawny flailing arm.

"Your sister said you were sick, Ronan Lafferty." Kevin's tone sounded severe, and even to Amber, his narrow-eyed glare looked scary. "Does she know you're following us?"

"Yes—no!" As Amber approached, the panicked boy suddenly went still, his eyes round with wonder. "Y-you've come for him, haven't you?"

Kevin eased his grip, but his voice remained hard. "Come for who?"

But the boy didn't shift his stare from Amber.

"The selkie prince," he whispered. "You've the same golden eyes."

She put her hand on his skinny little shoulder and mental images bombarded her.

A man lying facedown in the sand, his legs tangled in a dark shroud.

Blood oozing from his side and from a lump on his forehead.

Seals barking.

The boy and his sister rolling the injured man onto some kind of wooden sled.

"Parker!" she cried, staggering backward as if the child had struck her. "Oh my God, Parker!"

She would have fallen if Kevin hadn't let go of the boy and grabbed her by both arms.

"Yes," the boy, Ronan, said, blinking hard when she severed their mental link. "Prince Par-Ker. He'll be fine now that you've come for him."

Amber felt Kevin's concern and confusion wash over her. He hadn't exactly invited her, but she reached for the warm comfort of his mind for just a moment.

———

"He's alive?" Kevin asked the boy, who nodded eagerly, his pale eyes never leaving Amber.

All the color had leached from her face, and she

didn't seem capable of supporting her own weight. He could feel the sensual brush inside his mind that signaled her mental invasion. Her inner turmoil of shock, uncertainty, and a wild, unreasoning hope touched him, along with a jumble of images.

He couldn't shut her out. In truth, he didn't want to. Resisting the urge to pull her against him, he tried to send back calm, soothing thoughts.

"First he was hurt and couldn't wake up," the boy continued. "Then he got a fever, but 'twill be fine now that you're here."

Amber seemed to recover enough of her equilibrium to pull back from Kevin both mentally and physically. "Wh-where is he?"

"Our cottage, of course," Ronan answered. "This way."

While they followed the child back across the dunes, Kevin tried to sort out the facts. He found it far easier to fall back on the long ingrained habits of police work than to think about the amazing feel of Amber's mind touching his and the uncomfortable emptiness when she pulled away.

Ronan and his sister had found Parker in what they called the selkies' cave early Tuesday morning. Their father had been gone since Monday and taken his mobile phone, their only source of communication with the rest of the world.

"Does your father often leave you alone like this?" Amber asked, clearly upset at the idea.

The boy nodded but went on to explain, "But never for this long before. Meriol planned to go to the village today, until Mr. Coyle and then you came."

Even though he'd seen Meriol's open hostility, he asked the boy anyway, "Don't you like Mr. Coyle?"

Ronan blushed. "He argues with Da a lot. Da called him a bleedin' bastard last time."

Hardly the ideal partnership, Kevin mused.

"Why do you think my brother is a selkie?" Amber gave voice to his next question.

Strange how their thoughts ran so often on the same lines, even when they weren't mentally connected.

"Why else would he be in the cave with the seals, then?" the boy answered, slanting her a look that seemed to calculate her sincerity. "Me mum told us stories about selkies and how they lived as seals, but could also turn human. 'Tis one of the few things I remember about her."

Though Amber said nothing, the way she bit down on her bottom lip told Kevin that the child had stirred her sympathies.

Was it only sympathy she felt for him as well?

"'Twas how we knew your brother was a prince," Ronan went on, his bare feet shuffling through the sand. "His golden eyes."

The path to the cottage intersected their way. Ronan stopped long enough to stomp the loose sand off his feet. Then he gave Amber a long, appraising look.

"Don't worry, we'll not be telling your and Prince Par-Ker's secret."

Halfway down the path, the girl, Meriol, ran to meet them, her expression tight with distress.

"Ronan!" She jerked her brother by the arm to pull him close to her. "I told ya not to go!" She thrust her chin in Kevin's direction. "He's Garda!"

"But she's Prince Par-Ker's sister!" the boy protested in a stage whisper. "Look at her eyes."

The news made Meriol glance nervously between Kevin and Amber. So much for winning her confidence with his claims of being a policeman. She looked ready to bolt.

"Please, Meriol," Amber entreated. "If you know where my brother is, I need to see him."

Fingers twitching on Ronan's sleeve, the girl shifted her gaze back to Kevin and tried to sound defiant. "Are ya going to arrest us?"

He shook his head. "I'm PSNI, that is, Police Service of Northern Ireland, like the Garda, but in County Derry. I can't arrest anyone in County Donegal."

That stopped her nervous twitch, but she turned plaintive eyes to Amber. "We didn't hurt him."

"She knows that already," Ronan said, pulling free of Meriol's grasp. "C'mon, he's 'round back."

They covered the remaining distance to the cottage in double-quick time. Three brown chickens flapped out of the way as Ronan led them across the front yard and around the side of the cottage. A rough addition had been tacked onto the back of the house. Its low roof slanted down even with Kevin's head, and the foundation was a thin slab of concrete flat on the ground.

"He was too heavy to lift into the house," Meriol explained, defensive once more.

She opened the wooden plank door and darted inside, Amber right behind her. Kevin caught the door before it closed, and Ronan rushed in under his arm. As he ducked to keep from bumping into the frame he heard Amber's cry of distress.

"Parker!"

A mattress lay on the floor in the back corner. Amber knelt beside the reclining figure. Kevin recognized the same floppy brown hair from the picture he'd passed around Malin Head.

"He's burning up with fever!" Amber's voice sounded thick with tears as she ran her fingers down her brother's unresponsive face. "Parker, can you hear me?"

Meriol offered up a bowl of water and a tea towel. "He keeps getting hotter and hotter."

Amber dipped the end of the towel into the water and blotted her brother's forehead. Kevin saw a large purple contusion in the edge of his hairline. The injury practically shouted concussion, but it didn't look infected.

"Is he hurt anywhere besides his head?" he asked Ronan, who was peeking over Amber's shoulder.

"His side," the boy answered.

But when Ronan reached for the quilt covering the injured man, Meriol batted his hand away. "I'll show them."

The girl folded back the edge of the quilt to reveal Parker O'Neill's bare torso. A half-dozen small plasters were stuck in two lines to his lower ribs, just above the elastic band of his boxers.

Amber gave a strangled sobbing gasp, and at the same time, the image of the bullet hole in the oarlock flashed through Kevin's mind.

"'Twas already scabbed over," Meriol explained with the matter-of-fact manner of an experienced nurse. "I put on the plasters to protect it from the covers."

When Amber touched the nearest of the plasters, the injured man moaned. She jerked her hand away and went back to wiping his face with the wet cloth.

"What about his clothes?" Kevin asked.

"His shirt had a great bloody hole," Meriol said. She

motioned to a pair of clean khaki trousers folded over a crate. "Alls he wore were those and his knickers."

"And his big selkie skin wrapped round his legs," added Ronan. "I hid that, of course. Just like the people did in Mum's stories."

"Of course," Kevin agreed. "But can you go and fetch it now?" Then, as the boy rushed out, he turned to Meriol. "Have you any rubbing alcohol?"

"To bring down the fever," Amber finished for him, but the girl shook her head.

Kevin squatted next to Amber and gently lifted Parker's eyelids, one at a time. His skin felt hot and dry. His pupils were dilated and didn't react, whether from the blow to his head or the fever, Kevin couldn't be sure.

"That's why I couldn't find the link to his mind," Amber whispered so only Kevin would hear. "He couldn't find it either." Her hand clutching the towel trembled. "This isn't enough to help him. Do you think it's safe to move him?"

"I don't see any other options." Kevin wished he felt more confident. He addressed the girl. "Do you have a shower or bathtub?"

"A tub, just inside the back door."

"Go and put warm water in it. Not hot or cold, warm. Enough to bathe him." As Meriol edged her way out of the room, he turned back to Amber. "Looks like we'll have to carry him."

She gave a little nod of acknowledgment and patted her brother's cheeks. "Parker? Can you hear me? Please, Parker!"

Kevin took the bowl of water and poured it over the

unconscious man's head. He roused enough to give another low moan.

Before Kevin could do anything else, the boy, Ronan, ran back into the room clutching what might have once been a coat. But drenching in salt water and then drying out had left the heavy garment crumpled and twisted almost beyond recognition. To a child's eyes it might have been the hide of a selkie.

"C'mon, Parker!" Kevin smacked the other man's face with considerably more force than Amber.

Parker moaned again, and his eyelids fluttered.

"You have to get up," Kevin ordered.

He and Amber tugged and pulled until they managed to get Parker upright. He was almost the same height as Kevin, if a bit leaner, but being unresponsive made him a dead weight.

That the two children had managed to drag him all the way here was nothing short of a miracle. Kevin seriously doubted he and Amber would be able to carry him inside.

He commandeered the coat from Ronan and, one-handed, wrapped it around Parker in a kind of sling. At least they wouldn't have to lift him very far off the floor until they reached the tub. With himself at Parker's head and Amber at his feet, they hauled him like an eighty-kilo sack of potatoes out of the room and up the three wooden steps into the cottage. Ronan dashed between them, holding doors.

Luckily the loo was just inside and to the left of the back door. Panting and sweating, Kevin and Amber laid their heavy burden on the cold tile floor. Parker moaned again, but his eyes remained closed.

Thanks to the combined efforts of all four of them, they managed to wrestle Parker into the half-full tub. Water went everywhere, splashing all of them and finally rousing Parker, who began to thrash and splatter them even more. Amber finally grabbed both his wrists and stopped his flailing with some soothing sounds and no doubt a mental connection as well.

Meriol crouched on the other side of the tub, scooped tepid water with a dipper, and poured it over Parker's shoulders. Flicking aside his wet hair, Parker opened eyes that were lucid at last.

"Am-Amber? Is it really you?"

She let go of his wrists and rested her hands on his wet shoulders. Her voice sounded tremulous. "Of course it's me. You called and I came."

Her brother looked unconvinced. "I'm not d-dead? Two goons with guns are trying to kill me."

Amber traced her wet fingers over his stubbled cheek. "You're going to be all right, Parker. Don't worry. The men with guns are gone."

"No, they're not!" Parker contradicted, grabbing her by the wrist and splashing both their hands down into the water. "They're looking for me. I know because I heard their thoughts."

Chapter 7

AMBER STARED INTO HER BROTHER'S EYES, WHICH WERE still dull with pain and fever, and sent him a mental query.

Can you hear those men now? Do you think they can hear you?

The comfort of making the familiar link with Parker was overridden by his confusion and anxiety.

I don't know. The mindspeak is so different here. It's not just the two of us. I can read a lot of people, and some of them know I'm doing it. We have to be careful.

His gaze flicked to Meriol, then over to Kevin and Ronan.

I know, Amber sent back. *I can read all three of them, but not everyone.*

With a look that said he knew what they were doing, Kevin interrupted their mental tête-à-tête. "Do you know where the men with the guns are?"

"No," Parker admitted, shoulders sagging in defeat. "I haven't heard them since… Sorry, my memory is messed up. I don't even know what day it is."

"We have to get you to a doctor!" Amber stood, and in her resolute teacher voice addressed Meriol and Ronan. "We need his pants and some kind of shirt. Also a towel and possibly more bandages."

As Ronan raced for the door, Kevin added, "And pack a few things of your own. You're coming with us." Then he leaned over and addressed Parker. "Can you walk?"

"I—"

"No!" As she had earlier in the yard, Meriol stood and defiantly faced Kevin. "Da told us not to leave 'til he comes back."

"Ronan told us your father's been gone nearly a week," Kevin explained in a softer tone. "You can't stay here alone, not now."

"Da's coming back," she stubbornly insisted. "And if the welfare people take us, they'll split us up. I won't leave Ronan. I won't!"

The girl's panic touched Amber, and she tried to reassure her. "We won't call the welfare people. We'll just take you and Ronan someplace safe until we find your father."

Meriol looked unconvinced, but she handed Amber a towel from a nearby rack.

"Go and leave a note for your da, then," Kevin said in an unmistakably gentle undertone. "Tell him you and Ronan are with me, Kevin Hennessey."

"The plasters are in the cupboard under the sink," Meriol said. And with a toss of her head, she left the room.

With Kevin's help, Amber got Parker out of the tub and seated on the commode. He was too weak to do much, so she rubbed him on the back, chest, and arms with the towel, being careful to avoid the wound across his side. She was almost finished when Ronan reappeared with Parker's pants and a red flannel shirt he declared "an old one of Da's."

"But he won't mind if you borrow it, Prince Par-Ker," the child added, obviously still firm in his belief that he was in the presence of selkie royalty.

"When you found Prince Parker in the cave, how did you get him here?" Kevin asked the boy.

"In the sled," Ronan replied.

"Show me."

Kevin and the boy walked out, leaving Amber alone to help Parker get dressed. The sleeves of the shirt were too short for her brother's long arms, but it buttoned just fine across his chest and stomach. Parker leaned heavily on her shoulder as he pulled his pants on over his still damp legs and boxers. Once they were past his hips, he sat back with a shaky huff.

After a deep breath, he spoke, trying to sound flippant. "So if I'm the prince that makes you the princess." He nodded in the direction where Kevin had gone. "But who do you think he's supposed to be?"

She forced an indulgent smile at her brother's intended levity. "Kevin? He's the knight in shining armor."

Parker raised his eyebrows in a hint of his usual self. "Okay, guess that explains why you were kissing him."

"You'll be sorry for spying on me, Parker," she threatened, just like she'd done since they were young teens. But she fleetingly wondered if now that she and her brother were connected again, would she still be able to link mentally with Kevin?

Parker held up his hands in mock surrender. "I didn't mean to listen in. Besides, I already like this guy better than that asshole you married. At least this one's Irish."

She hid her relief by rolling her eyes and saying, "Hello? We are in Ireland."

Instead of sassing her back, Parker's expression went serious. "I know, and I think that might be what's going on with our mindspeak. It's enhanced here."

"More than enhanced," she agreed. "It's morphed into something beyond our link, something scary."

Kevin's reappearance cut off more discussion. Meriol hovered behind him.

"We're going to pull you down to the beach in a sled. Then take you in the curragh to a doctor." He gave Parker an appraisal as he spoke. "Think you can walk to the front door?"

"I'm pretty dizzy just sitting here," Parker admitted, and Amber knew even without their connection how much the disclosure hurt his pride. "Maybe if I lean on you…"

"To be sure," Kevin said, but he waited for Parker to hoist himself to his feet before he offered his assistance. Just like any good knight in shining armor.

The sled turned out to be a rickety cart that might have once been pulled by a pony. But the wheels had been replaced by two smooth wooden runners, one on each side.

"We use it to haul things up from the beach," Meriol explained. She had a small duffel bag slung over one shoulder, so in spite of her protest, she had obeyed Kevin's order.

"We can roll heavy things into the back." Ronan tilted the open end of the cart down to the ground to demonstrate. "Like we did with you, Prince Par-Ker."

"I know you're glad I can manage under my own steam this time." Parker tried to sound casual, but Amber could see that the short walk through the cottage and out the front door had left him badly winded.

With Meriol and her on one side, and Kevin and Ronan on the other, they pushed the cart to the curragh. Parker's weight made going down the path a challenge, but crossing the sand became a feat of sheer brute strength, largely on Kevin's part. While Parker had remained stoically silent at first, the rough jostling and banging around in the cart eventually reduced him to gasping moans and groans.

Midway between the dunes and the waves, a breath-less Kevin called for a rest break. All four of them collapsed on the sand, huffing and sweating. Parker lay silently in the cart, his knees curled to his chest.

Meriol pulled a bottle of water from her duffel bag, took a drink, and then passed it to Amber. Grateful, she took a big gulp.

"How did you ever get him up those dunes and to your house?" she asked, handing the water bottle to Ronan.

"It took us most of the day," the boy admitted. He swiped his sweaty brow with his arm before he sipped, then passed the water on to Kevin. "And Meriol swore a lot."

"Did not."

"Did too!"

Amber saw Kevin's mouth twitch as he tipped the bottle up to drink. When he finished, he got up to offer water to Parker.

"Well, you both did an amazing job," Amber said, struggling back to her feet. "And I can't thank you enough for saving my brother's life."

She looked over the edge of the cart at Parker and sent a whisper of reassurance to his mind. *Everything will be fine.*

We there yet? Parker sent back, but the thought was too weak to be humorous. A sliver of apprehension skit-tered across her mind.

From across the cart, Kevin capped the bottle and handed it to her. "His fever's rising. We need to get going."

Shoving aside worry, she nodded and gave the almost empty bottle back to Meriol. Now that she'd found her brother, she would not stop until he was all right, no matter what she had to do.

When they'd reached the dunes, Amber had followed Kevin's example and tied her rain slicker around her waist. Grimly determined, she readjusted the garment and tried unsuccessfully to dust the sand off her sweaty arms. She didn't even want to think about how bad her hair must look.

Looking quite appealing in his layer of sand and sweat, Kevin clapped Ronan's small, thin shoulder. "Heave ho, mate. We're nearly there."

Every muscle in her arms, back, and legs crying in protest, Amber positioned herself at the back of the cart and pushed. The vehicle plowed through the loose sand with uneven starts and stops. She definitely felt like swearing, but she was soon panting too hard to spare the breath for words. However, she refused to let herself stop. Her three companions seemed equally determined. Even Ronan kept his head down and never let out a whimper of protest.

When they finally reached the packed sand at the high tide mark, the sled almost flew out of their hands as it skidded easily toward the beached curragh.

Once they reached the boat, Parker rallied enough strength to get out of the cart. But it took Amber and Kevin's combined efforts to boost him up and over the side of the little vessel. Unable to stay upright on the seat, Parker drew himself into the pointed bow of the boat, his breath labored and raspy.

"In with you," Kevin ordered the two children.

Ronan obeyed, scrambling over the side like a monkey. But Meriol pushed the empty sled back toward the dunes.

"Leave it, Meriol! We'll come back for it later."

With a mutinous glare, the girl pushed the cart just beyond the high water line before she complied with Kevin's demand. While they waited, Amber rolled and pulled the legs of her pants up over her knees. Maybe that would keep them from getting wet.

Meriol insisted on helping shove the curragh into the surf. Again, the girl and Amber combined their efforts on one side with Kevin on the opposite. Ronan crouched beside Parker as the boat slipped backward through the wet sand.

"Get in!" Kevin shouted when the cold waves washed over their ankles.

Obviously she'd had a lot of practice, for Meriol gripped the top of the wooden frame and easily heaved herself up and inside. Kevin gave another shove and followed. Amber teetered awkwardly half in and half out for a moment, before she tumbled onto the floor boards. One of her muddy shoes smacked her in the forehead.

As Amber struggled to crawl onto the bench seat, Kevin used an oar to turn the curragh around so that they faced the waves. The first one broke over the bow and sent a chilly spray over all of them.

After their hot, sticky labors on the beach, Amber didn't mind the cold salt water. She and Ronan shrieked with delight while Kevin maneuvered the boat on top of the second cresting wave. As the third wave passed harmlessly under them, Kevin drew in the oar and scooted back to the outboard motor.

Then Amber realized Meriol didn't have her duffel bag. The girl had left it in the sled. She turned just as the engine sputtered to life, and a blast of rebellion and desperation broadsided her mind.

"Now Ronan!" Meriol shouted, and standing on the seat, she leapt into the water.

A loud splash sounded from the other side along with a wisp of regret as the boy followed his sister.

"Ronan! Meriol! No!" Amber's cry came too late. She saw her own surprise reflected in Kevin's expression. "We have to go back!"

———⁓———

Kevin shook his head. "We can't force them to come with us, even if we do catch them. Besides, your brother needs a doctor sooner rather than later."

Looking more than a little crestfallen, Amber nodded her head. That she had not known the two Lafferty children would make a break for it surprised Kevin even more than Meriol and Ronan's bold actions. He'd been certain she could read both of their minds, but apparently she hadn't. And he hoped that Parker's confused brain had not overheard the men with guns today, or even yesterday.

"They'll be all right for now." The reassurance was for himself as much as her. "I'll contact the authorities as soon as we get your brother some help."

"You told them you wouldn't call child welfare." Her rebuke stung more than he wanted to admit, and he had to look away from her sorrowful golden eyes.

"Can't be helped. They must have other relations somewhere who won't go off and leave them for days on end."

When she didn't reply, he sneaked a sidelong glance and saw that she was watching the passing shoreline. They were almost abreast of the cave where they'd spent yesterday with the seals. Where they'd kissed.

The memory sent Kevin's mind off on a risqué tangent.

"Isn't Malin Head the other direction?" she asked, interrupting his thoughts.

He hoped like hell she hadn't read any of them. Clearing his throat, he answered, "'Tis shorter to go straight away to Ballyliffin. They've a clinic, and Malin Head doesn't."

From the floor of the boat, Parker stirred suddenly. Amber slid off the seat and scooted toward the bow to comfort him.

A few meters to the left, Kevin saw flashes of brown just beneath the surface of the water—seals. He steered the curragh further out to avoid them, while Parker mumbled incoherently and struggled to sit up. Amber pressed her brother's shoulder back down with soothing words and dabbed at his face with the bottom of his flannel shirt. Within a few more minutes, they were out of sight of the cave, and Parker seemed to relax once more.

When it was clear she could do nothing more for her brother, Amber crawled back up onto the seat and donned her socks and shoes. Both her movements and words jerked erratically. "His fever's worse. How much longer until we get there?"

"Within the hour," Kevin assured, but she didn't meet his gaze. "And a round of antibiotics and fluids will fix him right up, I'm sure."

Then the pair of them would head home to America.

Why didn't that fact make him feel happy? Or at least relieved?

His sister and brother-in-law had forced this seaside holiday upon him so that he could make some decisions about his future. A future that most decidedly did not include a telepathic Yank, no matter how appealing. Helping her had been a way to absolve a few of his past transgressions, at least that's what he'd told himself. But as Kevin watched her untie the slicker from her waist and shrug it on, desire and longing washed over him and settled with an ache in his groin.

Amber was not like any woman he'd ever met and not just because of her mental telepathy. She'd aroused feelings in him he'd never expected to experience again.

Tenderness.

Caring.

The tentative stirrings of trust.

And when she left, he might never feel them again.

After the way he'd neglected Caitlin, he didn't deserve to have such a relationship, the stern, unyielding side of his conscience reminded him. Accepting the self-reprimand, Kevin concentrated on getting them to Ballyliffin with all possible speed.

Once they entered Trawbreaga Bay, the headwind disappeared and the water smoothed to faint ripples. Only the urgency of their errand spoiled the perfect boat ride. Amber had left him to his gloomy thoughts and tended to her brother. While she might not be able to do much physically, Kevin felt sure the two of them were mentally linked. And that must be an emotional balm for both of them.

She finally broke the long silence when they were within sight of Ballyliffin. "Is that old tower built right on the beach?"

Kevin nodded as he slowed the motor and angled the curragh for the small pier. "'Tis called an O'Doherty's Tower. Several of the villages 'round here have one. They were used for defense in the old days."

"It's easy to forget this quiet place can be dangerous," she murmured, her gaze straying back to Parker.

Cutting the engine completely, Kevin let them drift the last few meters to the pier.

"Ho there!" He hailed an idle fisherman. "We've an injured man here, and we need help."

The man shouted in Gaelic to a trio of men at the foot of the pier. By the time the curragh was secured, a half-dozen people bustled over to offer assistance. Amid more shouts and much talk in both English and Gaelic, they lifted Parker and carried him to a waiting car.

Amber hovered and anxiously directed the activities, then crawled into the backseat to hold her brother's head in her lap. Kevin got in front with the driver, a spry old gent named Tommy, for the three-block trip to the clinic.

Quick as their arrival was, the news of their coming preceded them. Two burly youths stood by the clinic door with a stretcher. The appearance of an injured Yank was no doubt the most exciting event to occur in sleepy Ballyliffin in a fortnight or more.

A house once occupied by a physician had been converted for emergency treatment, routine follow-up care, and an occasional overnight stay. The doctor rotated between this and his main practice in Buncrana, and a nurse practitioner saw patients in his absence.

Kevin turned down their chauffeur Tommy's invitation for a pint at the pub across the street and sat in one of the plastic chairs in the waiting area. Amber accompanied her brother and Nurse Casey into the back room.

After what felt like an endless twenty minutes, Amber reappeared, looking more relieved than since they first located Parker.

"She's taking some X rays just to be sure," she said, sinking into the chair next to him. "But she believes it's only a concussion coupled with infection and dehydration. She doesn't even think she needs to call the doctor."

She leaned over and rested her head on his shoulder. Her sigh sounded more content than weary. "You truly are a knight in shining armor, Kevin Hennessey."

Stifling the urge to grimace, Kevin wished he were so noble. And even more, he wanted to kiss her. How in the name of heaven could she have gotten so thoroughly under his skin in a few short days?

Then he felt a faint beckoning at the edge of his mind. A hint of gratitude laced with desire. And he knew how his sudden infatuation had happened. She wanted him too, in an irresistibly seductive blend of mental and physical fulfillment.

A pleasure that would ultimately bring pain to both of them. But like the drowning man who can't stop the water rushing into his lungs, Kevin opened his mind to her. The sweet flood of emotions momentarily robbed him of breath. With it came Amber's own sense of delight. She had feared that discovering and reconnecting with her brother might have affected the link with Kevin, but it hadn't.

He turned so that their foreheads touched, and he savored the wonder of melding their thoughts and feelings. The breath from her parted lips fanned his.

A loud cough pulled them apart. He turned to see the nurse who ran the place standing in the doorway.

"Your brother's X rays are fine, Miss O'Neill," she said, blue eyes twinkling while Amber blushed. "I've put him in one of our rooms and started an IV. You can come sit with him if you'd like."

Amber rose to her feet, her conflicting thoughts swirling through Kevin. "Yes, thanks, I'll just…"

"Second door on the left." The other woman nodded down the hallway behind her, and then pivoted on her heel.

"I need to return the curragh to Malin Head," Kevin said, even as Amber's thoughts protested. "I'll get the Rover and be back."

She trailed her fingers across his cheek. "How long will that take?"

Always the impatient Yank.

His silent admonition made her smile.

"Two or three hours, no more."

"I'll be waiting." Her lips brushed his cheek, but the blast of desire she sent into his brain shot straight to his groin.

And there it stayed for the entire trip back to Malin Head. Skimming over the water, all Kevin's thoughts were occupied with ways to prolong Amber's stay and postpone her inevitable return to California.

But on the even longer drive back to Ballyliffin, reality shoved its way into his mind, and he cursed himself for a fool nine ways to Sunday. No matter how many times he told himself this was only a meaningless fling, how many times he acknowledged that the pain of her leaving would be far worse if they spent more time together, it didn't make him want her any less.

Tea time was nearly over when he finally parked the Rover in front of the clinic and hurried inside. Mrs. Casey was on the phone at the front desk, and she motioned him toward the back with her free hand. He remembered her telling Amber second door on the left, but he rapped lightly before he opened it, just in case.

Amber lifted her head when he entered, her golden eyes meeting his as a wave of happiness and longing crashed into his mind. After only one look at her Kevin's pulse pounded loud in his ears.

She raised a finger to her lips and nodded at her brother, asleep on the hospital bed beside her chair. In spite of the IV in his arm, and the blankets piled on top of him, Parker looked, if not healthy, at least much improved.

He is. Amber's answer floated into his head. *He's going to be fine in a couple of days*.

Kevin couldn't let himself hope that she would spend those days with him. He banished that thought with the more practical matter of food. Neither of them had eaten since early this morning. After a word with Mrs. Casey to confirm Parker's condition, the two of them hurried to the pub across the street to fill up on tea, sandwiches, and scones.

While they ate, they planned. Mrs. Casey had agreed not to keep Parker overnight, and Kevin didn't need to do much convincing to persuade Amber not to stay in the little hotel in Ballyliffin. She and Parker would stay at Kevin's cottage tonight and tomorrow. Then on

Monday, she would go into Carndonagh for her car and check in with Constable Shanley.

She had already spoken to a Ballyliffin Garda officer and told him all she knew about her brother's incident and the Lafferty children. The officer had been eager to pass everything off to Shanley, since it all appeared to be in his jurisdiction.

"Nothing but the most dire of emergencies gets tended on Sundays." Kevin confirmed her mental query.

Concern clouded Amber's golden eyes. "But I'm worried about Ronan and Meriol."

Her concern over two children she hardly knew from Adam touched him, as did so many things about her, and he found himself making promises he didn't really want to make.

"Coyle wasn't back when I was in Malin Head, but I'll check in with him once we get your brother squared away. If he hasn't found his partner, I'll make him help me corral those two young ones."

She rewarded him with a smile and a touch that had him longing for more and half-believing he might deserve it.

―――

The last of the scones devoured, Amber and Kevin ambled back to collect her brother from the clinic. The fact that Parker got into Kevin's ancient Range Rover under his own power illustrated his rapid rate of recovery and lightened Amber's mood considerably. She wasn't even concerned when he opted to spend most of the ride sprawled across the backseat, saying nothing aloud nor in her mind.

Kevin kept their conversation on neutral topics, but he allowed their mental link to stay in place. So when she told him she had switched teaching jobs and moved a year ago, she wordlessly revealed the real reason. Her ex-husband had forced her to sell her home as part of their acrimonious divorce settlement. The settlement had left her seriously in debt.

Then when Kevin told her about being an officer of the court for his brother-in-law the magistrate, he trusted her enough to reveal that the PSNI had put him on administrative leave for drinking. The job had been a way to prove his sobriety was permanent, and now he itched to move on.

Amber poured forth her feelings of understanding and acceptance and received his surprised gratitude in return. Still, he shied away from her delving too deeply into his memories, and she respected his wariness. Her own wounds were too painful to be easily shared. But she felt cautiously optimistic that their fragile bond of trust would strengthen. If they only had enough time.

The sun poised low on the horizon and bathed Kevin's stone cottage in golden light when they finally pulled into the side yard. Parker heaved himself out of the backseat, but he was too unsteady on his feet to walk unaided. She and Kevin propped him between them to help him into the house.

If Parker felt up to it, tomorrow they'd drive to the hostel in Buncrana and retrieve his things. But for the moment, Amber helped him remove his pants and crawl into bed, while Kevin stayed in the kitchen brewing tea.

"Milk and sugar?" Parker joked after she gave him a steaming cup. "Meriol put whiskey in my tea."

After drinking less than half the mug, he pled fatigue, and Amber rejoined Kevin at the kitchen table. They sat and sipped in companionable silence for several long minutes before Kevin drained his cup and rose to his feet.

"I'd best go into Malin Head before it gets dark."

She sent a ribbon of supportive encouragement intertwined with sensual anticipation.

"Keep that up, and I shan't go a'tall," he vowed.

"Just a little something to think about while you're gone." Then she stood and kissed him, her hands framing his face while her tongue explored the warm sweetness inside his mouth. He pulled her close enough that she could feel his erection pressing against her while he took a taste of her too.

But after a moment he broke away with a frustrated groan. "That fecking gobshite Coyle better have found Lafferty."

Amber smiled slyly. "Now who's impatient?"

Kevin groaned again and muttered something about the patience of a saint as he headed out the door. She caught a fleeting, shadowy image of herself naked before she broke their mental link.

Giddy with excitement, she cleaned up the kitchen, Kevin's sentiments about finding Lafferty echoing inside her brain. The idea of making love with Kevin again fueled every sexual fantasy she'd ever had, and a few she hadn't allowed herself to imagine. Now that she knew their connection wasn't a fluke, she yearned to explore the depths, push the physical and mental boundaries.

Once everything was tidied up, she decided to undertake some improvements on herself, starting with a shower and clean clothes. She tiptoed into the bedroom to go through her backpack, hoping against hope to find something alluring in the few items she'd hurriedly brought with her.

Her brother slept, but fitfully. The jumbled bedclothes provided testimony to his restlessness. Worried that his fever might have returned, she reached tentatively for his mind while she approached his side.

Parker moaned low and guttural, his legs twitching free of the blanket. Amber sent soothing thoughts as she laid her palm on his forehead. But her touch made him gasp loudly, almost a shout, as he bolted upright in bed. She grabbed the headboard to keep her balance.

"Holy shit! No!" Parker cried out, and a blast of shock and terror surged into her mind like an electrical charge.

Reeling from the intensity, Amber fell to her knees while images of a sailboat and the two Lafferty children leapt in front of her eyes.

Ronan! Meriol! Oh, please God, no!

She wasn't sure if Parker had spoken aloud, but he panted, and his eyes rolled with fear and agitation. She pulled back from their mental connection. At the same time, he tried to crawl over her, but his legs were still too weak to support his weight, and he collapsed next to her on the floor.

"It's all right, Parker," she soothed, smoothing the hair out of his eyes. His forehead was damp with perspiration but not warm with fever. "It was just a dream."

"No!" He shook off her hand and pressed his palms against his temples. "I'm not dreaming. I saw them. The goons are coming for Ronan and Meriol!"

He rocked to and fro in distress as he had when they were very young. Then he sent images of three figures standing in the back of the sailboat. Evil intent enveloped the scene. Amber felt rather than heard the pistol shot, saw two of the men dump the third into the ocean. The image faded, but the malevolence remained, and it was directed at a beach where a thin column of chimney smoke rose above the dunes.

Bitter bile rose in Amber's throat as she read that intent.

Parker pulled himself up onto the mattress. "We have to save them!"

Amber stood as her thoughts and Parker's swirled chaotically inside her head. "But Kevin—"

"We don't have time to wait!" Parker insisted. Using the bedpost, he leveraged himself to his feet and then tottered the three steps to the bureau. Leaning across one corner so that he wouldn't fall over, he snagged his folded pants off the top. "Help me put these on."

Amber grabbed him by the arm and yanked the pants out of his hand. "You're not going anywhere. I'll go after Meriol and Ronan."

Chapter 8

AMBER DIDN'T WASTE TIME ARGUING. SHE SHOVED Parker in the direction of the bed and waited just long enough to see that he hit the mattress and not the floor. Then she was in the living room, shoving her arms into the sleeves of her windbreaker. As she paused at the back door, she snagged a flashlight sitting on an open shelf over the washer.

Her mind crowded with urgency, she operated on the same instinctive level that had brought her to Ireland. Everything else, her every conscious thought and feeling, was sublimated to her goal. Reaching Ronan and Meriol became her sole objective. They had saved Parker, now she must rescue them. Besides, they were a pair of innocent children.

Shoving the flashlight into her jacket pocket, Amber rushed down the back steps of the cottage and approached the edge of the bluff. She knew the children were close to the sea. Therefore, she must get to the shore in order to find them. Without a vehicle, the fastest way was over and down.

She trotted along the edge, peering into the fading light, searching for a trail down the steep face. After ten long minutes, several scraggly bushes and protruding boulders proved to be the most promising possibility. With the sound of the waves breaking far below her, she grasped the sturdiest branch, swung over, and skidded toward a boulder a good eight feet down the cliff face.

Amber landed butt first in the middle of the rock. Scrambling to her feet, she scooted across and down to a smaller piece of rock, and then to a large bush growing almost perpendicular on the steep crag.

Knowing it was impossible to climb back up, she inched her way along with agonizing slowness. At one point, her foot went out from under her in a shower of pebbles that almost took her with them as they rained down the precipice. More than once, she crawled like an insect, stretching her arms and legs to find secure spots to grip.

Full dark descended just before she reached the base of the cliff. She slid the last few yards on her rear and landed feet first in a pile of sand. Trying to get her bearings, she sat for a moment, and watched dark scraps of clouds float across a nearly full moon.

Ignoring the sand and dirt under her nails, Amber pressed her fingertips to her temples and tried to connect to Parker. A faint thread of panic and anxiety teased at the corners of her consciousness, and she sent reassurance back along the gossamer strand. It floated away before she could tell if he received it. Then just for the hell of it, she reached for Kevin's mind, but found nothing.

Determined to find the two children, she rose to her feet, brushed sand off her jeans, and searched her brain for the direction of Malin Head. She knew their home lay between where she stood and the village.

Then an image came to her, whether from her own memory or some place else, she wasn't sure. It shimmered as if floating underwater. She could see the shoreline, the seal cave, and the beach with the dunes that hid the Lafferty cottage.

Now sure of her way, Amber went first toward the breaking waves. The packed sand close to the water line made walking much easier, and she headed out at a quick pace. The moon shone with enough brightness that she didn't need the flashlight, but every so often she would gaze out at the open sea for signs of a white sail.

Twice she had to clamber over or around rock outcroppings. She used the flashlight once, so that she didn't have to slow her pace. When she reached the third rocky ridge, she recognized the place where she and Kevin had laid the ambush for Ronan.

The tide was low as she crossed in the spot where she'd stood earlier to inspect the starfish. As soon as she reached the open beach, a dark shape just above the water line startled her.

A curragh!

The same curragh that had been there this morning. Michael Coyle's.

The moment she recognized it, Amber's heart gave a thud of dread. She ran for the dunes without pausing to see if Coyle was anywhere near. Flopping onto her knees behind the screen of tall grasses, she crawled a dozen yards before she dared to poke her head up and survey the scene.

Just like this morning, a lone set of tracks marred the surface of the smooth sand in front of the curragh. Moonlight glinted off the metal of the outboard motor. But farther out on the water, something pale glided over the waves.

The unmistakable triangle of a sail.

Her heart leaping into her throat kept Amber from crying aloud, but her mind shrieked in terror. Parker was right, the goons with the guns were coming!

She scrambled across the dunes and ran down the path toward the cottage. Breathing hard, she ducked off the path just before she reached the yard and circled around through the brush toward the back of the house. After several long, tense moments of surveying the moonlit area, she made a mad dash for the storage room where they'd found Parker this morning.

Flattened against the rough plaster, she held her breath, then edged her way to the door. Finding it unlocked, she slipped inside. She pulled the flashlight out of her pocket and switched it on, running the slender beam around the room.

Seeing that nothing had been moved since this morning, Amber backed slowly out of the room, internally debating whether to go ahead and try the back door or go around to the front. As she eased her way out the door, she stumbled into Michael Coyle.

A yelp of surprise erupted from her lips before she could stop it. When she turned to run, Coyle grabbed her arm.

"You? What the devil are you doing here?" he demanded in a gruff voice.

She snatched her arm from his grasp and gave him a challenging glare. "Looking for Ronan and Meriol."

"They ain't here."

Amber's mind screamed a protest, while the words scraped out of her constricted throat. "Oh, God! Do the men in the sailboat have them?"

Coyle looked surprised at her question. "What do you know about those men?" Harsh lines of fatigue and worry marked the skin around his deep-set eyes.

She still couldn't read him.

"They shot at my brother, tried to kill him." A chill ran through her as she spoke the words, and she ran her hands up and down her arms.

Something sticky on the sleeve of her windbreaker made her jerk her hand in front of her eyes, and she saw an unmistakable smear of blood across her palm. Then she noticed a dirty rag wrapped around Coyle's fingers.

"What happened to your hand?"

He twitched it behind his back. "Pinched it on the outboard."

She knew he was lying without any mental connection. *What was he hiding?* She also knew they couldn't waste more time talking, so she reached out frantically with her mind for anyone.

"We need to get out of here," she declared. "I just saw the sailboat."

Her words made him flinch. "Shite! I've done me best to find those two hellions. God forgive me, but I don't want them on me soul!"

As he spoke, Amber caught a brief glimpse of a thought… from Ronan.

Giddy with hope, she grasped Coyle's shoulder. "I think I know where they are. Can you call the police?"

But Coyle only grew more agitated. "Don't be such a feckin' neddy. Shanley's in the thick of this, same as half the village. Smuggling's been the only way to turn a penny in Malin Head since God himself was a boy."

Her mouth fell open in shock as she digested this information.

Smugglers in this day and age?

What did they smuggle?

But she had no time to ask. With a shake of his head, Coyle strode rapidly away.

She sprinted after him and caught up as they reached the path to the beach. "But what are we supposed to do? Are these guys locals?"

Coyle kept walking, shoulders hunched. "They're suppliers, and a nasty bunch at that. We were just middlemen, Silas and me." He paused long enough for a shudder to run through his compact frame, his bandaged hand cradled by the uninjured one. Then he seemed to reach a decision, for he straightened his shoulders and met her gaze. "I'll distract that lot. You find those kids. They've an aunty down in Sligo Town. Take them there."

He shied away from her and broke into a jog, as if being too close to her caused him pain. Amber hurried after him, not giving voice to the dozens of questions crowding her mind. She knew Michael Coyle wouldn't answer her.

When they reached the dunes, they could see the sailboat drawing closer to the beach.

"They can't come all the way to shore, can they?" Amber whispered.

Coyle shook his head. His own tone was low. "They'll have to use an inflatable dinghy. I'll try to outrun 'em. Which way you goin'?"

Amber still didn't completely trust the man, but she had no other choice. Biting her lip, she inclined her head in the direction of the seals' cave. "That way."

"I'll go t'other," he said, giving her one last measuring glance. "Stay behind the dunes for as long as you can. Go now!"

Crouching so that her head was below the tops of the high grasses, Amber turned and ran. From the corner of her eye, she saw Coyle bounding down the side of the dunes and across the open expanse of beach. But he was out of her line of vision before he reached the curragh. Keeping her head down, she continued to run.

By the time she heard the curragh's outboard motor start, it sounded faint and far away. Moments later, she heard an even more indistinct sound of a second outboard. Someone was going after Coyle. Maybe he was trustworthy after all.

Soon she couldn't distinguish the whining hum of the engines over her own harsh breathing. Picking her way over rocks and uneven ground slowed her down, but Amber didn't dare use the flashlight. Finally, she had to turn toward the sound of the breaking waves before she lost her way completely.

When she reached the beach, she strained her eyes but saw no sign of the sailboat. With some of the weight of worry lifted from her shoulders, she hurried down close to the water line. Then she jogged across the hard-packed sand toward the seals' cave.

—*∾∾*—

Parker wasn't sure how long he'd lain senseless on the hard tile floor, but he knew for certain that he couldn't get up. He had tried and failed and was now so weak he would have to crawl on his belly like a worm.

The scream from Amber's mind, complete with the images of the sailboat, Meriol, and Ronan, had catapulted Parker out of bed. He staggered across the bedroom only to keel over in the tiled entry as he passed out.

When he came to, he rolled over and saw that he was too far from anything that he might use to pull himself up. Taking a deep breath, he struggled as far upright as his hands and knees before his shaky arms collapsed and he found himself facedown on the tile once more. Like a moron, he immediately tried again, with the same disastrous results. At least the second time, he believed he was only senseless for a few moments, because the ache of his wrist, which was trapped under him, startled him to full consciousness.

Fighting the pain and fatigue, he reached out and tried to mentally connect with Amber. But all he got was an image of a cave filled with seals.

Just as he marshaled the last of his waning strength to inch his way from the entry hall into the living room, he heard a vehicle screech to a halt outside. A moment later, the key rattled in the lock, and the door flew open, scraping Parker's bare leg in the process.

"Amber?" The big Irishman's voice rang with alarm, while behind him, lighter footsteps pounded on the gravel path. Hennessey almost stumbled over Parker in his haste. "Jaysus! What are you doing on the floor? And where's Amber?"

"Gone. After Ronan. And Meriol." Parker huffed out as Hennessey nearly dislocated his shoulder hauling him up.

"Shite!" exclaimed a young teen boy who nearly collided with both of them. "Are we too late, then?"

"We can't be too late," Hennessey declared in a tone that Parker didn't need a mental connection to interpret.

He scarcely got his feet under himself before Hennessey dragged him back into the bedroom and deposited him on the edge of the bed. The man had the strength of a solid brick shithouse.

While Hennessey rummaged in a bottom bureau drawer, the dark-haired boy shoved a pillow under Parker's shoulders to keep him from falling flat.

"You heard her too." It wasn't a question, and neither was Hennessey's next demand. "Can you find her with your mind, then?"

"I don't know." Parker put a hand to his forehead and pressed to help center his concentration. The pain inside his skull pounded like a pile driver. He winced. "All I keep seeing is this image of a cave full of seals."

Both Hennessey and the boy erupted with several colorful swear words. Parker craned his neck to see Hennessey squatting on the floor of the closet. The big man shoved something into his jacket pocket, stood, and then regarded the boy and him.

Though Parker thought he resembled a bull elephant ready to charge, Hennessey's voice was quiet, the deadly kind of quiet. "I'll go back for the curragh. Stay here, the pair of you."

"Awww, Kevin!" the boy whined, seemingly oblivious of his peril.

Crossing to the bedroom door, Hennessey turned and glared, his eyes blazing like laser beams. The air around him vibrated with urgency and determination. "Both of you need to stay inside this cottage. You hear me?"

Lower lip jutting, the boy nodded.

All Parker said was, "Hurry."

In three strides, Hennessey was out the front door. A moment after it banged shut behind him, Parker heard the engine of the Range Rover roar to life. Then the tires squealed and gravel pelted the ground as the vehicle tore away from the house.

Parker collapsed against the mattress and tried to contact Amber one more time. He got nothing at all. Apparently his concussion was interfering with their mindspeak. He sighed in frustration.

"So you're Amber—I mean, Miss O'Neill's brother, then," the teen said, sticking out a grubby hand for Parker to shake. "I'm Connor Magee. Are ya really a selkie?"

"Parker O'Neill." He gripped the boy's hand for a brief second and knew all about the kid's infatuation with Amber. "And as far as I know, I'm not a selkie. Neither is my sister."

A whisper of relief shot from Connor's mind to Parker's, while a blush stained the boy's neck and ears. "Ah well, you would be the one to know, wouldn't ya?"

Parker shifted his weight to a more comfortable position before he admitted, "Actually, I'm not even sure what a selkie is. Can you fill me in?"

The teen looked askance, like he couldn't believe a grown man could be so ignorant. "Why they're seals, of course. Enchanted ones who can shed their skins and look like humans." He crossed his arms and huffed out a dismissive breath. "Can't believe someone named O'Neill never heard of selkies. Even if ya are a Yank."

"Clearly my education has been sadly lacking," Parker said, sorting out this newly discovered information. "Why would a selkie want to be human?"

Connor's brow furrowed, as if he'd never considered such a question. "I expect they're curious. Or maybe even bored. The thing is, if you find their selkie skin and hide it, they can't turn back. They're stuck in human form, but they pine for the sea forever."

Parker made a sour face. "Too tragic. Nope, definitely don't want to be a selkie. I don't even like the ocean that much."

The boy appeared unconvinced. Or perhaps something else was bothering him. An uncomfortable silence stretched between them.

"But what about this other thing?" Connor finally asked, shifting his weight from foot to foot. "A few minutes ago when Kevin asked ya to find your sister with your mind. Can ya really do that? Does it hurt?"

Parker sensed the earnestness in the boy's question, read his deep need to be treated like an adult instead of a child.

He decided to take a chance and be honest with Connor Magee. "My sister and I are twins. We communicated telepathically even before we were born."

"How bleedin' deadly!" Connor exclaimed. "Can you do that with other people too?"

"No, not until we came here. Apparently being on the auld sod of our ancestors has increased our abilities." Parker had developed this theory back in junior high school when pictures of Ireland stirred something powerful inside him. He had waited over half his life to test his belief, but never imagined just how intense the reality would prove to be.

Connor bit his lower lip as he mulled over the knowledge Parker had imparted to him. "So Amber must've talked to you and Kevin inside your heads, didn't she?"

"Sort of," Parker replied, cringing with the recent memory. "But not in words, in feelings. Something scared her, and she blasted her fear into my mind. I'm guessing Hennessey experienced the same thing."

"No shite!" Though the teen tried to sound sarcastic, his anxiety was palpable. "One minute Kevin's asking about me Uncle Michael, then all of a sudden he goes bloody mad ouva."

With hardly any effort at all, Parker reached into Connor's mind and saw the whole scenario—the pier on the right, the line of small black boats on the left, Hennessey's jaw going suddenly slack...

"He yells, 'Something's wrong with Amber!'" Parker could hear Hennessey's voice overlaying Connor's, and then he felt the boy's own frightened response, the worry he still felt. "I scarcely got me arse inside the Rover before he took off for here."

"He cares about my sister." Funny, how that little twinge of possessiveness Parker always felt when it came to Amber wasn't as strong as usual. "A lot. Same as you."

Connor hunched his shoulders like a turtle pulling into its shell. His ears glowed bright red. "Your sister..."

"Is the best," Parker filled in. "I know. And don't bother trying to deny anything, Connor, because I'm reading you right now."

~~~

The tide was still out far enough for Amber to walk right up to the mouth of the cave, but the moonlight didn't reach into the dark interior. She pulled out the flashlight and switched it on. The small beam shone feebly in the vast darkness.

Holding her breath in anticipation of the stench, she stepped inside the cavern. She played the light across the sand and over the humped shapes of dozens of sleeping seals. The creatures littered the sandy floor, lying singly or in groups of twos and threes.

Still attempting to ignore the overpowering smell, she cast about with her mind.

Ronan?

Suddenly, the beam of light glittered back at her, flashing from the eyes of one of the creatures. A jolt of alarm snapped through the silent air a second before the seal called out a challenge. The sound reverberated off the walls and ceiling, causing grunts and snuffles among the other animals, and then another bark.

The light swinging wildly, Amber clutched her temples and transmitted calm reassurance, broadcasting all around herself in a sweeping arc. A few more scattered yaps echoed from the far reaches of the cave, but for every thread of fear and anxiety that came to her, Amber sent back soothing thoughts.

Safe…

No harm…

I've come for my young.

After several long moments, she could feel the tension ebb gradually from the air.

"Ronan?" she called softly. "Meriol? Where are you?"

Pointing the light down, she ventured farther into the cave, still sending tranquil thoughts. A few of the seals sat up or rustled in their sandy beds, but Amber detected no feelings of fear or threat. Not even when she slowly ran the light across them.

Plenty of large shapes littered the ground in and

around the pool, but she could distinguish nothing that looked remotely human.

"Ronan? Meriol?" she ventured again, and when she received no response, she very gingerly cast out with her mind.

Again, no human thoughts came to her through the haze of sleepy animals as she picked her way along, staying close to the cave wall. Then a faint, hesitant thread that had to be the boy reached her. Mentally, she grasped it and sent back.

Ronan!

I've come to protect you and Meriol.

She sent an image of the sailboat and didn't dampen her fear.

We need to run. Now!

Stand up so I can find you.

Amber sensed resistance, but from an outside source. Must be Meriol. She reached for the girl's mind, but couldn't connect, so she tried Ronan again, all the while shining the light in the direction where she guessed the thoughts originated.

A large hump lay alone and slightly apart from the other animals. Too far for her flashlight to discern clearly. She took a step closer, then another. Before she could take a third, a pale hand shot out from one end of the shape and waved.

Ronan!

She sucked in her breath through her teeth and tempered her mental shout of triumph as she rushed forward. The dark shape looked familiar even as its movements suddenly became very un-seal-like.

Two round, white faces appeared. Then Amber

recognized the misshapen coat she and Kevin had used to carry her brother. The coat Ronan had insisted was Parker's selkie skin.

While she stood frozen in astonishment at the effectiveness of the disguise, the boy rose, shook off sand, and mentally cried out his relieved greeting. A moment later, his still sand-coated arms went around her waist, and he pressed his dirty face against her windbreaker.

With disjointed mental images, Ronan revealed how he and Meriol had watched the curragh carrying Amber, Kevin, and Parker head out for Ballyliffin. Then the children had gone back to the cottage, changed clothes, and prepared to go after their father's secret cache of money.

Amber had a hazy picture of another cave piled with crates and containers. A spectacular array of coins and jewelry spilled on the ground, all products of Ronan's imagination.

But the fanciful representation gave way to the very real scene of Ronan and Meriol rolling their cart along the path between their home and the beach. A small curragh rested precariously on top of the vehicle, and Amber could feel the straining ache in the boy's arms and legs as he struggled to help his sister move the over-burdened cart. The distant sound of an outboard motor halted their progress.

The white sail and the hum of the motorized launch leapt from Ronan's terrified mind to hers. Through a frenzy of fear, Amber saw the curragh and cart crash into the undergrowth on one side of the path, while the two children ran the other way. The duffle bag thumped against Meriol's side while Ronan carried the heavy coat bunched in his arms.

"Did you come alone, then?" Meriol's sarcastic query ended Ronan's mental tale.

The girl stood a few feet away, brushing sand off her jeans.

"Yes," Amber confirmed, feeling decidedly inadequate under Meriol's measuring glance. "The men in the sailboat are back. We need to get to Kevin's house."

"They didn't find us before."

"They only searched the cottage," Ronan interrupted his sister. "They didn't come here to the cave."

Meriol's expression grew more annoyed as did her tone. "'Tis the other cave they want. They won't come here."

Desperate to end the argument quickly, Amber seized upon the one thing that might sway the girl. "Prince Parker thinks they will. He's heard their thoughts, and he sent me to find you. He's still too weak to come himself."

Her gamble paid off. Meriol literally wavered at the mention of Parker's name. Tender concern laced with adulation seeped from her slender frame as she rocked ever so slightly from side to side.

Amber clutched eagerly for the girl's mind, sending images of feverish Parker calling out.

"Please," she whispered. "We have to hurry."

A soft, dreamy vision of Parker floated along the link for a brief moment before Meriol snapped her head up, obviously aware of Amber's presence in her mind. With an outraged gasp, the girl broke their mental connection.

"I need to get our things." She pivoted on her heel and tramped to the side wall of the cave where she squatted to move aside a pair of flat rocks.

"Will Prince Par-Ker be all right?" Ronan asked, staring up at Amber with wide-eyed distress.

Amber rubbed a dirty smudge off his cheek, just like she'd done for dozens of her former students.

"He'll be fine. Don't—" But her words suddenly dried up as a sound drifted over the lapping of the waves. The unmistakable hum of an outboard motor.

Chapter 9

WHOEVER WAS IN THE BOAT KNEW ABOUT THE CAVE because they pulled to the side of the entrance with the strip of sandy beach. The same beach with her footprints still marking the otherwise pristine sand, Amber realized.

She crouched behind a boulder at the back of the cave, not far from the rock shelf she and Kevin had previously occupied. The duffle bag with Meriol and Ronan's meager belongings sat at her feet. The children themselves had hastily resumed their hiding place beneath Parker's old coat on the opposite side of the cavern.

From the moment Amber first heard the outboard motor, the other occupants of the cave began to stir. Grunts, groans, and the sounds of heavy bodies moving restlessly echoed from walls to ceiling. An undercurrent of tension buzzed inside Amber's mind. The seals sensed both the impending intruders and her own fear, and they were reacting.

Amber's first thought was concern for Meriol and Ronan's safety. She tried to mentally sooth the animals and steer them around the hidden children. Peeking around the boulder, she saw the animals' focus was clearly elsewhere, and that's when she recognized the protectiveness within the heavy layer of tension among the creatures.

They perceived her and the children as part of their group, and they would defend their own against trespassers.

The first bark of warning sounded at the same time Amber saw the beam of light shine into the entrance of the cave. A dozen more cries echoed the call, and the larger animals began to move toward the entrance.

The lone figure of a man stood silhouetted at the mouth of the cavern, a light swinging from his hand. A score of barking seals scuttled out to challenge him.

"Amber!" His voice was nearly obliterated by the barking, but she heard and knew it immediately. "Amber, are you in there?"

"Kevin!"

He jumped to the side as a large seal lunged at his leg, teeth snapping.

"Christ Jaysus!" He swore, backpedaling fast as the big galoot and two of his mates came after him. "Amber?"

Sweet Holy Mother, he hoped she was all right!

A mob of enormous bodies surged toward the opening of the cave.

Just when he thought he'd have to use the lantern to defend himself, the seals suddenly ceased their onslaught. Instead of charging, they milled about in confusion. Over the din, Kevin heard his name. He shined the light into the moving bodies and saw one taller figure far in the back.

She cried his name again and waved her hand over her head as she bounded between the creatures. Icy apprehension seized his throat as she stumbled her way toward him, bumping into two or three seals as she went. If she angered them, they could very easily turn and attack.

"Careful!" he croaked out.

But by then, she'd reached him. The lantern fell onto the sand beside his feet as her arms went round him. He saw the two children near the wall of the cave in the moment before he cupped Amber's face in both his hands.

A torrent of relief poured out of him and into her, leaving his legs rubbery. From the moment he'd dashed from the cottage, he'd refused to let himself think he might fail, even with the possibility hammering away at the back of his mind.

Kevin swayed against her as she sent back his feelings coupled with her own. Awash in their combined flood of thankfulness and joy, he feathered his lips across first her eyelids and then her cheeks, and finally her mouth. The briefest whisper of a touch…

It was enough for him… Enough to know that the endlessly torturous rush to get here hadn't been in vain. That for the time being they were together, safe.

But she wanted more.

Before he could lift his head, she slanted her mouth across his and devoured his gentleness with a hot jolt of desire. The touch of her demanding tongue momentarily vaporized his restraint, and he eagerly tasted the silky heat inside her mouth. Passion and possession flared through both his mind and body for one gloriously invigorating moment before he broke the kiss with a groan.

"We shouldn't be giving the young ones an advanced education," he muttered, all too aware of Meriol and Ronan's open scrutiny.

"Luckily, I'm a teacher," Amber whispered back, and gave him one more quick kiss.

Around them, the seals shuffled back into the cavern, paying the four of them no heed at all. Had Amber been the one to spur them into action? Maybe Ronan and Meriol's idea that the O'Neills were selkies wasn't that far-fetched after all.

"Where have you been, Kevin?" the boy asked, plucking at his sleeve.

"I've been looking for your da and Michael Coyle." Kevin looked into the child's dirty face and saw far too much knowledge for one so young.

"But then the princess called for you, didn't she?" Ronan smiled and cast a quick sidelong glance at Amber. "Same as she did to me."

Meriol clicked her tongue in a dismissing sound. "I s'pose you left our bag in the back of the cave," she said to Amber, rolling her eyes. "I'll fetch it."

Kevin reached down, picked up the lantern, and handed it to the girl. "Take this so you don't trip over anything."

With a long-suffering sigh, Meriol took the light and tramped off into the cavern.

"I ran into Coyle at the cottage," Amber murmured. "He led the sailboat in the opposite direction."

In spite of her low tone, Ronan heard her anyway, for he piped up, "Did the men in the sailboat hurt Prince Par-Ker? I think they hurt my da too."

"Don't worry," Kevin quickly assured the boy. "We won't let them touch you or Meriol."

As he spoke, he met Amber's worried gaze. Pressing her lips tightly together, she supplied a quick mental recap of her meeting with Coyle.

Smugglers…

"…and a nasty bunch at that."

"Shanley's in the thick of this, same as half the village."

"…find those kids. They've an aunty down in Sligo Town. Take them there."

None of it came as a surprise to him. The illegal activities going on in the area were one of the many reasons his father had kept to himself in all his years of living at Malin Head. Far easier to turn a blind eye when you knew nothing.

The PSNI had a special task force to investigate smugglers and contraband, but Kevin didn't know if the Republic had an equivalent. Not that he was certain they could be trusted either.

He tried to comfort Amber by sending her a healthy shot of reassurance. "I know someone in Malin Head we can trust."

"Hurry up, Meriol!" Amber called, glancing nervously out to sea.

She was looking for a white sail. So was he.

The girl trotted up, the duffle bag slung over her shoulder, and the sand-covered coat clutched under her other arm. She must have guessed at the substance of their conversation, for when she handed him the lantern, her fingers trembled a little.

Good! She needed to believe the threat was real. This was no game.

Kevin turned off the light and herded the pair and Amber to the beached curragh. The incoming tide already lapped at the back of the boat as he tossed the lantern inside. He positioned himself at the prow and nodded to the two ragamuffins.

"Get in, and so help me Meriol, if you jump out this time, when I catch you, I'll drown you."

"I won't," she promised contritely. Then she tossed her things over the side before giving her brother a boost and climbing in herself.

One healthy shove and the curragh slid into the surf. Kevin vaulted over the side while Amber scrambled after him. In only a few moments, he had them past the breaking waves and was able to start the outboard. The sputtering hum sounded loud in the still night air.

Compared to earlier, the sea had grown quite calm. A sailboat without auxiliary power wouldn't be going much of anywhere with so little breeze. Still, he steered the curragh as close to the shore as he dared and kept a sharp eye out for any trace of another watercraft.

Meriol and Ronan spread the dirty coat on the floor near the prow and curled up on it. Amber squeezed close to his side on the back bench.

"I just connected with Parker," she murmured into his ear. "He knows we're all okay. You left Connor with him?"

"We didn't know Coyle's whereabouts, so I couldn't just abandon the little gobshite," Kevin explained. Then he added, "Has he talked your brother's ear off yet?"

The little spurt of laughter inside his mind warmed Kevin clear down to his toes. All the places where she touched him—arm, side, thigh—tingled with heightened sensation. No woman had ever affected him in quite this way, inside and out.

For a brief moment, he looked into her eyes, dark and fathomless in the moonlight. What a pity they couldn't have met back in the day when he'd been stupidly optimistic about the future, back when he'd still had hope.

"Thank you, for everything," she said, putting her arm around his waist and snuggling closer still.

The swirl of her gratitude, mixed with desire and ardor, made Kevin feel ashamed of himself and a little ill. Amber wasn't some loosebit to knock back with no regard for her feelings. But heaven help him, he'd pretty much done just that.

And wanted to do it again.

Having her near made every shred of decency he tried to preserve fly right out the window.

"Don't thank me just yet," he replied, concentrating hard on the passing shoreline so that perhaps she couldn't discern his thoughts quite so easily. "We're not quite home free."

"What will we do if the sailboat…" She stiffened and didn't finish the question.

So much for keeping his thoughts to himself.

But she didn't move away either. "You have a gun, don't you?"

He nodded. After more than a dozen years with the PSNI, he'd never once discharged his weapon except on the firing range. He hoped like hell that tonight wouldn't be a first.

When the white foam against the breakwater came into view, Amber finally relaxed a little. They'd made it all the way to the village of Malin Head without seeing another vessel on the water. She suspected they had Michael Coyle to thank for that, but she wouldn't let herself speculate on what he might have done to divert the sailboat and its occupants. More pressing matters required her attention at the moment, and two of them were asleep in the floor of the boat.

Moving reluctantly from Kevin's warmth, she crawled to where the two children lay. Gently, she shook Ronan's shoulder.

"Wake up, we're in Malin Head."

Meriol sprang instantly awake, but Ronan rubbed his eyes and groaned softly.

The whine of the motor went suddenly silent, and Amber saw they were coming abreast of the wooden pier. No sign of life stirred in the dark, silent harbor.

"Secure us next to the ladder, will you, Meriol?" Kevin called out.

Grabbing a short length of rope, the girl did as he asked with quiet efficiency. Then, slinging the duffel bag over her shoulder, she climbed out of the rocking boat and up onto the pier. A still drowsy Ronan followed, dragging the remains of the coat behind him by one dirty sleeve.

"Meet me on the beach," Kevin instructed.

Awkwardly, Amber clambered after the boy, the flashlight in her pocket banging against the side of the iron ladder as she climbed. By the time she stood on the pier, Kevin had untied the boat and shoved away. She watched him row the few dozen yards to where several other dark shapes sat in a line on the pebbled shore.

A small hand clutched hers, and, startled, she looked down into the owlish face of Ronan. "C'mon then, Princess Amber."

A pair of gulls flapped noisily into the air as she and the children plodded down the pier. Kevin met them a few steps from the foot and led the way up the street past darkened, silent cottages and shops.

The bungalow porch he mounted wasn't far from the waterfront and had no lights visible in any of its windows. But the profusely blooming red geraniums growing next to the steps left Amber's tired, aching bones with a homey and comforting feel. Still holding Ronan's hand, she and the two children stood on the path in front of the house.

The woman who answered Kevin's persistent knock wore a faded blue bathrobe. She peered myopically through the glass-paned storm door before she exclaimed, "Kevin Hennessey, as I live and breathe! What are you doing here at this hour?"

As if he were not much older than Ronan, Kevin dropped his gaze and shuffled his feet. "So sorry to disturb you, Mrs. Fitzpatrick, but I've a very big favor to ask."

Opening the storm door, she squinted in Amber's direction. "What do you and your Yankee girlfriend... But surely those are Silas Lafferty's children?"

Amber saw understanding and apprehension chase across Mrs. Fitzpatrick's features. "Come inside, all of you. Quietly now, so's we don't wake the mister."

She ushered them inside, through a tidy, if crowded, front room into a spacious kitchen and dining area. Ronan, who had seemed asleep on his feet, perked up as soon as Mrs. Fitzpatrick mentioned food.

With the children off to the loo to wash up, Kevin got directly to the point. "Their da's gone missing almost a week, and his partner, Michael Coyle, thinks he's met with foul play. Coyle told Amber to get the children to their aunty in Sligo, but for now I believe they'll be safer here." He shifted his weight like a guilty teen again. "Besides, with Amber and her brother at my place, I've no room for Ronan and Meriol to sleep."

Expression never changing, Mrs. Fitzpatrick stood at the sink, silently peeling potatoes during Kevin's recitation. She finished with the potato in her hand before she replied. "My own dear sister Marie lives in Sligo Town, as do both her daughters. I'll call them first thing in the morning and see if they've heard of the aunty. Do you know her name?"

Kevin's negative head shake didn't seem to disturb Mrs. Fitzpatrick. She merely shrugged and picked up another potato. "No harm will come to them here to be sure."

Amber felt the wave of relief and gratitude roll from Kevin's shoulders as he said thank you and asked to use the telephone.

"You'll be calling the authorities then?" Mrs. Fitzpatrick rinsed the potatoes and put them on the cutting board. When Kevin answered with a tight-lipped nod, she added, "Not Jamie Shanley, I hope."

So the woman knew perfectly well about the smugglers and who was involved with them. Amber hoped her surprise didn't show on her face.

Kevin's expression remained neutral, and his tone betrayed no emotion. "No. A Garda in Ballyliffin who talked to Amber this afternoon." He moved his steadfast blue gaze from Mrs. Fitzpatrick to her. "Do you have his name and number, luv?"

After a momentary search through her pockets, Amber found the officer's card. Kevin took it and disappeared into the sitting room just as Meriol and Ronan came back.

"Sit yourselves down, all of you," Mrs. Fitzpatrick instructed. "I'll have some fish reheated and fresh chips fried in two shakes."

True to her word, the woman had food on the table in short order. Ronan downed almost a full glass of milk in one long guzzle. Meriol was only slightly less enthusiastic, but the lump of worry in Amber's stomach pretty much killed her appetite. She picked at a few pieces of potato while she waited for Kevin to come back into the kitchen. Mrs. Fitzpatrick set aside a plate of food for him.

The children finished their fish and chips and started on new glasses of milk and shortbread cookies, but Kevin still hadn't returned. Amber wanted to reach out mentally to see what was going on, but she didn't feel comfortable doing it, so she distracted herself with a cookie.

With the cookies gone, Mrs. Fitzpatrick went off to make up beds while Amber helped Meriol and Ronan get ready to go to sleep. They passed Kevin, phone still at his ear, as they headed into the washroom. After a look at his tense expression, Amber found it even more difficult not to link into his mind, but she continued to resist.

Ronan was almost asleep on his feet, so Amber decided to just wash his face and hands instead of insisting on a bath. He never uttered a protest when she scrubbed behind his ears and then combed sand out of his hair.

At first, Meriol was openly hostile about not needing Amber's assistance. But by the time she'd finished with Ronan's hair, the girl took his place, though rather half-heartedly. After several long moments, she met Amber's eyes in the mirror. "Does your hair curl like that all on its own?"

Amber gave a little shudder at the sight of her own unruly mop and nodded. "I'm afraid so."

"I wish mine did," Meriol said on a sigh.

"Well, I wish mine was straight like yours," Amber replied. Then, when the girl rolled her eyes with skepticism, she added, "Next time you wash it, braid it while it's still wet. It'll be wavy when it dries."

Meriol turned around, her expression wary as a cornered animal, her voice a hoarse whisper. "What's to become of us, then?"

Laying the comb aside, Amber put her hand on the teen's stiff shoulder. "Tomorrow we'll get in touch with your aunt in Sligo."

She tried to link into the Meriol's mind, send her reassuring thoughts, but the girl jerked away and stood up. "We've not seen Aunt Cara since Mum died. She doesn't want us."

"Where's Sligo?" Ronan interrupted.

"'Tis the end of the bloody world!" Meriol snapped.

"Watch your language, young lady," Mrs. Fitzpatrick warned from the doorway. "The beds are ready, and I've some make-do nightclothes for the both of you."

Ronan gazed up at Amber with sleep-heavy eyes. "Can't we just stay with you and Prince Par-Ker?"

The boy's plaintive question sliced deep into her mind and left Amber awash in guilt and remorse. "We have to go back to America in a few days."

"And that really is the end of the world," said Mrs. Fitzpatrick. "So we can't have you going there."

Even though Amber knew the woman's words were true, she didn't feel any better about leaving the two children to their plight.

The upstairs guestroom obviously doubled as a sewing room for Mrs. Fitzpatrick. Pieces of colorful fabric lay on one end of a worktable, and a portable sewing machine occupied the opposite end. One of the woman's old nightgowns lay across the foot of the trundle bed along with one of her husband's T-shirts, makeshift nightwear for the two children.

While Meriol changed behind a fabric screen, Amber helped Ronan out of his dirty outer clothes and into the oversized T-shirt. He gave her hand a squeeze and then crawled under the blanket on the smaller part of the trundle.

"G'night Princess Amber," he breathed on a soft sigh.

Meriol climbed over her brother and snuggled down with her face toward the wall. She said nothing.

"Sleep tight," Mrs. Fitzpatrick said, and turned out the light. As she shut the door, she murmured, "I only hope their aunty does better by them than their father has." Then she paused at the top of the staircase and regarded Amber with a shrewd and speculative gaze. "'Tis a pity you're going back to America so soon. Not for the sake of those two, but because of Kevin. You're the first woman I've known him to take any interest in since... Well, I'm sure you'd know."

The image of the petite blonde woman and the tiny infant attached to tubes and wires flashed through Amber's memory. She squirmed with discomfort. "You mean since his wife and baby?"

"'Twas a cryin' shame about that baby," the older woman mused as she paused at the top of the stairs. However, she wasn't done discussing Kevin's private business. "But Kevin was not to blame any more than anyone else."

Bristling from Mrs. Fitzpatrick's scrutiny as well as her nosiness, Amber couldn't stop herself from asking, "So why wouldn't Kevin's father have approved of me?"

The other woman gave a dismissive shrug. "Because you're a Yank, of course. Kevin's sister Leonore took off with a Yank, and they never heard from her again. Broke her parents' hearts. Declan made Sharletta and Kevin swear they would never run off to America."

Without giving Amber a chance to respond, she turned and walked down the stairs. Not that there was much to say, Amber reflected, as she followed their garrulous hostess.

Downstairs in the kitchen, Kevin had wolfed down most of his food. When he saw Amber, his hint of a smile curled her toes and made her momentarily forget everything else. She automatically sent a ribbon of warm pleasure and anticipation from her mind to his. He looked away and went back to eating, but not before she caught an answering strand of longing from him.

"I spoke to your Officer Reynolds in Ballyliffin," Kevin said between bites. "He'll be taking the report to Garda headquarters in Letterkenny first thing in the morning. Shanley reports there too."

Amber recalled the earnest face of the younger officer who'd spoken to her and then Parker at the clinic. He had seemed trustworthy and not at all cynical and impatient like Shanley. She only wished she could be sure.

Kevin rose and took his dishes to the sink. "I also put a call in to a couple of PSNI fellas I know in Derry. Malin Head may not be their jurisdiction, but the border is very close."

Mrs. Fitzpatrick's face puckered in disapproval at his last comment, but she intercepted his plate and silverware, deposited them in the sink, and asked, "More tea, then?"

He shook his head. "'Tis very late, and Amber's brother is quite ill. We need to get back to him and young Connor."

Amber had temporarily forgotten about the boy, and she didn't want to think about his missing uncle. "Still no luck reaching Coyle?"

Kevin shook his head again, not meeting her eyes. She could clearly see that Coyle's status was a worrisome point for him also.

"Don't worry about the two upstairs," Mrs. Fitzpatrick reassured. "I shall be making calls early and wager I'll find their aunty before noon."

"Thank you, Bridget." Kevin paused for a moment after using her given name, and his spine seemed to stiffen. "I trust you same as my father trusted you, and I appreciate all that you've done this night."

The woman gave a brusque toss of her head. "'Tis what any good Christian woman would do, especially for the son of an old friend."

"Well, thank you all the same," Kevin insisted.

The woman dried her hands on a tea towel and escorted them to the front door. "Good night then, and we'll be in touch."

"Thank you," Amber repeated, wishing she could come up with more adequate sentiments.

Guilt, worry, confusion, and a few more emotions she didn't want to identify tumbled around inside her exhausted brain as she followed Kevin off the porch and down the path to the main road.

"The Rover's parked up by the pub," he said, reaching for her hand. "We'll be back at the cottage soon."

She linked her fingers with his, and his touch felt warm and earthy, like the fragrant smoldering peat fire he kept burning in his fireplace. In spite of all the scary uncertainty surrounding them, when she was close to Kevin, she felt safe.

With the undeniable tingle of attraction sizzling from his palm to hers and right up her arm, she reached for his mind. But instead of comfort, she found the tangled images of all that had happened in the past few hours, interspersed with memories of his father, his pregnant wife, his soul-robbing drunken binges...

Bewildered, Amber severed the connection, stopped in the middle of the empty road, and stared at him.

"I warned you," he said by way of apology.

He tried to let go of her hand, but she wouldn't let him.

"I'm not sorry." She continued to gaze into the dark wells of pain that brimmed in his eyes, but she left him the privacy of his thoughts. Finally she asked, "What do we do now?"

He looked first in the direction of the waterfront, then up the road where the car was parked before he said, "We wait."

It was close to midnight when at last they reached the cottage. Amber sat next to him in the Rover, drooping with weariness.

She hadn't said much, and she'd stayed out of his mind, for which he was grateful. Her one brief glimpse inside him had apparently been more than enough.

Kevin himself had been too done in to keep her away from the dark agonies buried in his soul. Memories and events he would rather not examine too closely, much less share.

When they pulled into the yard, he saw her put a hand to her temple and knew she'd called to her brother. So once they were inside, he wasn't at all surprised to find Parker awake, though still in his bed.

Connor, who'd been draped over the sofa, sleeping, woke up a bit more slowly. Since Amber went straight away to her brother's bedside, telling the teen about his still missing step-uncle fell solely to Kevin. He didn't spare the youth any bit of the graveness of the situation.

"The morning will be soon enough to sort everything out," Connor agreed with a stoical acceptance that confirmed Kevin's belief there was no love lost between the boy and Coyle.

When Amber returned to the sitting room, Kevin sent her off to shower while he and Connor figured out the sleeping arrangements. Since Parker occupied the only bed and couldn't be moved, the remaining options were limited. Luckily the night was mild, so most of the extra sheets and blankets went to make pallets for himself and Connor on the floor of the kitchen and back porch. As was proper, they agree to reserve the couch for Amber.

However, when she emerged from the loo, hair still damp and face flushed from scrubbing, Kevin almost threw propriety out the window. Perhaps the back of the Rover was a better option for him after all. Bidding her a quick good night, he ducked into the loo for his own go at the shower, and considered it divine intervention when the hot water ran out halfway through.

Shower finished and clothes changed, Kevin opened the bathroom door and nearly swung it into Connor. Curled on his pallet opposite the washer, the youth slept soundly facing the wall.

Kevin didn't fare nearly so well in his own spot close to the kitchen door. The hard tile floor seemed to bite into his spine and arse, and no matter how hard he tried not to think about Amber asleep on the sofa in the next room, visions of her kept popping into his too alert brain.

Receiving her mental distress call earlier tonight had affected him far more than it should have. And when he'd learned she went after the Lafferty children on her own, feelings of helpless terror like he hadn't experienced in years burned through his soul.

Once he'd finally gotten himself sober, he'd sworn that he would never care so deeply again. He had destroyed the person he cared for most in the world, and had come precariously near to destroying himself. He couldn't risk that happening again.

But Amber, with her insidiously seductive mental connection, forced him to tread too close. What she gave and what she demanded were more than he could handle, no matter how much part of him wanted to.

After what felt like hours of tossing, turning, and cursing himself for a fool, Kevin finally drifted into a fitful dreamless sleep. He awakened with a start when something warm and soft pressed against the length of his back. Jerking to a sitting position, he swallowed back the half-formed expletive as cool fingers settled across his lips.

"Shhh," Amber whispered in his ear.

Then her moist mouth trailed down the side of his throat and paused at the neckband of his T-shirt.

The breath rattling in his parched throat sounded loud in the pre-dawn stillness. "Please, Amber, don't—"

"Shhh!" She hissed again, lifting her head. Only a tiny rim of gold showed around her wide pupils. "I sent Connor to the couch twenty minutes ago. I've waited long enough."

Chapter 10

IN THE GRAY LIGHT FILTERING THROUGH THE WINDOW, Amber's hair shone like a banked fire, dark with a deep red glow of smoldering heat. Kevin's fingers ached to touch the silky strands, just as his bone-dry mouth longed to taste the wet sweetness inside hers. But he didn't dare touch her, kiss her. If he did, he knew he wouldn't be able to stop.

"We can't do this," he groaned, shoving her hands aside.

She gave a sigh of disappointment that made her breasts rise and fall enticingly under the thin knit fabric of her nightgown. Looking away, he fought his rapidly rising desire by thinking about Connor and her brother asleep only a room or two away without so much as a closed door between them.

He thought seriously about pulling the covers over his head, as if that would cure the problem. Instead, she was the one who lifted the blanket and shoved her bare legs next to his. The feel of her skin against him cranked his libido close to the limit.

Snuggling beside him, Amber put her arm across his stomach and laid her head on his chest. "We don't have to do anything, if you don't want to."

"'Tis not that I don't want to," he gritted out. "I do. But your brother and Connor are bound to hear us."

"Not if you're extra quiet," she murmured with the faintest hint of amusement. "Just shout inside your head."

Then Kevin felt the intimate touch inside his mind, the sensual brush of velvet that signaled her presence. Unable to resist the connection, the chance to share every pleasure between them, he surrendered with a groan.

Her hand slid down his side.

"Sweet saints!" he swore softly as her fingers inched across his hip and worked their way under the elastic waistband of his boxers.

When her hand encircled him, he bit his lip hard to stifle the moan. She absorbed the shock and the sharp pang of pleasure and sent it back to him over their mental link, while she began a slow stroke up and down his hard length.

"You'll be... the death of... me!" he panted.

And all the while, her deft fingers continued to squeeze, pull, and stroke him in the most exquisitely torturous way.

A sanguine smile curled the corners of her mouth. "Not quite yet," she whispered. "But soon."

Her dark head disappeared beneath the blanket, and she stopped her erotic caresses long enough to tug at his boxers.

Surely she didn't intend to...

Kevin felt rather than heard her little mew of satisfaction as his erection sprang free. Her fingers claimed him, leaving trails of fire as they explored. And after them came her hot, wet tongue, swirling molten flames around and down.

You taste wild, like the sea.

Her thought floated to him on a smoky haze of passion.

She was nothing like the sea.

She was heaven.

Or as close as he would ever come to it.

But if she didn't stop now he would most certainly die, just as he surely would if she did.

Involuntary and inhuman sounds worked their way from his constricted throat while Amber's lips inched back up his shaft to settle lightly on the swollen tip.

Before he lost his last shred of control, Kevin grasped her forearms and pulled her up to his mouth, drowning his guttural moans in a hard, deep kiss. His tongue thrust boldly inside, taking possession of her mouth the way the rest of him would take—*must take* possession of her.

She answered him with the same rough urgency. With her lips fixed firmly to his, she plastered her breasts against him and rubbed with the same demanding rhythm that would very soon consume them both.

He wrenched his mouth from hers and struggled to his feet, one hand jerking up his boxers, the other dragging her with him. Her mind gave a startled protest while he kicked away the blankets entangling their feet.

"The loo," he explained in a hoarse whisper. "It has a door and a lock."

Instead of answering, Amber leapt, hooking one leg around his waist as her greedy mouth fastened atop his.

Stumbling for a moment, Kevin put one steadying hand across her back while he gripped her thigh with the other, lifting her completely off the ground. He could feel the hot wet center of her arousal burning through the satin crotch of her knickers and the cotton layer of his boxers as he tangled his tongue with hers and staggered toward the door.

Combined with hers, his own blazing need bombarded

his overloaded brain. He swayed into the door frame
and spun crazily into the utility room, banging against
the washer.

Crap!

Amber swore inside his head just before she dragged
her lips from his. With what seemed excruciating slowness, she slid down his body, lingering for an agonizing
moment on top of his erection. Then, feet on the floor,
she twisted and shoved open the door to the loo. Panting,
they both tumbled inside.

As soon as the door banged shut, Kevin clicked in the
lock, then dug frantically through the cupboard under
the sink in search of the box of condoms. Beside him,
Amber drew her nightgown over her head and flung it
into the corner. Her knickers swiftly followed. Her skin
shone like milky satin in the dim room.

Shower…

Water…

Noise…

Scarcely coherent, blood thundering in his ears, he
sent the words.

She tugged his boxers to his ankles before she turned
away to comply. Meanwhile, he shredded the lid right
off the box when he found it at last.

Kicking away his pesky underwear, he joined
her in the shower. The water was only a trickle, but
he couldn't wait. He needed to touch her breasts,
thighs, everywhere.

Kevin pulled her against him and claimed her mouth.
With equal fervor, she kissed him back, shoving him
against the tiled wall. She clawed at his T-shirt, raking
her nails over his chest and down his stomach. The

shared intensity drove them like a pair of wild animals propelled into a frenzy by their need to mate.

He broke the kiss long enough to rip the T-shirt over his head, and then he grasped her by both thighs and lifted her, whirling so that her back was against the wall. Grasping his shoulders, she inched herself up high enough to wrap both legs around his waist.

Taking full advantage of her position, he sucked one of her nipples into his mouth. He wasn't sure if her moan of pure pleasure was only in his mind or not. But the potency of the combined sensation made him see stars. She writhed against him, her body like hot silk as she descended down his length.

She pulled her breast away from his mouth and replaced it with her lips and tongue. Tangling with his, her tongue set a rhythm their joined bodies quickly moved to imitate. Oblivious to everything but the primal need to thrust and withdraw, Kevin could no longer distinguish the boundaries between their minds nor bodies.

Every nerve ending, every fiber trembled on the brink of completion. Then he felt her spasm with joyous release and found himself exploding with the same glorious abandon, the orgasms shuddering and echoing between them.

Long moments later, he became aware of the cool, smooth surface of the tile sliding across his knuckles. Amber's rapid gasps fanned against his collarbone while his own knees wobbled a bit.

Somehow, he managed to step out of the shower and sit on the closed lid of the commode with her on his lap, their bodies and minds still united. With a sated sigh, she nuzzled his neck and drew lazy circles in his chest hair with her index finger.

Part of him longed to stay like this forever. But from some distant place in his subconscious came the thought that he shouldn't be using her in such a selfish way. They could have no future together.

As her finger paused in its movements, the rush of memory swept away the niggling wisp of Kevin's guilt. Instead the desire to have her all over again bloomed in his mind.

Or was it her thought? Her own recently quenched need stirring?

Her fingers brushed across his nipple, and she withdrew from his lap, but not his mind.

Shower.

Amber mentally answered his unformed question as she reached for the knobs to increase the water flow.

Join me?

Laughing as the spray of water hit her, she held out the bar of soap in invitation. No selkie had ever beguiled a human more effectively. Completely in her thrall, he stepped into the shower and slid the curtain closed behind him.

In spite of the fact that mere minutes ago Amber had experienced the most incredible orgasm of her life, she could feel the unmistakable stirrings of lust deep inside her. Looking at Kevin's nude form sent warm sparkles fizzing through her blood. His physical beauty rivaled any statue she'd ever seen in a museum. And far better, he was real.

Being connected to him mentally and physically was unlike anything she'd ever felt. Sex had never been this good. Not even on her honeymoon. She couldn't get enough of it.

Of Kevin.

Playfully, she backed him into the spray. The water ran in streaming rivulets down his arms and glistened on the wide expanse of his shoulders. He looked like some sea god rising from the waves.

Tipping his head back, he closed his eyes while the water soaked his thick black hair. Her breath momentarily caught in her throat. Then he stepped away from the spewing nozzle and shook his head like a dog, spattering her with droplets.

"Hey—" she protested as he swung her around and directly under the water.

Sputtering with laughter, she flipped her wet hair in his face. Like naughty children, they splashed each other a few more times. Then Amber grabbed the bar of soap and lathered Kevin's back.

Starting at his shoulders, she leisurely worked her way down his spine. She spread the foamy bubbles across the wide, muscled width that tapered down to his hips. By the time she reached his tight buttocks, her scrubbing had changed to caresses. But when she tried to move her hand from his back to his front, he grabbed her wrist and took away the bar of soap.

"Turn 'round," he said, making a circle with his fingers. "And I'll wash you."

"If you insist." She obediently showed him her back, but not before she noticed his erection had already started to grow again.

Not getting enough wasn't just her problem.

As his big hands skated over her skin, she purposely leaned backward enough to feel his arousal brush against her skin.

He groaned into her dripping hair. "Sweet saints! Still impatient?"

"Only when it comes to you." She could hear the ragged edge in her amused tone.

How could she want him again so soon?

But she did.

Another half-step back and Amber pressed her entire length, shoulders to hips, against his chest and torso. The bar of soap hit the tile floor as his arms encircled her, and his growing desire entwined with hers inside her mind.

Water pounding the center of his broad back, he cupped her breasts with his soapy hands and fastened his lips onto her neck. This time the groan of pleasure was hers as Kevin raked his thumbs over and over her nipples while his ever hardening erection thrust between her legs.

She was about to bend forward to give him better access when he suddenly stopped. Before she could form a question, she heard it, too. Connor calling his name.

Kevin let her go and turned to face the shower nozzle just long enough to rinse off the excess lather. Then he pulled open the curtain and grabbed a towel.

With Kevin's silent curses echoing inside her mind, Amber did the same quick rinse in the rapidly cooling water. Adding a few swear words of her own, she twisted the faucet handles to off just as Connor hammered on the bathroom door.

"Kevin! You in there?" the boy demanded. "Your mobile's ringing off the bloody hook."

"Well, answer it then!" he snarled in reply.

"I did! 'Tis Mrs. Fitzpatrick, and she said 'tis urgent."

The flare of alarm surged between their minds as Kevin grabbed his discarded boxers. Amber snatched a towel for herself.

"Tell her I'll be right there." Kevin instructed through the door, his voice still gravelly.

They both heard Connor's bare feet slapping against the floor. He'd obviously left the phone in the other room. A quick spurt of relief from Kevin mingled with their shared anxiety. With a towel hanging over his damp shoulders, he reached for the door knob.

Lock it again! he sent as he slipped out of the room.

But Amber was far more worried about Mrs. Fitzpatrick's urgent call than Connor's opinion of Kevin and herself in the shower. Toweling her hair, she finger-combed the wet strands away from her face. Then, towel wrapped firmly under her armpits, she scampered into the utility room just long enough to snag one of Kevin's T-shirts off the drying rack.

A minute later, she emerged wearing the T-shirt with the towel wrapped around her waist in a makeshift skirt. Clutching her rolled nightgown and soiled undies in one hand and holding up the towel with the other, she tip-toed toward the kitchen.

Phone to his ear, Kevin sat at the table. Connor faced him, his back to the rest of the room. As she slunk across the far wall, Amber noted that Kevin's brows were drawn together in a fierce scowl.

Bedroom, he sent, his eyes not moving so much as a flicker in her direction.

This time Amber obeyed, not even daring to breathe while she inched her way out. Once she reached the still-dark living room, she could see a light coming from the bedroom, and she forgot about stealth.

"What's going on?" her brother queried as soon as she rushed in. "Who's on the phone?"

Parker looked so much better, she wanted to give a rousing cheer, but then his mental thread of apprehension hit her.

"Mrs. Fitzpatrick," she explained. "The woman who has Ronan and Meriol."

The thread morphed into a full blown torrent of panic. Parker threw his legs over the side of the bed to stand.

"Are they…?"

"I don't know. Don't get up! Wait a minute!" Hiding behind the open closet door, Amber flung on clean panties and her jeans.

"I'm fine," her brother snapped.

Struggling with her zipper, Amber kicked the closet door shut. Parker stood at the foot of the bed, looking pale but steady. Before she could rush to his side, Kevin walked in wearing boxers and minus his towel. A few tiny beads of water still clung to the hair on his chest.

"A fisherman found Michael Coyle adrift in his curragh," he said, pulling a T-shirt from the bureau and shrugging it on. "He'd been badly beaten and most of his fingernails pulled out."

She gasped and fought the urge to gag. Parker sat abruptly on the end of the bed.

"They called paramedics, but they have to come from Carndonagh," Kevin continued in a tight, clipped voice.

Reaching behind her, he opened the closet door and extracted jeans and a wool shirt. "Coyle asked for Connor. I'm taking him now."

As if Kevin had summoned him, Connor walked in, completely dressed and with his hair combed out of his eyes.

"There's no hot water," he said in an uncharacteristically subdued tone.

Silently, Kevin buttoned his jeans, but not his shirt. Amber followed him across the room where he sat on the bed next to Parker and put on clean socks. Though the tension emanating from him was palpable, he'd grown quite adept at shielding his thoughts.

"Meriol and Ronan?" Parker asked. Amber could feel his panic seething close to the surface.

"Are fine." Expression grim, Kevin pulled his shoes from under the bed, put them on, and stood. His eyes, filled with haunted shadows, fastened on her. "Stay here. I'll leave the mobile."

She nodded, reluctantly severing their mental connection because she thought he wanted her out. But then he unexpectedly hooked his arm around her and kissed her fast and hard. The fingers of his left hand burrowing into the wet hair at her temple while his tongue swept between her lips. He didn't give her a chance to reciprocate, but pulled away and let her go as brusquely as he'd grabbed her.

"Let's go, Connor." He turned and stalked away without looking back. Wordlessly, the boy followed.

Amber blinked twice in utter amazement, her finger-tips rising to lightly touch her mouth. Thoughts spinning incoherently, she felt water ooze from her hair and soak the fabric at the neck of the T-shirt she wore.

From outside, she heard the slam of the Rover's doors, the crank of the engine as it started, and finally, the tires crunching the gravel as it drove away. But she couldn't force herself to move or think.

At last, Parker spoke. "That was… interesting."

His words dissolved her paralysis. She turned toward him and saw the clock on the nightstand. A few minutes before seven…

"Do you want some breakfast?" she asked, wondering how long she could keep herself from going stark raving crazy until Kevin returned.

Her brother shook his head. "Maybe later. Not sure I can eat right now."

The image of fingers with torn and bleeding tips flashed between them. Her stomach gave a queasy lurch. She absolutely couldn't think about that!

She looked at Parker, still dressed in his filthy, torn canvas pants and the too-small flannel shirt, and came up with Plan B to keep herself occupied. "Give me your clothes, and I'll do a load of laundry."

"Connor said there's no hot water," he said with a meaningful lift of his eyebrows.

"Cold works better than nothing." Rather than rise to her brother's mocking challenge, Amber crossed her arms and put on her stern teacher persona, quite a trick considering the circumstances. "Just give me your clothes. All of them."

"What am I suppose to wear in the meantime?"

Parker complained, but he unbuttoned the shirt all the same.

Amber opened the top bureau drawer. "You can put on some of Kevin's clothes."

After rummaging around and finding nothing but socks, she closed the drawer and opened the next one.

"A shirt's okay, but I draw the line at wearing some other guy's underwear." Parker paused for two heartbeats before he added, "Even if you are in love with him."

Parker watched Amber recoil as if he'd struck her.

She grabbed the top of the bureau to steady herself. "Wh-what did you say?"

Ignoring her rhetorical question, Parker tossed the soiled shirt on the end of the bed and crossed to the closet. His head still throbbed a little and being upright made him dizzy, but not to the point that he couldn't function or think. And Amber was definitely right about him needing clean clothes. His could probably stand upright in the corner based on scent alone.

"I felt pretty damn guilty when I thought you'd slept with Hennessey so he'd help you find me," he admitted.

What he didn't own up to was how much the idea had haunted him for most of the drive from Ballyliffin yesterday. The sexual tension between his sister and the Irishman had bombarded his mind. He had known all too well what had gone on between them.

What a difference a few dozen hours could make.

But he kept that thought to himself as he snagged a dark blue polo shirt off a hanger and pulled it on.

"Kevin wouldn't—" she sputtered.

"I know that," he interrupted, unfastening his pants and letting them drop to the floor. "Mr. Knight in Shining Armor is a lot easier to read than you. Not that I even needed mindspeak last night when he charged in here looking for you."

She sent a bolt of outrage directly between his eyes. "Stay out of my private thoughts, Parker Anthony O'Neill! And Kevin's too."

"Touchy," Parker muttered, feeling the same twinges of jealousy and possessiveness he had the first time Amber had noticed a boy and vice versa. "I didn't even mean to do it."

And that brought up an entirely different issue. Taking a shaky breath, he voiced what had been bothering him since that awful day in the curragh. "I seem to catch thoughts from everyone whether I want to or not. Do you?"

He felt his own bewilderment and uncertainty mirrored in her. They had shared this sometime gift and sometime burden for all their lives. Their ability had bonded them closer than any other two people. But now everything had changed.

"Not everyone," Amber answered pensively. "They have to be connected to you or me somehow. I think they have to care about one of us."

Silently, Parker digested this tidbit. That their abilities might be different had never occurred to him. They'd always accepted mindspeak as a part of themselves, an extra limb or body part. But here in Ireland, their abilities had branched and spread so unexpectedly. And at least in his case, uncontrollably.

He pulled a pair of sweatpants from the far side of the closet. "Turn your head," he ordered his sister. "Unless you want a peep show. I'm about to go commando under these sweats." He dropped his boxers and jerked the pants on fast, nearly losing his balance in the process. "All right, you can look now."

Knotting the drawstring tight, Parker scooped his dirty pants and boxers off the floor and tossed them onto the bed with the flannel shirt. Then he sat down heavily on the side of the bed. Just changing clothes had left him winded, he noted with dismay.

Clutching an armful of her own clothes, Amber gathered his up too. "These people you read, do they ever send back?"

"Not exactly. Definitely not like you do." He scratched at the bandage on his forehead. "Do they with you?"

But he was afraid he already knew the answer. He could feel the subtle changes when he touched her mind.

She nodded, quickly adding, "But not the same as you either."

He wasn't buying it. "Not even Hennessey?"

Her golden eyes leapt to meet his, and he knew without trying that she'd retreated behind the mental barriers they'd both perfected almost twenty years ago.

"Kevin and I have something that's unlike anything I've ever experienced before," she murmured. "It's mental, but physical too. He and I…"

She looked away, blushing from her neck to the roots of her hair. The only other time Parker could recall her acting like this was after she'd lost her virginity. She definitely didn't act the same way when she got engaged to her jerk of an ex-husband. In fact, her lack of a strong reaction had led Parker to suspect the marriage was a mistake, but Amber had refused to listen to his misgivings. Damn her stubborn hide!

"You know, of course, that the big lug doesn't think he's good enough for you," Parker mused. "And he's probably right."

"That's not true," she shot back. "Kevin's a far better man than he gives himself credit for being."

Parker threw up his hands in mock surrender. "Then what are you going to do about it, Amber? I've learned all too well in the past few days that life's short. If he's that special, you can't just walk away."

Chapter 11

"DO YA LOVE HER, THEN?" CONNOR BLURTED AFTER they'd driven in dead silence for fifteen long minutes.

"Huh?" Kevin shot the boy a quizzical glance as he steered the Rover around a large pothole.

Connor rolled his eyes and gave a long suffering sigh. "Amber, of course. After the way ya kissed her and all, I figured ya must. Love her, I mean."

This was a conversation Kevin most decidedly did not want to have with Connor or any teenage boy.

"She's a Yank," he said shortly.

"What's that got to do with anything?" Connor demanded.

Everything.

But aloud, Kevin said, "She'll be going back to America in a day or two."

"Not if ya asked her to stay," the boy insisted with typical kid logic. "Or better yet, go with her. California's got to be bleedin' deadly, 'specially compared to here."

Kevin couldn't deny that he'd thought about doing that very thing, ever since she'd crawled under the blanket with him this morning. Only six or seven hundred times. But he wasn't about to admit that to Connor.

"'Tis not that simple," he stated instead.

The boy crossed his arms in obvious exasperation. "Why the bloody hell not? If I thought she loved me, I'd follow her to the feckin' ends of the earth!"

If only it were indeed so simple.

Gripping the steering wheel hard, Kevin said nothing for several long moments. Then, without taking his eyes from the road, he asked, "Exactly how old are you, Connor?"

The boy's face twisted into a resentful pout. "I'm not a child. I'll be fifteen in a fortnight."

"In another dozen years, you'll be surprised how complicated life can be."

"I don't care," Connor shot back. "You'll still be a feckin' neddy if ya let her go."

Unfortunately, that was probably the truth. However, Kevin was saved from further conversation by their arrival in the village.

Everyone in Malin Head seemed to have gathered at the pier where a body that must be Michael Coyle lay on a makeshift cot, swathed in blankets, awaiting the arrival of the paramedics. After parking the Rover, Kevin hung back and let Connor work his way to Coyle's side.

Far in the distance, Kevin could make out the sing-song wail of a siren. He wondered if anyone had bothered to call Shanley along with the ambulance and decided he wouldn't wait around and find out. But first, he focused his attention back to Connor and watched the boy motion with his hand for people to move back. Then he bent close to Coyle's face, which, even from where Kevin stood, resembled nothing so much as a bloody, mangled pulp.

Whatever Coyle said seemed to agitate the boy, who went round-eyed, shook his head, and pulled away. But Coyle raised a hand wrapped in bloody bandages and forced Connor back down so he could whisper more into his ear. In spite of his unhappy expression, the boy nodded this time.

While Kevin lingered a few additional moments to watch the scene play out, the sound of the siren grew more distinct. A ripple of anticipation moved through the bystanders.

Unnoticed, Kevin turned and walked to the side street where he'd parked the Rover.

Something significant was about to happen.

Every PSNI officer who served more than a few months developed a sense for such things, especially those in Derry or Belfast where troubles always seethed close to the surface. Everyone on the force knew beforehand even if they couldn't stop it. They came to recognize the feeling in the air or the gut.

Kevin hadn't experienced the feeling for over four years, but there was no mistaking it. And he felt it here and now in Malin Head.

Five minutes later, the ambulance roared down the main street alone. Either nobody had called the Garda station, or more likely, Shanley didn't think Coyle's mishap was serious enough to miss breakfast. Obviously the feeling hadn't hit him yet. But the constable would be singing a very different tune when Garda HQ called him in an hour or two.

In a few more minutes, Connor materialized beside him.

"You're not going with him, then?" Kevin asked, taken slightly aback that the boy hadn't ridden along in the ambulance with Coyle.

The teen shook his shaggy head. "I need to call me mum and step-da in Sligo, tell them what happened.

Besides, Michael asked me to finish up a couple of things here." The boy paused and shifted in obvious discomfort. "And then he told me to get the hell out of Malin Head and stay out."

Kevin cocked one eyebrow and waited, but Connor didn't elaborate further.

"Do you want me to go with you?" Kevin finally asked, but Connor emphatically shook his head. "Then I'll wait for you at the Fitzpatricks' cottage. I need to check on Lafferty's young ones."

Connor gave an involuntary twitch, then blurted, "Ya know Parker and Amber read minds, doncha?"

"I do," Kevin admitted, crossing his arms and studying the boy's tense expression. "What of it?"

"Can you do it too?"

He watched the boy draw circles in the dirt with the toe of his trainer before he answered, "Only hers, and only the thoughts she wants me to know."

This reply didn't ease Connor's anxiety, for his brow furrowed and he chewed his bottom lip for a moment. "How far off can she be and still know, do ya think?"

"I'm not sure." Whatever the boy wished to conceal, it concerned him deeply. Contemplating the possibilities, Kevin added, "I think it depends on the circumstances. But I know when she's reading my mind. I can feel her. Dunno about him though."

"He was in my mind last night," the boy said in a hoarse whisper. "And I'd have never known, except he told me."

The harsh wail of the siren temporarily interrupted their conversation.

Kevin waited for the noise to fade away sufficiently so that he didn't need to raise his voice. "Did Coyle make you promise just now not to tell something?"

Red splotches stood out on the boy's face as he nodded without meeting Kevin's gaze. "He made me swear on all that's holy."

Kevin gripped the youth's bony shoulder. "Connor, if 'tis something illegal or 'twould put someone in danger—"

"No! God, no!" Connor twisted away, eyes round. "I wouldn't do that!"

If only he could believe the wee gobshite. But he couldn't force the boy to tell what he knew.

Kevin took a deep, steadying breath. "You need to tell your parents in any case. If you won't tell me, promise you'll tell them or someone else."

"I will. I seriously will." Then Connor turned and dashed away.

Kevin had to dredge up every speck of self-control he possessed in order not to chase after the little knacker and try to shake some sense into him. Fuming at his own powerlessness, he stalked up the lane toward the Fitzpatricks' cottage.

Mrs. Fitzpatrick reached her own gate only a few steps ahead of him. Obviously she'd been down at the harbor along with everyone else in the village, watching the little drama play out. She welcomed Kevin warmly and asked if he'd eaten any breakfast.

Before he could reply, the cottage door banged open, and Ronan flew out and down the steps to meet them. The child grabbed Kevin about the waist in greeting, and Kevin surprised himself by patting the boy on the head.

"Did Prince Par-Ker and Princess Amber go back to America yet?"

Kevin shook his head, but Mrs. Fitzpatrick interrupted Ronan before he could say anything else. "Go and wash up for breakfast now, and give the poor man a wee bit of peace."

As the boy hurried ahead of them, Kevin caught a glimpse of Meriol inside the house, though the girl seemed intent on keeping her distance.

"Any luck with finding their aunty?" Kevin asked in a low tone.

Mrs. Fitzpatrick shook her head. "I was about to call my sister when all this business with Michael Coyle started. But surely another thirty minutes won't matter whilst I get a nice hearty meal for you and those two young ones."

An hour later, Kevin pushed away from the table, comfortably stuffed with what back in Armagh they called an Ulster Fry. Meriol, who had eaten her meal in sullen silence, busied herself with washing the dishes. Ronan helped by clearing the table. Mrs. Fitzpatrick had retired to the sitting room after filling all their plates, and her voice could be heard as a low murmur as she spoke to someone on the phone.

A knock on the front door startled everyone. With Mrs. Fitzpatrick still on the phone, Kevin rose to answer.

Connor stood on the porch, a pair of dusty duffel bags at his feet. Kevin ushered him in, setting the bags just inside the door.

By the time they reached the kitchen, Mrs. Fitzpatrick joined them. In very short order, Connor had a plate of eggs and toast in front of him. Between gulps he recounted that his step-father would be round to fetch him sometime this evening. Though the teen wasn't happy, Kevin and Mrs. Fitzpatrick decided it would be best for Connor to remain at her cottage along with Ronan and Meriol.

Even though he joked with Ronan, Kevin noted that Connor seemed a bit more restrained than usual. But whatever was bothering him had not slaked his appetite in the least. Rather than bring up the subject again and perhaps risk an argument over the decision to leave Connor here, Kevin slipped quietly away from the kitchen and toward the front door. Mrs. Fitzpatrick followed him.

"They shall all be just fine," she reassured. "And I'll ring you as soon as I learn anything about the two younger ones."

Trying to ignore the stinging of his conscience and lingering unease that urged him to do more for the three ragamuffins, Kevin thanked her and left. His footsteps dragged down the lane, his body balking at what his mind knew he must do. But in the course of eating breakfast, the inescapable reality had become clear to him.

Now he must be the biggest fecking neddy in the bloody world.

He had to send Amber away.

<hr />

Amber heard the Rover before it arrived. She was outside hanging wet clothes on a line she'd spied earlier strung below the eaves across the back porch. Between fighting with the washer and fixing breakfast for herself and Parker, she'd kept herself distracted from the real issue.

Kevin and her.

She'd refused to discuss it any further with Parker after his annoying pronouncement. What did her brother know about love anyway? He'd never been in a relationship that lasted more than a month or two, usually by his own choice.

The dusty vehicle stopped beside the cottage, and half the real issue got out and strode toward her. Her heart did an unexpected loop-de-loop at the sight of him.

Good grief! She felt like a teenager in the throes of her first crush. How stupid was that?

Kevin wore a stern expression, but he exuded an almost melancholy air. She stifled her automatic inclination to connect with his mind.

Use your words! she reminded herself as if she were one of her eight-year-old students.

"Is everything all right?" she forced herself to ask.

He paused a short distance from the bottom step and gazed up at her, his expression grim. "Coyle looked like the devil held him up by the heels and shook him, but I expect he'll live. I didn't speak to him, but Connor did."

She smiled a little in spite of herself, but even without a mental connection she could sense Kevin's concern. "But Connor's okay, isn't he?"

"I hope so," Kevin said, turning away so that he no longer looked at her. "He wouldn't tell me what Coyle said to him other than to get out of Malin Head. I almost wished you were there, so you could…"

Amber squeezed her eyes tightly shut and willed herself not to reach for his mind. "So Connor's gone?"

"Not yet. His parents will fetch him later today. No word on Meriol and Ronan's aunty yet either."

She opened her eyes to find him looking at her again, but he seemed aloof, almost standoffish. Something within him seemed to have shifted. The dynamic between them had changed.

He cleared his throat. "So how's your brother then?"

Exhaling the breath she only just realized she'd been holding, Amber draped the last shirt over the line and opened the back door. "Much better. Come in and see for yourself. He's on the phone with the place he was staying in Buncrana."

She wanted to touch Kevin.

Mentally and physically.

So badly she ached.

But obviously that was not what he wanted. And if she looked at him right now, Amber knew she wouldn't be able to restrain herself, so she marched through the house without turning around.

Parker lounged on the couch, his legs stretched out, bare feet hanging over one upholstered arm. The cell phone sat on the top cushion next to his shoulder. Amber thought he looked pale under the dark stubble of his beard, and she sent a little ribbon of questioning worry to his mind.

Though he greeted Kevin jovially, Parker didn't get up. To keep herself from doing something stupid, Amber put her brother and the sofa between her and Kevin. Whatever was bothering Kevin, she wouldn't push him to tell her. Also sensing the change, Parker raised one eyebrow but said nothing to her. Internally or externally.

"Sorry about borrowing your clothes," Parker said to Kevin. "But someone insisted mine were too aromatic to continue wearing. Of course she was right, as usual. But the good news is that my stuff is still sitting in Buncrana, and I've convinced them to let you pick it up."

Kevin spoke to her at last. "What about your car?"

She huffed out a frustrated sigh. "The mechanic said he couldn't fix it, so I called the rental company. They're sending a replacement, but it won't get here until tomorrow."

This information seemed to trouble Kevin, for a fleeting expression of distress crossed his face. She gave herself the equivalent of a mental slap to keep from reading him.

Before anyone could say or do another thing, the phone rang. Parker handed it to Kevin, who turned away to answer.

Don't! Amber gave her brother a mental reprimand when Parker leaned curiously in Kevin's direction.

What's up with you two? Parker sent, eyes narrowed.

She shrugged and tried for a noncommittal air as Kevin stepped into the other room.

Go to Buncrana, her brother sent, along with an image of her and Kevin in the Rover, then a blanket spread in a deserted meadow.

Mind your own business! Amber snapped an arrow of annoyance at him just as Kevin came back into the room.

"Mrs. Fitzpatrick located Meriol and Ronan's aunty, Cara Mulrooney." A weight seemed to have lifted from his shoulders, but the shadows remained in his eyes. "She's coming from Sligo as quickly as she may."

"Good!" Parker exclaimed a bit too heartily. "Now you two can go to Buncrana for my stuff."

Though Amber slanted her brother a censorious look,

fifteen minutes later, she and Kevin were in the Rover, bouncing down the rutted lane.

Staying out of Kevin's mind had been pure torture, especially when he mentioned that she and Parker might be more comfortable in Buncrana. Parker had quickly proclaimed himself still too weak to travel, but Amber knew he had ulterior motives and suspected he had no scruples about reading Kevin against his wishes.

"Please tell me what's wrong," she said, unable to bear the silence any longer. "I know you don't like for me to read you, and I haven't, but I need you to talk to me, Kevin. Did I do something wrong?"

Jaw tightly clenched, he turned the Rover onto the main paved road before he answered. "'Tis not you, 'tis me. I'm afraid I've done nothing right when it comes to you, Amber luv."

"Oh, bullshit!" she declared, crossing her arms. "You didn't do anything except what I wanted you to do." She caught a little burst of surprise at her profanity, but refused to connect with him. Instead she said, "It's the mental thing that's scared you, hasn't it? Well, it scares me, too."

"No," he began, then cleared his throat. "I mean, yes, being connected mentally is… disconcerting, but not in a bad way."

She uncrossed her arms and leaned toward him. He flinched. So even if he said it wasn't bad, he still didn't want her in his mind.

"Then what—" she began, only to have him interrupt.

"You and me together can never be, luv, and I'm sorry I let you think it might." The car bounced into a particularly large pothole. Kevin swore under his breath, then continued, "No woman deserves the likes of me, certainly not you."

As he spoke, anger seethed from her stomach to her chest, nearly smothering her. Finally catching her breath, she managed to choke out, "I'm perfectly capable of thinking for myself, and nobody, including you, Kevin Hennessey, lets me think anything. Likewise for what I deserve, I'll be the judge of that!"

"I didn't mean…" He paused, then huffed out a sigh. "You don't understand."

Narrowing her eyes, Amber glared at him. "I understand just fine. There is something between us, or we wouldn't have this mental connection. Maybe I imprinted on you like a baby duck or maybe it's something more. But whatever it is, I intend to get to the bottom of it, so pull this car over. Right now!"

He started to protest, but a glimpse of her fierce expression obviously changed his mind. Pulling off the pavement, he stopped the vehicle at a wide spot that bordered a rock-strewn field.

She waited just long enough for him to turn off the ignition before she began. "I've been a freak my entire life. Me and my brother. We didn't really know it until we were ten and our pediatrician discovered we could communicate telepathically."

Amber reached to form a mental connection with Kevin, but instead of reading, she sent him images of herself and Parker as children. "Once that happened, every neurologist, psychologist, psychiatrist, and every other 'ist' wanted to take a poke at us. We became lab animals."

A shudder ran down her spine at the memories and

images she sent to him—electrodes, sensory depriva-
tion, blood and tissue samples. But then her tone hard-
ened. "After three years, we decided we'd had enough.
Between the trauma of our parents' divorce and the onset
of puberty, Parker and I convinced all the doctors and
researchers our abilities were gone. And in the process,
we learned to trust no one except each other."

She felt his indignation on her behalf, his compassion, and worst of all, his pity. All the air seemed to have
evaporated from the inside of the Rover. Unsnapping her
seat belt, Amber opened the door and slid out of the seat.
With gravel crunching under her shoes, she walked to
the front of the vehicle and leaned against the substantial
bumper, inhaling deeply.

A moment later, the driver's door slammed, and Kevin
joined her. At first he said nothing, just took several deep
breaths of the salt-tinged breeze along with her. Finally
he said, "But you learned to trust again eventually. Surely
you trusted your ex-husband, at first anyway."

With a rueful sigh, she shook her head. "Josh and
Parker had an instant and intense jealousy of one
another. I never told Josh everything, and I'm glad I
didn't. Parker was right about him. He only wanted to
use me."

Remembering Josh's betrayal, how completely
he'd taken advantage of her, made Amber squirm. But
she dug deep to retrieve the memories and send them
to Kevin. He needed to know how important this link
between them was to her, how significant that she had
placed her trust in him.

"Don't, please." Both his tone and his posture went
rigid with the issue of her trust. "I don't deserve it."

"Well, I happen to think you do." Before he could protest further, she gripped his upper arm. "Prove me wrong, Kevin."

He pulled away from her and squeezed his eyes shut. Her anger started to waver and with it her resolve. She'd pushed him too hard, demanded too much. Regretfully, she pulled back on her mental connection.

Wait!

Amber wasn't sure if he'd spoken aloud or not, but she felt him lower his previously unyielding defenses. She peeked inside his mind and saw the images of the petite blonde woman and the baby in the incubator with the tubes and wires.

Kevin spoke in a detached tone. "Caitlin and I were uni sweethearts. She was a year younger. We got married after she finished her degree. I was newly hired by PSNI and busting my arse to make inspector by the time I was thirty."

She glimpsed the wedding, a few dozen people in a large stone church. A younger version of Kevin, serious in a dark suit, watched the bride in an ivory sheath dress and short veil. A redhead in teal green stood next to her.

The disconnected timbre of his voice slipped a little, and Amber felt his growing agitation, but she didn't want to physically touch him for fear he'd break their mental link. "She was keen on having kids, but she had two miscarriages early on, and we decided to wait a while. I transferred from Belfast to Derry and was right in line for the promotion. We bought a townhouse, and she got pregnant right away."

The two-story row house sat in the center of the block with identical connected houses on both sides. Amber watched blonde Caitlin, wearing a blue maternity top, snip wilted blossoms from the plants on the porch. But a dark pall hung over the scene, Kevin's subconscious foretelling the disaster about to happen.

"Even though she was high risk, everything was going so well that we kind of forgot about the danger, or at least I did."

Amber could almost taste the bitterness as the threads of his memory unraveled in jerky starts and stops.

Kevin arriving home late at night.

Kevin in the pub with his mates.

All of them roaring with drunken laughter.

"That's where I was the night it happened." His voice was a hoarse whisper. "At the pub swapping pints."

He sunk down and sat on the bumper of the Rover, one hand shielding his face.

Lightly brushing his shoulder with her fingertips, Amber sent soothing feelings into his mind in an effort to comfort him. "Kevin, you don't need to go on. You don't have to put yourself through…"

"No!" He shook off her hand and fixed her with a steely-eyed glare. "I've started, and I'm going to tell you everything."

She wasn't ready for the blast of images. Pregnant Caitlin tumbled down the stairs. Bright red blood soaked through her clothes and spread across the floor as she screamed and cried but didn't get up.

More screams.

More blood.

And overlaying the scene was Kevin with his mates, drinking and laughing.

Amber staggered and grabbed the bumper for support.

Gasping, she slid down to sit next to Kevin, who gazed out at the distant sea.

"We knew the baby was a boy," he murmured in a faraway voice. "And had even named him. Patrick for her father. Declan for mine."

Caitlin's cries became weak sobs. Through Kevin's perceptions, Amber heard the paramedics arrive and bang on the front door. As she watched them rush inside the townhouse, the scene jerked back to the pub.

Someone in a police uniform burst in with a cell phone in hand and shouted for Hennessey. Kevin staggered to his feet but was too drunk to stand. His mind refused to accept what he was told. One of his drinking buddies poured a cup of hot coffee down his throat, almost choking him. Then two of them dragged him out to a car. One held his head out the open window so the cold air could revive him.

Inside the hospital, a sour-faced nurse greeted him with a gruff, "So they finally found you then? Your wife's in surgery these past two hours. She's lost a lot of blood and might not make it."

Amber felt the terror and guilt that had ripped through Kevin, heard the anguish as he whispered, "The baby?"

The nurse shook her head. "Too much trauma. He's alive but won't last 'til morning."

Elbows braced on his knees, Kevin buried his face in his hands and moaned low in his throat as he relived the ordeal all over again. Amber knew it wasn't the first time or probably even the twentieth, but this time was because of her. Tears sliding unheeded down her cheeks, she flooded his mind with solace and empathy, but before she could form any words, he lifted his head.

"There's more," he snapped, and sent her the image of the baby, small enough to hold in one of his palms but for the tubes and wires. His raspy voice accompanied the mental memories. "My son lived thirty-eight more hours. I scarcely remember any of it. Caitlin never got to see him until after…" He choked back a sob and added, "I had to tell her our baby was dead and there'd never be another."

This time Caitlin's screams were grief.

"No, no, no! Not my baby!

"Please God, no!"

She hammered on his chest with weak, ineffective blows, and he didn't make a move to stop her.

"Where were you, Kevin? This never would have happened if you'd been there!"

"That's not true!" Amber's outraged exclamation severed her link to Kevin's mind. She raised her hand to her face and stared dumbfounded at the moisture from her own tears.

"Yes, 'tis." Kevin's face was a dry, harsh mask, and his tone matched it. "I never should have left her alone. 'Twas all my fault just as she said."

Amber fished in her pocket for a tissue and blotted her eyes. "It was an accident. Nobody's fault." The set of his jaw told her that all the logic in the world wouldn't matter, so she asked, "What happened to Caitlin?"

"They had to keep her sedated, so she wouldn't hurt herself or anyone else."

Gingerly, she reconnected and peeked at the images of Caitlin, now a wraith with hollow eyes and disheveled hair who stared in mute pain and contempt. Once again, Amber nearly doubled over with the intensity of Kevin's agony.

An intensity he did not allow to leak into his measured tone. "The doctors told me she needed to go to a psychiatric facility, so I signed the papers to send her there. She didn't speak to me, wouldn't take my calls, just stared at me like a zombie when I did go see her. When she was finally released, she went to her father's. Two weeks later she talked to me. She said, 'I want a divorce.' So I gave her one."

He rose to his feet and turned his back on her. "We need to go. There's a storm brewing, and the sooner we get to Buncrana and back, the better."

The scattered clouds overhead and on the horizon didn't look threatening to Amber, but she didn't argue. She pulled away from his mind and got into the Rover. However, as the vehicle picked up speed on the lonely stretch of road, she ventured another question. "Did you ever see Caitlin again?"

Kevin gave a slight nod. "Fourteen months ago, when I finally dried myself out, I went to Belfast to ask for her forgiveness. She'd remarried, and they'd just started the adoption process. She said perhaps after she had a child of her own she could find it in her heart to forgive me."

Amber didn't need to ask. She knew he hadn't gone back. And he'd never forgiven himself either. Somehow, she had to convince him that he deserved forgiveness and so much more.

Could she accomplish such a daunting task? She had to try. Maybe if they were in a completely different environment?

After a long, uncomfortable silence, she cleared her throat. "How much longer is your vacation—I mean holiday?"

He gave her a suspicious glance. "Another fortnight or so, maybe longer."

"Why don't you come back to California with Parker and me?" she blurted, and then rushed to continue. "Just for a visit. We both have another month before school starts. I know you promised your father you wouldn't go to America, but a short vacation wouldn't hurt. Would it?"

Kevin made a derisive noise in the back of his throat. "America doesn't need another bloody fecking Irishman..."

But before he started with a litany of excuses she didn't want to hear, she cut him off.

"Then give me a reason to stay."

Chapter 12

"THEN GIVE ME A REASON TO STAY," AMBER CHALLENGED, as if all those ugly revelations hadn't just happened.

And the worst part was Kevin wanted to give her one, or a dozen. However many it took to get her to stay. Not that he deserved to have her. No more than he deserved to sprout wings and fly.

"Weren't you paying attention?" he asked a bit more sharply than he intended. But perhaps he needed to be blunt for his own good as well as hers. "I'm damaged goods, a drunken lout who killed his innocent child and nearly killed his wife too."

"No, you're not," she stubbornly countered, totally ignoring all his evidence to the contrary. "Besides, that's all in the past, Kevin. And no matter how much we might want to, we can't change it."

Heaven knew how many times he'd wished he could change it. How many times he'd drowned those wishes in a bottle of whiskey.

"Don't be a bloody fool," he argued, letting his ire at himself seep out. "All it would take is one drink and I'm right back in the gutter. I'd have no future, and you'd have none with me. I could destroy you just like I did Caitlin."

"Nobody's future is guaranteed. I could be hit by a truck tomorrow." Amber looked at the narrow empty road stretching in front of them. "Okay, maybe not here, but in California I can, and all the mental telepathy in the world won't make a difference."

Kevin shifted in his seat at the mention of her telepathy. The knowledge served as another reminder of how very special she was. The only reason she wasn't reading his every thought was her own sense of honor and fair play. He laid his hand on her arm and felt the featherlight caress of her mind whispering over his thoughts. But when he glanced into her golden eyes, they brimmed with sadness.

"Being special ruined my life. It robbed me of my childhood, wrecked my marriage, and made me live in fear of being found out." Then a ragged edge of hope tinged her melancholy tone. "But I don't have to worry about that with you, and that's why I want to stay. For a little while, at least."

From the moment he'd first kissed her in the seals' cave, he'd found it nigh on impossible to deny her anything. But this time was different. This time her safety might be involved.

He felt her probing query and surrendered with a sigh. "I don't want you and your brother to stay in Malin Head because something is about to happen."

"You mean with the smugglers?" The image of the white sailboat slashed from her to him.

"Yes, and I'm afraid I can't keep you safe because I don't know how widespread 'tis." To emphasize his point, he sent another image and added, "If you can climb down the cliff face near the cottage, someone else can climb up."

Her uncertainty echoed hollowly through his thoughts along with jumbled likenesses of her brother, Shanley,

Donahue, and a couple of the other villagers she'd seen in the pub. Then the picture of the little seaside hotel in Ballyliffin settled in his mind.

"If Parker and I go there, will you come with us?"

Kevin fought the temptation to say yes. "I can't, luv. Coyle made Connor promise to do something. He wouldn't tell me what, but I have to make sure the little knacker is all right."

A ripple of amusement and understanding accompanied her chiding. "Even though he's not your responsibility?"

"We both know he hasn't anyone else, and at the moment, there's nobody I trust except Mrs. Fitzpatrick."

"And you don't think she can stop him?" She paused for only a brief moment before she acquiesced. "You're probably right. Connor can be very determined."

Not half so single-minded as Kevin knew Amber could be. With a rush of relief, he saw the town of Buncrana on the horizon. Perhaps between fetching her brother's belongings from the hostel and finding a place for a quick lunch, he could forestall the argument he knew was coming.

~~~

The elastic waistband of Parker's boxers was still damp, as were the waistband and seams of his tattered canvas pants. But he pulled them down off the clothesline anyway. He'd worn Hennessey's sweats long enough.

In spite of eating everything in the kitchen that did not require firing up the monstrosity of a cookstove, four days without food had left him leaner than usual, and he could barely keep the pants from sliding off his hips.

Parker stiffened when the light breeze that ruffled his recently washed hair carried the approaching whine of a car engine.

Could Amber and Kevin be returning already?

He'd expected it to be closer to dinnertime, not the middle of the afternoon.

His mind automatically reached for his sister even as he realized the high-pitched sound was definitely not that of Hennessey's ancient Range Rover. He was about to have company. Clutching the clothes in his left hand, he hurried into the bathroom to change.

He came out just in time to see a red and white Mini Cooper screech to a halt near the kitchen window. Cautiously, he sent a mental probe toward the unfamiliar vehicle and detected Ronan's childish thoughts.

Rushing to the front door, he threw it open as the boy emerged from the car and bounded in his direction shouting, "Prince Par-Ker! You're all well then?"

"Yep, almost good as new, my man," Parker assured his pint-sized rescuer, who grabbed him around the waist in an unexpected hug. Peeking into the boy's mind was like gazing through a chaotic kaleidoscope.

Dizzy, Parker broke the connection in time to see a well-dressed, dark-haired woman hurrying toward them. Her pantsuit jacket was too long to get a good look at her ass, and the fact that he wanted to check it out confirmed how near he was to a complete recovery.

"She's me Aunty Carrie from Sligo," Ronan informed him with a hint of pride.

Acutely aware of his oversized polo shirt, threadbare pants, and bare feet, Parker extended his hand in greeting. "I'm Parker O'Neill."

"Cara Mulrooney," she replied, giving his hand one firm shake. "Please tell me my niece Meriol is here with you."

Though her voice was husky, her upturned nose and the spray of freckles across it gave her an almost childish look. Her clear moss-green eyes held Parker momentarily spellbound.

"M-Meriol?" he finally managed to stutter. "Why would she be here?"

Grim lines bracketed Cara Mulrooney's full lips. "I'm afraid she's run away. When Ronan told me she was quite keen on you, we thought she might have come here."

"Oh, shit!" Parker muttered, then bit his bottom lip. "Sorry. Please, come in. Tell me what happened."

He ushered the woman and boy inside. Since the living room was heaped with sheets and blankets from the night's crazy sleeping arrangements, he led them into the kitchen.

"I know I'm supposed to offer you tea, but I'm afraid I don't know how to make it." Parker apologized, feeling more than a little oafish.

"I know how to do it, Prince Par-Ker!" Ronan eagerly volunteered. "If you'll just put water in the kettle."

"Thanks, my man." Parker filled and plugged in the electric teakettle, then pulled the teapot and canister where Ronan could reach them.

"My nephew tells me you're a selkie prince who reads minds," Cara Mulrooney said, her hands folded primly in front of her.

Suppressing a grin, Parker plunked three mugs onto the table before he sat down. "Afraid I'm just a science teacher from California. But your niece and nephew saved my life."

Just for the hell of it, he took a peek inside her mind. Her emotions were almost as chaotic as Ronan's. Confusion and concern were tantamount. Then, when she glanced at the little boy standing on tiptoe at the kitchen counter, Parker felt the wash of newfound maternal love and pride. Her luminous green eyes drifted back to him, and he got a healthy dose of skepticism and mistrust.

Fair enough, considering how flakey he knew he looked. He sent her a thread of reassurance and said, "Please, tell me what happened. I want to help."

Her confusion increased a notch, and she broke eye contact. "I hardly know where to start. When Mrs. Fitzpatrick called me out of the blue this morning, I... I was shocked, but I called my boss and came here straight away."

He resisted the urge to pat her arm, settling instead for another soothing ribbon of thought, and what he hoped was a trustworthy expression.

"I guess you didn't have a close relationship with your brother-in-law?"

Her gaze brushed over Ronan's turned back, and she dropped her voice. "Silas and I never got along. Not since he married my little sister in a rush, if you get my meaning."

Actually, he got the full technicolor memory. Little sis bore a striking resemblance to Meriol with dishwater blonde hair pulled into the same messy ponytail. The two sisters shared a similar slim build and were near the same height.

"Holy Christ Jaysus!" Cara shouted. "You're only eighteen years old, Bree. You can't throw away your future like this."

"You're but twenty yourself, Carrie, and not everyone wants to go to university like you." Little sister's hand curled protectively across her stomach. "I really want this baby, and I happen to love Silas, too."

Ronan plunking the heavy teapot onto the table interrupted Parker's mental eavesdropping.

"I'll fetch milk and sugar," the boy said, and Parker realized the child had the same upturned nose as his aunt.

While Ronan opened the refrigerator, Cara Mulrooney confided in a hoarse whisper, "I wanted to get custody when my sister died, but the attorney told me I'd not have a legal leg to stand on."

"I see," Parker murmured, but before he could more fully "see" Ronan returned with a carton of milk and the sugar bowl.

The boy's anxiety and eagerness to please overrode the feelings Parker could discern from the woman. Reading everyone wasn't as easy as reading just his sister. But then, he'd done that all his life. He hadn't yet mastered this newly discovered skill.

"Thank you, Ronan." Cara's green eyes sparkled with fondness. "Sit down, and I'll serve then."

Still contemplating the intricacies of reading two or more minds at once, Parker waited impatiently for the tea to be poured and the milk and sugar dispensed. The ritual seemed to soothe the woman and the boy, but it drove him bonkers. Rather than stirring, he used his spoon to break apart the two sugar cubes in the bottom of his cup and rashly lifted the hot beverage to his lips.

"When you got to Mrs. Fitzpatrick's, is that when you discovered Meriol was missing?" The moment he touched his lips to the tea, he regretted it. He quickly set the mug back down and poured in more milk.

Cara nodded. Little wisps of her hair had escaped her elaborate braid and framed her face, making her look young and vulnerable. "Mrs. Fitzpatrick sent a boy named Connor off to the bakery an hour before, but she saw Meriol at least once after that. She called the bakery, and the boy had been and left, but Meriol wasn't with him."

Parker caught a sudden thread of guilt from Ronan, and he reached out for the child's mind at the same time he asked, "Did you wait for Connor and question him?"

"No, because Ronan was sure she'd gone to say good-bye to you. That she didn't want to leave without seeing you one more time..." No doubt guessing what Parker already knew, her voice trailed away, and she gave her nephew a suspicious glance.

"You didn't exactly tell the truth, did you Ronan?" Parker asked, while he filtered the images jumping through the boy's mind. Likenesses of Meriol and Connor predominated.

Ronan stared into the murky depths of his cup and gave a reluctant shake of his head. Then he lifted pale, pleading eyes to Parker's. "Please don't be angry, Prince Par-Ker! I knew you were the only one who could find them. You and Princess Amber."

"Ronan!" Cara admonished. "This man is hardly out of his sick bed."

Parker ignored her and focused on easing the boy's shame. "She and Connor are together, aren't they?"

While Ronan nodded, his aunt cried, "We need to contact the authorities."

"No!" Parker and the boy countered in unison.

"Just let me handle this first," Parker added, in what he hoped would reassure the obviously startled woman. Her growing agitation kept bumping into his mind and upsetting his control.

Meanwhile, the boy nervously chewed his bottom lip before he spoke again to Parker. "I overheard the two of them. I looked and listened to everything so I could show you."

Parker reached over and laid his palm across Ronan's skinny forearm. "Okay, show me, and be sure you remember everything. Now when did you hear them?"

"A-after lunch. Mrs. Fitzpatrick washed all our things. She sent Meriol upstairs to pack them." Ronan gripped Parker's wrist with clammy fingers and stared into his eyes. "I stayed in the kitchen to help, but it didn't take long…"

The kaleidoscope in the boy's mind coalesced into a single thread of images. Parker watched a plump, gray-haired woman fold a tea towel over her arm and tell Ronan to "…go upstairs and help your sister."

He climbed the steep staircase with Ronan, taking the steps two at a time. The door on the right side of the landing stood ajar. Meriol and Connor's voices floated out.

"Ya need both to open it." Connor sounded a bit exasperated. "So just give it over and I'll bring back your share."

Meriol made a familiar impatient noise in her throat before she replied, "Give me your key then, and I'll do the fetching."

Parker felt Ronan's breath catch. Then, the boy sank to his knees and crawled close enough to the door to peek inside. Meriol and Connor stood toe-to-toe arguing, oblivious to being observed. Connor straightened to his full height, which wasn't much over Meriol, but registered as enormous in Ronan's perception.

"A wee slip of a girl such as you can't handle the curragh by herself," Connor declared. "And this place isn't easy to get to like the seal cave."

"Mr. O'Neill," Cara Mulrooney's voice cut through Parker's connection with Ronan, but didn't quite sever it. "What's going on? Are you hurting my nephew?"

Belatedly, Parker realized the boy's breathing was ragged and his pulse fluttered visibly in his throat. But he didn't break eye contact and kept sending Parker the images—Connor reluctantly agreed to let Meriol come along...

"Hang on for one more minute," Parker chided the woman. "I'm just extracting information."

Wrong answer.

She shoved back her chair and stood, jerking Ronan's arm from his grasp. "What are you? Some kind of sideshow hypnotist?"

Unfortunately, her demand disrupted Ronan's concentration and broke the link.

"Not exactly," Parker muttered, while mentally he reconnected and commanded Ronan. *Don't tell her! Our secret.*

Eyes bulging, Ronan stared from him to his aunt.

"Do you know the place they were talking about?" Parker asked aloud, shoving aside the emotional interference created by Cara Mulrooney. "Where they were going?"

"I-I think so..."

The image looked foggy but was unmistakably a cave. Surf pounded on the rocks at the entrance.

"What's there?" Parker prodded.

"Da's treasure."

This image was too clear, almost cartoonish. Treasure chests full of gold coins and jewelry lay strewn across the cave floor like pirate booty.

"Mr. O'Neill, we must contact the authorities," Cara Mulrooney insisted.

Good thing she was cute because she was as irritating as hell. Parker blew out his breath in annoyance and decided he would have to tell her at least some of the truth.

Connor Magee wasn't the only one who knew how to play the height card. Parker stood and glared coolly from his six-foot-two-inch vantage point.

"Miss Mulrooney," he said as if addressing one of his unruly junior high students. "Cara. We can't contact the authorities because some of them are involved. At least that's what Kevin Hennessey, who lives in this house and happens to be an ex-cop, believes. And I think he's right. Whatever kind of mess your brother-in-law is in, it's ugly, and it's widespread."

Her pretty mouth opened and closed twice, but no sound came out. *Well shit!* If that little factoid left her speechless, what he was about to do would probably knock her right onto her shapely ass. Better just do it and say nothing to her.

He squatted so that he was eye level with the boy and gripped his shoulder. "Okay, I need you to think hard now, Ronan. Show me the outside of the treasure cave."

The youngster squeezed his eyes closed and sent Parker a perfect postcard image.

Blue-green water dotted with dark boulders.

Roiling white foam.

Rugged cliffs.

The cave entrance was difficult to pick out because of the rock formations surrounding it. Some of the outcroppings were partially submerged while others were constantly lashed by the waves. One rock looked like a gigantic round haystack, while another near the cave entrance resembled a blocky palace guardsman.

"Good job, my man!" Parker encouraged. "Now try to picture how you would get there from the village."

Ronan's brow furrowed with fierce concentration. Parker could see the small pier at Malin Head as the boy imagined the two of them in a motor-driven curragh. They rounded the breakwater, and Ronan headed them northeast. On their right, the coastline flew rapidly by. On their left, they passed a small, low island with seals sunning themselves. Then the haystack rock jumped into view, and finally the rock guarding the cave entrance.

Parker absorbed the image then broke the link. "Excellent!" He praised the boy as he straightened and nearly collided with Cara Mulrooney, who stood close behind him.

She shot daggers into Parker as she grabbed Ronan in a smothering embrace. "Are you hurt, my darling?"

The child shook his head, and she sagged with relief.

"I need to borrow your car," Parker blurted, while to himself he muttered. "Shoes. Gotta find some kind of shoes."

"Wha…" She trailed after him into the laundry room where he spied a pair of rubber flip-flops under the stationary tub. "Mr. O'Neill—"

"Parker," he interrupted, fishing the flip-flops out and shoving them on his feet. "Call me Parker, and give me your car keys."

She stared at him for a moment, mouth agog, before she said, "What are you doing?"

"Going after those kids before they get hurt, or worse." He brushed past her, headed for her purse on the floor next to the kitchen table.

"But Mr. O—Parker," she spluttered in protest. "You're not well."

She probably meant his mental condition, not his physical, but he didn't stop to argue. Instead he simply stated the obvious. "There's nobody else, and we can't wait."

He snatched the wad of keys from the outside pocket of the purse. Easier to ask forgiveness than permission, he rationalized.

She tried to grab them out of his hand. "I'll drive you to the village!"

"Sorry, I need you to wait here for Hennessey and my sister." He held the key ring out of reach and snapped off the one that looked like it fit an ignition. "Ronan, when Princess Amber gets here, I need you to show her the treasure cave, exactly like you just showed it to me. Can you do that?"

The boy nodded eagerly, and Parker ruffled his hair as he hurried past him. He also tossed the rest of the keys on the floor at Cara's feet, and as he expected, she fumbled after them.

Hennessey's dark green rain slicker hung on a peg next to the back door. Too familiar with the temperamental weather, knowing it would be a freaking miracle if it didn't rain, he snagged the garment and loped down the steps.

Just before the door slammed behind him, he heard Cara screech, "Wait! You can't do this!"

Hopping into the Mini Cooper, he didn't bother adjusting the seat, but jammed in the key and started the engine. Cara ran down the back stairs as he threw the car into reverse and tore backward out of the yard.

Glancing out the windshield, Parker watched her stamp her foot. She really was cute. And he hoped like hell she got a chance to forgive him.

―∾―

After stopping at the Buncrana hostel and stowing Parker's luggage in the back of the Rover, Amber and Kevin ate a strained and silent lunch of sandwiches and potato chips from a local deli. She stayed discreetly out of his thoughts, while Kevin seemed determined to avoid physical as well as mental contact with her.

When she purposely brushed his hand with hers, he sucked his breath in through his teeth as if burned. But the longing in his eyes was unmistakable. As far as she was concerned, Kevin's claims of safety were a smokescreen to cover his own ambivalence over their growing relationship. But in spite of all his protests to the contrary, he wanted her to stay. She just needed to find a way to make him admit it.

They were back on the road with the cottages of Buncrana receding behind them when she finally voiced the question that had been niggling at the back of her mind. "If you're afraid Connor might be in trouble, why didn't you stop him before we left?"

"He swore to me 'twas nothing illegal nor dangerous," Kevin replied a bit defensively.

Amber rolled her eyes. "Oh please! I know you didn't actually buy that."

After a long, contemplative pause, he murmured. "For the sake of his male pride, then. Coyle made him promise, and if he didn't at least try, I suppose 'twould make Connor feel less of a man."

"How positively medieval. Besides, he's just a kid."

"Not to himself. And you're the one with all the medieval talk about princes and knights," he reminded.

Crossing her arms, Amber searched for a snappy comeback. When none came, she muttered more to herself than him, "Wish I'd been there. Then at least we'd know what he planned to do."

"Funny thing is, Connor was worried you would know. Apparently Parker told him about the pair of you." Kevin shifted in his seat. "Connor asked me how far away you could be and still read someone's mind. I told him I didn't know."

She took her own turn at silent pondering. "I don't even know myself. I told you, everything is different here."

The understatement of the year!

"You were dozens of kilometers away when you saw that sailboat, and I heard you loud and clear." Kevin's tone grew speculative. "Perhaps you could read Connor right now."

"I was scared." But when she remembered the enormous surge of adrenaline that had fueled the transmission, Amber wondered if she could indeed reach mentally across a long distance.

Maybe to Parker, but to Connor?

"I expect you know he has a crush on you the size of Trawbreaga Bay, if that makes a difference," Kevin said, as if sensing the reason for her hesitation.

"I know." She sighed. And regretted that her longing for Kevin was even larger. "I suppose it couldn't hurt to try."

"Shall I pull the car over?"

"No, I think every bit closer I get might make a difference."

Closing her eyes to eliminate any passing distractions, Amber breathed deeply and cleared her mind. Then she pulled up the memory of the morning at the pier when Connor had wanted so desperately to go with them to search for Parker. When she had linked into his thoughts so easily…

She examined what she remembered of Connor's mind, absorbed every detail of how it felt.

The contours.

The rifts.

Every unique aspect she could recall of how he processed thoughts and memories.

Then, taking one final deep inhale, she cast out across the dark plain of her consciousness, searching for a thread, a hint of thought that might be his. After long, futile minutes, she pulled back. But she knew intuitively that she was on the right course.

"I'll try again," she told Kevin, rubbing her temples. "Tell me when we've gone ten kilometers."

While she waited, she tried to relax and not think about anything but Connor's mind. A few moments before Kevin told her they'd gone the distance, she caught a glimpse of the sea and decided to focus on that direction.

This time Amber felt the tendrils of her search skimming low over the surface of the shiny water, like a sea bird hunting for prey. On and on she went, stretching her mind farther and farther.

Suddenly, a faint wisp of thought floated by her. *Success!* She grasped and followed to its source.

When she recognized the familiar recesses of Connor's mind, she settled in to explore. But her triumph was short-lived. She knew the instant Connor realized she was there. His thoughts jerked abruptly and apprehension slammed through his mind and into hers.

No, no, no! Leave me be!

Amber knew he clutched his head and shook it violently, felt him pull his own hair and slam the heels of his hands against his skull. Fearful that he might physically harm himself, she quickly severed the link.

Maybe a little too fast, for she experienced the unsettling sensation of tumbling over and over through a long, dark tunnel. Like she'd fallen off a carnival ride that had gone terribly wrong.

Moaning low in her throat, she tried to open her eyes but couldn't. From outside her being, she watched her body sway and jerk as the Rover came to a rather precipitous halt. Then Kevin's arms were around her, and as he pulled her against his chest, her mind snapped back where it belonged.

"Are you all right?" he demanded, his tone hoarse and a bit shaky.

His wool shirt prickled against her cheek as she nodded and inhaled the warm scent of him—peat, sunshine, and a hint of the salty sea.

"I-I found Connor," she said, surprised her voice sounded so weak and unsteady. "He's in a curragh... But I don't think he's alone."

Kevin tightened his hold, and she could hear his heart thumping against his chest wall. "I don't give a bloody tinker's damn! Don't you ever do something like that again."

Then his lips claimed hers.

Chapter 13

THE SILKY HEAT OF KEVIN'S TONGUE INVADING HER mouth made Amber sigh with pleasure. But when she reached for their mental connection, his fierce, almost desperate possessiveness slammed into her with unexpected force.

Almost lost you, he sent.

Somewhere in the midst of the swirling turbulence of his emotions, she caught the image of Caitlin, disheveled and vacant-eyed with her mind broken. Raw panic that Amber might meet the same fate tore though him.

Safe, she sent back with a wash of reassurance. *No harm done.*

Kevin broke the kiss, embarrassment and self-recrimination flooding from him to her. "Sorry, I shouldn't have..." He panted, struggling to explain. "'Tis just that for a moment, you didn't seem to be there. In your body, I mean."

"I... I guess I wasn't," she admitted, suddenly aware of her own rapid breathing. Perhaps her body reacted to the danger even if her mind didn't. "But you brought me back, so don't apologize."

His hands trembled as he scooted behind the wheel and refastened his seat belt. While he restarted the engine she sent another thread of comfort into his mind.

"I shouldn't have asked you to try," he murmured as he pulled the Rover onto the paved road once more.

"You didn't know," she said, dismissing the whole incident lightly. "Neither did I. I'll be more careful next time."

"There shall be no next time!" he declared, and the accompanying roar of his emotions severed their mental link with the force of a lightning bolt. "I won't let you risk harming yourself that way."

She lowered the hand she'd raised reflexively to her temple. "But I'm only going to send to Parker at the cottage—"

"No need," Kevin cut in. "Your brother can't go haring off across the countryside, and we'll be there soon enough as 'tis."

He revved the engine and forced the vehicle to move faster to prove his point. With an exaggerated humph, Amber leaned back and stared ahead while they bumped and rattled down the badly paved road. Outwardly she appeared perturbed at Kevin's contradictory and autocratic behavior, but inwardly, she rejoiced. All his explosive feelings in connection to her could only mean one thing.

He cared about her.

Every bit as much as she cared about him.

Kevin maintained their bone-jarring pace right on through Carndonagh, and Amber kept quiet, watching the progress of the summer sun as it sunk steadily toward the sea. But when she recognized passing land- marks and knew they were less than a half-hour from the cottage, she surreptitiously sent out a mental call for her brother.

Unfortunately, Parker didn't respond, and she didn't dare cast about trying to locate him. Instead, she forced herself to wait ten minutes before she secretly tried again.

Still unable to connect with Parker, she fretted that her long distance probe for Connor might have somehow damaged her abilities. How ironic would that be?

Growing up, she had wished countless times that her telepathic ability would go away. But since being here in Ireland, it had morphed in ways she never imagined, and for the first time, she wanted to develop and explore these new possibilities.

"I'm going to contact my brother now," she informed Kevin in a tone that broached no arguments.

Then, in spite of his answering glower, she launched an all-out mental search of the cottage she knew lay just beyond the range of her physical sight. But instead of Parker, she discovered the familiar presence of Ronan Lafferty. Startled, she pulled back and didn't complete the link.

"Something odd is going on," she informed an anxious-looking Kevin. "Parker's not answering, and Ronan is at the cottage."

"Ronan? Are you sure?" But he didn't wait for her answer to push the Rover even faster.

Minutes later, they careened into the side yard in a flurry of dust and screeching brakes. Before the Rover completely stopped, Ronan barreled out the front door, a dark-haired woman right on his heels.

"Princess Amber!" the boy cried. When he reached her, he grabbed her around the waist in a death grip and babbled. "Meriol ran off with Connor, and Prince Par-Ker's gone to find them. He said I need to show you the treasure cave exactly like I showed it to him—"

"Slow down, Ronan!" Amber interrupted, patting him on the back. "Stop talking and just breathe."

Kevin rounded the Rover, but before he could say anything, the dark-haired woman spoke. "Are you Miss O'Neill and Mr. Hennessey? I'm Ronan's aunt, Cara Mulrooney." She grasped Kevin's hand and shook vigorously. "I'm so glad you're finally here. We've been waiting almost two hours."

"Where's Meriol?" Kevin demanded, his hand coming to rest on Amber's shoulder. Warm protectiveness flowed from him to her.

Cara Mulrooney's face crumpled. "When I arrived at Mrs. Fitzpatrick's she was nowhere to be found. Ronan convinced me she might be here saying good-bye to Mr. O'Neill. But it turns out she and this boy Connor have run off—"

"They went after Da's treasure," Ronan interrupted.

Straightening her shoulders, she shot the child a look of reproach, and then continued. "Apparently my brother-in-law and his partner had a cache of money that my niece and the boy knew about."

While Kevin stifled a groan, Amber quickly asked, "But what about my brother?"

"He dashed out of here as if the devil himself were nipping at his heels!" The woman's voice rang with indignation. "He even stole my car."

"He what?" She felt Kevin's astonished exasperation mirror her own.

"Well, took it over my objections at least," Cara Mulrooney amended. Then she narrowed her eyes and gave Amber a long, harsh look. "And he did some very strange things before he left. I'd half believe my nephew's claims that the man can read minds, except that's ridiculous."

"'Tis not, Aunty Carrie," Ronan insisted, and he looked up for support. "Tell her, Princess Amber."

Shifting with discomfort, Amber avoided the woman's skeptical gaze. "Ridiculous as it sounds, I'm afraid it's true. My brother and I have what most people call mental telepathy."

Cara Mulrooney went noticeably pale, the freckles on her nose standing out boldly. "Holy blessed Mother."

"It doesn't work on everyone." Amber tried to reassure. "But your niece and nephew seem to be quite sensitive."

"I think I need to sit down," the woman whispered. She lurched to the front of the Rover and sat down hard on the dirty front bumper.

Ronan let go of Amber and hurried to his aunt's side. "Do you need a cuppa, Aunty?"

Shaking her head, she waved him away and addressed Kevin. "Mr. O'Neill feared for my niece and young Connor's safety." She drew in a deep breath. "He also said not to contact the authorities because you, Mr. Hennessey, believe they are involved in illegal activities. So I've been waiting here all this time for your return. Is this all true?"

Kevin nodded, and his gaze seemed to radiate power. "This whole area is rife with smugglers and has been for years. Surely you know that, Miss Mulrooney."

Amber thought the woman shrank back a little from the strength of his scrutiny. She must have at least suspected her brother-in-law of breaking the law, or she'd have called someone.

"But I happen to know," Kevin continued, "that PSNI has tried to crack an Albanian ring near this area for quite some time."

The thought of Parker trying to fight off Eastern European thugs sent icy shivers up and down Amber's spine. She bit her lip to stifle an exclamation at this new and scary revelation.

"S-so s-sorry," Cara Mulrooney stuttered, looking equally appalled.

Ignoring both of them, Kevin squatted to focus on Ronan. "Tell me about your da's money."

"'Tis his treasure," the boy corrected. "And he keeps it in a cave. Meriol has one key and Connor has t'other. I showed Prince Par-Ker where 'tis, and he told me I must show Princess Amber exactly the way I showed him."

"With your mind, you mean?" Kevin asked, and Ronan nodded eagerly. "Go ahead, then."

"Don't worry, Aunty Carrie," the child said when his aunt reached reflexively to shield him. "It doesn't hurt or anything." Standing erect as a soldier, he took a step toward Amber. "I'm ready, Princess."

She smiled in spite of her worry and brushed a lock of hair off his forehead. Then she closed her eyes, opened the link, and looked inside Ronan's mind.

A perfect photographic image of the pier at Malin Head sat ready for her inspection. Amber paused to examine everything before she realized the boy was waiting for her go ahead.

All right, she sent. *Show me everything*.

As if someone had pushed the play button on a video, the scene moved. From her vantage point inside Ronan's mind, Amber traversed the pier, got into one of the black curraghs, and the outboard motor magically started.

While she continued to observe, the boat puttered past the breakwater and turned right, picking up speed as it skimmed over the sparkling waves. Unfamiliar coastline flew by on their right, open ocean on their left. She lost track of time and distance, but noticed first a flat island and then rocky outcroppings sticking up out of the water near shore. The boat slowed to a halt near a large stone mound.

Haystack, Ronan sent, and she realized it was an echo of Parker's thought.

Sentinel guarding the door.

She looked at the tall narrow column of rock and saw the dark opening beyond it.

Treasure cave!

This last thought was Ronan's, for accompanying it was an image of chests spilling out coins and jewelry.

Enough? Ronan sent.

Once more, Amber answered. *Just to be sure.*

What the bloody hell was taking so long?

Kevin clenched his fists tightly enough to gouge his nails into his palms and silently cursed himself for being the stupidest fecking neddy on God's green earth. After the near fiasco in the Rover, he should never have let Amber do her mental connections with the boy.

But how else were they to locate those two wee eejits? Not to mention her cursed gobshite of a brother? He'd made a right hames of everything by not locking Connor in the nearest boathouse when he had the chance.

Instead, Amber and little Ronan had been standing like stone carvings for what felt like forever. Both had their eyes closed, her right hand on his forehead, him clutching her left. Only the rhythmic rise and fall of that luscious chest of hers told him she was alive.

Or at least her body was alive. What might have happened to her mind put the fear in him something fierce.

He crushed a clod of dirt with the toe of his trainer and earned a scathing look from Cara Mulrooney. She'd reached for Ronan once, and Kevin had stayed her hand. If looks could kill, she'd have sent him to the devil nine times over already.

Just as she moved to reach for her nephew again, the boy's eyes popped open, as did Amber's. The breath he didn't realize he'd been holding whooshed from Kevin's lungs; at the same time Cara gave a little cry and pulled Ronan against her.

Amber's golden eyes locked with his, and her tongue flicked across her full lips. "Let's go. We need to hurry."

"I need my pocketbook," Cara exclaimed, and raced for the cottage door.

"I need the loo," Ronan announced, and scampered after her.

"Get in." Kevin ordered Amber, and when she shot him a startled look, he added, "Don't worry, I'm not leaving them. The only safe place hereabouts seems to be Mrs. Fitzpatrick's. We're going there."

As she got into the front seat, a dark corner of his mind urged him to take her to a nice quiet hotel and the hell with everything else. Thank all the saints in heaven she wasn't reading his thoughts right now!

"We could call Officer Reynolds or the Garda head-quarters," Amber suggested. "From Mrs. Fitzpatrick's I mean."

"And tell them what? That Connor and Meriol ran off in search of buried treasure and your brother's gone after them?" He pulled his jacket from the backseat of the Rover and slid behind the wheel. His Glock weighed heavily in his jacket pocket. "No, at the moment this is my mess, and I'll set it to rights."

Her sigh sounded sad and tinged with frustration, while her golden eyes glistened with remorse. "Actually, none of this is your mess, Kevin. Most of it is mine. Well, Parker's, and he's my brother."

He wanted to argue, and he most certainly did not want her to go along. But the truth was that it might take twice as long for him to find this "treasure cave" without her. And he didn't require mental telepathy to know that they needed to hurry.

Right on cue, Ronan bounded out the door, his aunt on his heels. The pair of them hopped into the backseat of the Rover, and they were off.

Kevin pushed the old rust bucket as fast as he dared. He attempted to question Amber about the location of the cave, but Cara Mulrooney kept interrupting with questions of her own. The woman could drive Saint Patrick himself mad.

For her part, Amber answered with few words, if she answered at all. However, after Cara's third interruption, he did catch a whisper of amusement inside his head, and the fleeting image of himself throwing a thunderbolt.

Mrs. Fitzpatrick rushed out to meet them when Kevin pulled the Rover to a halt in front of her cottage.

"Saints be praised!" she cried. "Any news of the young ones?"

Kevin shook his head. "We hoped you might know something. Amber's brother took out after them a couple of hours ago—he'd have been in a curragh."

He could tell from the tight, pinched look on the woman's face that she shared his opinion of Parker's harebrained behavior, so he muttered for her ears only, "The man has no fecking clue what he's about. I need to go after him."

She gave a slight nod of understanding while casting a nervous glance down the lane. "Come inside for a wee drop of tea, all of you. My mister's down at the pub, but he did say when he was headed in a while ago he saw some fool headed out to the northeast. I expect that would be Miss O'Neill's brother."

"Why would that make my brother a fool?" Amber asked, a hint of pique in her tone.

"Because the fishing's usually poor that way," Mrs. Fitzpatrick replied. She gave Kevin a meaningful lift of her eyebrow. "And there's a storm brewing."

Not necessarily a rainstorm, Kevin knew, and from the expressions on both Amber's and Cara's faces, they knew as well. When the four adults entered the cottage's sitting room, Mrs. Fitzpatrick shooed Ronan off to the kitchen to plug in the kettle and fetch the biscuits from the pantry.

"What's the latest on Coyle?" Kevin asked.

Still wearing her tightlipped concern, the older woman replied, "Doctor Walsh in Ballyliffin shipped him off to hospital in Letterkenney, but I expect he'll be fine."

"Anything from the Garda?"

"Nary a word."

The undertone in her response told him more than he wanted to know and none of it good.

Mrs. Fitzpatrick reached for a key hanging on a peg near the front door. "You'll want to take my mister's curragh. 'Tis the only one at the harbor right now with an outboard."

"Thank you again, Bridget." He took the proffered key and motioned to Amber. "Sorry we can't stay for tea."

"Wait!" Cara Mulrooney leapt to plant herself between him and the door. "She's my niece, and I'm going with you."

She'd already made this argument on the way here. Kevin was sorely tempted to shove her in the coat closet and lock her inside. "For the last time Miss… Cara, you have to stay here."

"If Miss O'Neill can go, so can I," the impertinent chit insisted.

"The only reason she's going is her mental link with her brother. She can find him far quicker than me mucking about by myself." He nodded toward the kitchen where Ronan rattled dishes. "Besides, you're all he has left. If anything should go wrong…"

Green eyes going completely round, Cara Mulrooney sucked in a sharp breath and stepped aside. He grabbed Amber's arm and pulled her out the door in case the annoying woman changed her mind again.

"You don't really think something will go wrong, do you?" Amber asked once they were out the gate and halfway down the lane.

"I wish I could be sure," he answered honestly. "But I do know we'll find them."

What he didn't know was the condition they might be
in. The image of Coyle's bloody pulp of a face flashed
across his mind. He banished it quickly and hoped Amber
hadn't caught a glimpse. She seemed to pick up stray
thoughts and feelings from him when they were close,
even without being directly connected to his mind.

A moment later, the pier came into view, and
Kevin concentrated on finding Fitzpatrick's curragh.
Overhead, clouds blew across the sun and cast every-
thing into gray shadows.

He knew the rain would start any minute. Amber
had on her waterproof jacket, but he wore only a light
cotton thing. Only a stupid townie went about without
rain gear.

He prayed that wasn't a bad omen for the rest of their
ill-conceived enterprise.

⁓

Amber crawled into the weather-beaten boat that smelled
strongly of fish and waited while Kevin shoved it into
the water. He made several attempts to start the engine
before it finally caught with a gurgling cough.

Once the outboard got going, they picked up speed
and headed for the breakwater. She scooted close to him
on the rough, peeling seat just as fat raindrops started
to fall.

Cursing under his breath, Kevin pulled a greasy-
looking hat from the cubbyhole next to the engine and
jammed it on his head, tying the string under his chin.

"Northeast then," he said.

She nodded and reached to form a link inside his
mind. Connecting with him came easily now and felt

almost as natural as being joined with Parker. Slowly, she unwound the ribbon of memory she'd read from Ronan, examining each image along with Kevin while she watched the passing landscape.

Once they were out on the open sea, he tried to rev the engine to a faster speed, but it sputtered and wheezed so badly, he was forced to remain at a sluggish pace. Amber felt his aggravation and unease brimming close to the surface and tried not to add her own to the emotional brew.

Peering from beneath the hood of her windbreaker, she squinted at the dark, rainy shoreline and tried to match it to the bright images Ronan had shown her. After ten long, futile minutes, she gave up with a frustrated sigh.

Relax, Kevin sent, with a soothing tendril of warmth in the growing chill. *We're on the right trail. Any traces of your brother?*

I'll check.

She savored the warmth of his mental caress for a moment before she broke their link and cast about in a brief search for Parker. The increased spluttering of the engine interrupted her.

"Shite!" Kevin muttered as the outboard grated and ground to a complete halt. "Can you check for petrol?"

While mentally casting out for her brother again, Amber located the heavy plastic gas container. Only a small amount of liquid remained in the bottom.

Kevin poured all of it into the proper receptacle, and after tinkering around for a few moments with a wrench, got the thing to start again. But their triumph was short-lived, for within a hundred yards, the engine choked and died again.

"Fecking bugger," he swore, along with several other colorful phrases.

In spite of his efforts, he had no more luck restarting the thing than she did at locating Parker. And to make matters worse, the rain grew harder and the ocean choppier.

"Now what?" Amber asked, holding back her own urge to curse.

"We row," Kevin replied, brushing past her to the bench closer to the bow. "No luck with Parker?"

She shook her head as she watched him unfasten the oars and position them in the oarlocks. "I'm going to try Connor."

Ahead on the left she saw white foam roiling across a rocky surface. The island Ronan had shown her. At least she knew they were still headed in the right direction.

Placing her fingertips to her temples, she closed her eyes and concentrated on Connor's mind. She could hear Kevin grunting as he pulled on the oars. Meanwhile, rain blew in under her hood and ran in rivulets down her neck.

Connor, where are you?

With the teenager's likeness flitting through the back of her brain, she cast out in every direction. Suddenly, Connor's image washed in front of her on a shining fluid stream.

Jerking mentally and physically at the unexpected sight, Amber almost broke the connection. She grasped for the watery ribbon of thought as it floated away. Securing her hold, she followed it.

The boy's likeness grew more distinct. Dark hair plastered against his head, he shivered in the rain, half in and half out of a green plastic rain slicker. Then Amber saw why he wasn't wearing the garment.

Another figure huddled next to Connor, also seeking shelter under the garment. Immediately, Amber recognized Meriol's striped T-shirt.

"What the bloody hell?" The images dissolved as Kevin's exclamation broke the link.

Her eyes popped open, and she grabbed the edge of the plank seat to keep from falling off.

"Something just ran into the left oar," he explained. "Nearly knocked it out of my hand!"

Still somewhat disoriented, she saw that Kevin had lifted both oars out of the water. They stuck out level with the side of the boat. She peered through the gloomy rain and saw a brown shape swirling next to the curragh, not far from the surface of the rough water.

Before Amber could say or do anything, the creature's sleek brown head broke the surface a little more than an arm's length from her. Huge liquid brown eyes stared into hers, and the whiskered snout twitched.

"Sweet Mother of God, a seal?" Kevin sounded thunderstruck.

The same one from the cave?

Amber couldn't be sure, but she sent a tentative mental probe in the animal's direction. The image of the two wet, shivering youngsters floated back into her mind.

"Holy crap!" Her voice came out a raspy croak as she struggled to maintain the link. "It knows where Connor and Meriol are."

"It fecking wh—" Kevin's oath was interrupted by a yip from the seal as it dived under the waves.

A moment later it popped back up a few feet in front of the curragh.

Amber blasted the image of Connor and Meriol at the animal with all the mental force she could muster.

Where? she sent. *Lead us!*

The seal gave another bark, turned, and started swimming on the surface of the water. After a dozen yards, it paused and looked back at the curragh.

"Follow it, Kevin!" she cried, astounded that the creature might actually be obeying her commands.

The oars smacked the water with an audible splash, and Kevin, rowing like a mad man, propelled the bobbing curragh forward.

Over his shoulder, his thought drifted to her with mingled amazement and amusement.

Just like fecking Lassie Come Home!

Chapter 14

PEERING OVER THE SIDE OF THE CURRAGH, AMBER SOON lost sight of the seal in the watery mixture of rain and waves. She stared at Kevin's back in front of her. The rain had soaked into his cotton jacket, and where the wet cloth plastered itself against him, she watched the sensual ripple of muscles across his shoulders and upper back. Even if he made the effort look easy, she knew it wasn't.

Feeling like useless cargo, she asked, "Can I help you row?"

"No, I'm… just hitting… my stride," Kevin huffed out in time with his stroking of the oars.

Long minutes dragged by with him methodically huffing and pulling the oars. Occasionally, she caught sight of the seal as it circled in front of them, raising a flipper in the air as if to urge them on.

Amber tried to reach out for Parker, but had no more success than earlier. Plus, the intense mental images from the seal seemed to interrupt her attempts to contact Connor.

Through the increasing darkness, she recognized the looming shape of the haystack rock, white foam curling where the waves churned against it. Although they must be near the treasure cave, the seal didn't hesitate and neither did Kevin.

As the round rock receded behind them, Amber squinted at the shoreline. The surf pounded the rough cliffs, and jagged rocks dotted the nearby sea. If a boat ventured too close, it could easily be dashed upon one of those rocks and destroyed.

Could that have happened to Connor and Meriol? To Parker?

She shivered and tried to banish the disturbing thoughts. Automatically, she reached for the comfort of Kevin's mind and quickly discovered he'd channeled all his anxieties and frustration, along with his energy, into rowing.

Tired? she sent, wondering if she could somehow direct some of her pent-up energy to him.

Not yet, he answered on a thread of reassurance. *Must be halfway to the bloody Antrim coast by now.*

He flashed her an image of a much greener and less forbidding shoreline. Definitely more appealing than their current location.

Show me Connor and Meriol, Kevin sent, and she quickly obliged, transmitting the watery image to him.

Recognize anything?

She felt his mental shrug. *Could be a dozen different spots.*

I'll try Parker again. But before she could break the link, Amber got a sudden jolt of surprise from Kevin. Gazing over his shoulder, she could make out a darker shape bobbing on the side of a partially submerged rock.

A curragh!

The very thing she'd feared.

Amber sucked in a noisy breath.

Rain gleamed on the slick metal of the vessel's outboard motor.

THE WILD IRISH SEA

Parker? Or Connor and Meriol? She knew she wouldn't like either answer.

Kevin angled them closer for a better look.

"Doesn't appear she ran aground," he mused, ceasing to row as he craned his neck to see inside the other boat. "Looks more like she drifted over and stuck there."

"But what about the passengers?"

He slammed down a mental barrier, but not before she got a quick impression of another image she did not want to see—a body tumbling over the side.

"No way to know," he said in a flat, emotionless tone.

She started to tell him he was a rotten liar, but the seal popped up next to them. It blinked its large eyes twice as if to question the delay.

"All right, you wee bugger," Kevin muttered, pulling on the oars once again.

But the creature didn't head back into the open sea. Instead, it dodged around the rock and angled toward the cliff face. Amber could see at least a half-dozen more outcroppings protruding from the water ahead of them.

"You can swim, then?" Kevin asked, no doubt sensing her apprehension.

Reluctantly, she pulled completely away from his mind. "Yes."

She could, but he didn't need to know exactly how much she wanted to avoid that particular activity.

She needn't have worried. In spite of the persistent rain and the growing darkness, Kevin steered them unerringly through the obstacle course of rocks and outcroppings and brought them ever nearer to the looming cliff face.

They heard the clamor of the seals before they saw them. The creatures' throaty barks and snorts carried over the roiling water. Their own guide paused long enough to give an answering yip before it arrowed toward a long finger of rock protruding from the cliff and pointing into the sea.

"About bleedin' time," Kevin groused, easing off on the oars.

While Amber chewed the inside of her cheek, he fought to maneuver the curragh parallel to the rocky jetty, but at the same time, keep them from getting too close to the jagged sides. When they were even with the end, which was partially submerged underwater, she could see that one side of the formation angled steeply a good six to eight feet above the surface. Waves pounded and foamed against the sharply vertical surface.

Several seals dove into the water at their approach, but at least twenty more sat arrayed upon the high slope, trumpeting out what sounded like angry warning calls.

"Looks like we've got a welcoming committee," Kevin observed, as a half-dozen sleek brown heads broke the water beside them.

Placing both palms against her temples, Amber sent out a mental call to Connor.

A thin vocal cry floated down in answer. "Amber! Kevin! Up here!"

"Thank God!" Her shout was both mental and physical. Then she sent. *We're almost there. Are you all right?*

But interference from the seals swimming under and around the curragh disrupted her connection to Connor.

Kevin leaned heavily on the oars and propelled the craft backward.

"Shite!" he declared. "We can't land here anyway, even if these buggers would let us. I'll row to the other side."

Shutting her eyes, Amber concentrated on the seals and sent out a broadcast to let them through, that they intended no harm. She immediately felt the agitation and tension ebb and opened her eyes to see the animals swimming around them headed back to dry land.

Within a few minutes Kevin rowed around to the opposite side of the rocky finger. Scores of barnacles, urchins, and other sticky creatures dotted the outcroppings close to the surface of the water. The upward slope was gentler, but the waves barely skimmed over a wide expanse of rock.

"Too shallow here," he explained, steering clear and continuing to row in the direction of the cliff face.

Amber could see and hear more seals on the rocky slope, but the guttural mutterings no longer sounded threatening. She again tried to reach out mentally for Connor and this time was able to link into his mind.

Are you and Meriol all right?

Meriol's fine. My ankle… She got a picture of Connor falling as he crawled from the curragh, and the sharp pain as he went down on the slippery rocks. She cringed.

Broken? she sent.

Dunno. Can't walk. She felt the youth's embarrassment as she saw the memory of Meriol helping him inch his way up the rocky slope.

Stay there! We're coming after you.

Connor sent an image of a dozen seals standing guard all around him and Meriol.

Careful, he cautioned.

Kevin's voice interrupted her reply. "This is likely the best place we'll find."

Pulling in the oars, he reached to secure a short rope to a pointed knob stone. She flinched as the curragh scraped against the unforgiving rocks.

"Connor can't walk," she reluctantly informed Kevin. "His ankle might be broken."

Muttering a curse under his breath, Kevin cinched and knotted the rope to the curragh's bow. Much to her chagrin, the stern still bobbed erratically in the choppy waves.

"Best I can do. 'Twill be bleedin' tricky. Maybe you should stay here."

While she appreciated his concern, Amber had a few of her own. "There are at least a dozen seals guarding Meriol and Connor. I'm not sure they will let you approach them by yourself."

His expression grew even more grim. "Fine, but let me go first so I can catch you if you fall."

Balancing precariously on the front plank seat, he scrambled from the curragh onto the rocks and extended his hand for her. Gripping his wrist, she followed.

<hr />

Could this fecking night get any worse?

As the rain dripped from the brim of his hat into his eyes, and his feet slipped and skidded on the wet rocks, Kevin marveled at just how wretched their luck kept growing. He struggled to find his next solid foothold while Amber clung to his arm like a drowning woman. Next, he'd have to bodily carry Connor back to the curragh, if he didn't have to fight off a passel of angry seals first.

And they still had to locate her crazy brother Parker. Not to mention avoid whoever had attacked Coyle and probably killed his partner Lafferty.

Yes indeed, 'twas one helluva night.

"Connor! Meriol! Hallo!" he bellowed to make sure he and Amber were still headed in the right direction.

A chorus of seals barked in answer. But in between their racket, he caught an answering hallo from the boy. Then an especially large creature loomed directly in front of them. Kevin's free hand strayed to the pocket with his Glock and ammo, and he cursed himself for not having the gun loaded. But at the same time, Amber released her hold on his other forearm.

She no sooner placed both hands to her head than the big bugger backed off. All the other seals also went suddenly silent. It was bloody spooky the way she could command them with her thoughts.

Carefully, he picked his way around the animal only to be greeted by the sight of two more a short way ahead. But like oversized lap dogs, those two scooted aside at Amber's approach, their adoring gazes firmly fixed on her.

A dozen more meters and he finally caught sight of Connor and Meriol huddled together under a green rain slicker that looked suspiciously like his. The two young-sters occupied a flat rock and were flanked by five more seals who silently watched their every movement.

"Kevin! Amber!" the boy called, and gave a slight wave of his hand. Relief was plainly evident in his voice. "Thank Jaysus, Mary, and Joseph you found us!"

"Prince Par-Ker said you would," Meriol added, and even her usual acerbic tone seemed subdued. No doubt because she was wet, cold, and scared.

"Where is—" Amber began.

"Let's have a look at that ankle," Kevin interrupted. He really preferred to deal with the issue at hand— Connor and Meriol—before he confronted the next—the whereabouts of Parker O'Neill.

Under the continued scrutiny of the seals, he squatted to get a closer look at Connor's injury. Amber bent next to him.

He quickly decided against removing the boy's shoe, for the joint was swollen almost twice its size with the flesh on the inside an ugly bluish-purple. The sight made Amber suck in her breath in an audible hiss, and he almost did the same. If it wasn't broken, the sprain was one of the worst Kevin had seen, and he had no way to bind it.

"'Twas such a stupid bleedin' accident," Connor mumbled, shamefaced. "Foot went right out from under me. Cost us the curragh too."

Straightening to his full height, Kevin nodded in understanding. "We saw it wedged against a rock about a hundred meters out."

"'Twas out of petrol anyway," Meriol muttered, locking eyes with Amber. "Prince Par-Ker told us to get as far from the cave as we could and not to worry because you would find us, which you did."

Confusion and worry chased across Amber's face. "Parker told you? I don't understand. Where is he?"

Meriol squirmed with discomfort, and tears suddenly welled in her eyes, so Connor answered. "He lit out in the other direction to draw off those buggers in the inflatable."

"Wait!" Kevin interrupted before a shocked Amber could utter a sound. "Go back a bit. Did Parker find you in the cave?"

Nodding, Meriol seemed to draw inward, cowering against Connor. Kevin wondered if she feared either he, or more likely Amber, was about to unleash unholy wrath upon her. Not that she didn't damn well deserve it.

When she spoke, her voice sounded childishly small, not at all like her usual caustic self. "We were arguing about the money and didn't even hear him until he was nearly beside us."

Before Kevin could ask about the money, Connor took up the tale. "I nearly jumped clean outta me skin when this voice right behind me suddenly says, 'Doesn't matter if it's a feckin' million dollars, you two morons won't live long enough to spend a dime.'"

Kevin saw the hint of a smile curl the corners of Amber's beautiful mouth at the words, which did sound like something her brother would say, though with a Yankee accent, of course.

"I turned 'round, and there he was," Connor continued. "He pointed to the cave entrance where the sun was sunk halfway to the horizon. But in the glare, I could make out a triangle of a sail. He nodded toward it and said, 'If they catch us, we're all dead meat.'"

Amber's lips pressed in a tight line. She edged closer and reached for Kevin's hand. Hers felt cold and clammy, and he knew it wasn't just because of the rain.

Meriol hiccupped back a sob. "I started stuffing money into my hat. Prince Par-Ker jerked me up and said, 'Don't ya get it? They already killed your father for this and the other stuff in here. They'll kill ya too, even if ya are a little girl.'"

She clamped her hand over her mouth, no doubt to stifle another sob.

"What else was in the cave?" Kevin broke in while he had the chance.

"Lots of crates," Connor said. "I saw guns in some of them, ammo too. And I think there was that stuff, ya know, to make bombs."

Weapons and explosives. Kevin honestly wasn't surprised.

"Tell me where my brother is!" Amber ordered, her patience obviously at an end.

"He'd beached his curragh beside ours," Connor explained, and his eyes got a glassy look, which Kevin interpreted to mean that Amber was reading his thoughts. His voice suddenly sounded soft and far away. "By the time we got there, we could hear the outboard on the inflatable, so we knew they were coming. Parker told us to give him a five-minute head start, then take off in the opposite direction as far and as fast as we could go."

"He told us not to worry because you would find us," Meriol added, her voice still thick with tears. "He went toward Malin Head."

Amber's grip tightened like a vise around Kevin's fingers, and her face lost all color.

"No," she whispered, and Kevin knew without any mental telepathy that she was thinking Coyle had done the same thing. He'd drawn the smugglers away from the Lafferty cottage, and when they caught him, they'd all but killed him.

"I saw at least three seals chase after Prince Par-Ker," Meriol finished. "I know they'll protect him."

Amber must not be inside Connor's mind any longer, Kevin observed, because the boy's tone sounded normal again. "When we ran outta petrol, I rowed us toward shore.

By the time we got here, I saw a couple of seals in the water, and when we finally got up to this rock there were about a dozen of 'em. 'Twas like they were guarding us."

He eyed the five remaining creatures, who were still silent but no less attentive. Then the youth looked at Amber, and Kevin realized she'd loosened her hold on his hand. Her breathing sounded rapid and shallow.

God in heaven! She was trying to contact her brother.

In a not-so-subtle attempt to stop her, he jostled her shoulder. "We need to get the hell out of here, now."

But he was too late. Gasping with horror, Amber doubled over as if in pain.

"They have him." She moaned. "Oh God! Parker…"

Meriol burst into fresh tears as well. Great sobs shook her slender shoulders. "We have to save him!"

Kevin pulled Amber against him and forced her to stand upright. "We've no time for any of this."

His harsh tone only made Meriol cry harder and cover her face with her hands. But Amber straightened up and fixed him with an urgent expression.

"You're right because they're coming for us." Her pronouncement made Meriol stop in mid-sob. Behind her, two of the seals shifted restlessly.

"Shite!" Connor declared, his own eyes round with fright.

"How close? How many?" Kevin demanded as he pulled out his Glock and shoved the ammo magazine into place.

Connor's eyes went even wider, and Meriol choked. One of the seals yipped.

Amber moved so that she wasn't touching him, then squeezed her eyes shut and put both hands to her temples.

Everything went deathly silent for a dozen heartbeats. Kevin fought the panic gripping him by the throat.

Giving a long exhale, Amber's eyes fluttered open. "They have Parker on the sailboat. He's not sure, but he thinks there's only one guard with him. Two other men are in the inflatable speedboat searching the area. They're all armed."

"Just fecking dandy," Kevin muttered. They'd be sitting ducks out in the curragh without an outboard. But if they stayed here, sooner or later they'd be found.

"If we go back to the cave, there's plenty of guns for all of us," Connor began.

"Have you ever used one?" Kevin challenged. The boy shook his head, still eying the Glock. Kevin shoved it back into his jacket pocket. "Then you've no business with one."

"Can we set a trap for them somehow?" Connor persisted, his injury apparently forgotten.

"No! If we hurt them, they'll kill Parker," Amber declared, settling the matter.

"What we need is a way to get on that sailboat," Kevin mused aloud.

He could feel Amber's anxiety hovering on the edges of his mind. From the corner of his eye, he saw one of the seals move a flipper, and an idea started to take shape.

"Can Parker persuade his guard to move the sailboat closer to us?" he asked Amber, who looked perplexed by the question. "With his mind. Can he mentally order him like you do with the seals?"

Doubt clouded her golden gaze. "I-I don't know. We've never done anything with other people."

Mentally, Kevin reached for her, felt the tingling comfort of her presence as she settled into that empty space in his mind that only she filled. He opened the vision of his half-formed plan for her inspection.

"Tell him to try." He attempted to shield his misgivings as he looked at her and the two bedraggled youngsters, all depending on him. "And while you're about it, send the big bruiser behind me for some reinforcements."

I know you can do it. He sent a hearty burst of confidence toward her mind. *And so can your brother.*

An instant later, her eyes snapped shut, and he felt her withdrawing. But a tiny sweet seed of warmth lingered.

He reached out a hand to Connor. "Up you go! I hope there's nothing wrong with your arms, boyo. Meriol, help me get him down to the curragh."

As he hoisted Connor to his feet, the closest seal uttered a grunting bark. Shuffling to the edge of the rocky shelf, the big animal flung itself at the water two meters below in a perfectly executed dive. The other four creatures stared expectantly at Amber, who still had her eyes closed and fingertips to her temples.

"I don't need your help," Connor fussed at Meriol, who draped his arm across her shoulders. But the girl refused to budge from his side.

The three of them began to pick their way across the wet, slippery rocks. Moments later, Amber appeared on Kevin's other side, the four seals shuffling after her. The seed inside his mind blossomed.

So far, so good. But anxiety laced her attempt at optimism.

It'll work, Kevin reassured—not that they had any real choice. His crazy scheme had to work.

I showed Parker where we were as best I could.

In the few minutes it took them to get to the curragh, three more seals joined them. Kevin saw several others nearby swirling though the water. At least that part of the plan was going smoothly.

Getting Connor into the boat proved tricky indeed. Meriol leapt in first and steadied the bobbing vessel as best she could. Amber followed, bracing herself to take part of Connor's weight as Kevin helped the boy heave himself over the side.

Though the lad obviously tried not to, he grunted, groaned, and actually yelped once with pain before Amber got him settled on the plank seat. Kevin felt a portion of her mental attention transfer from him to the boy.

"Are you all right?" she asked, smoothing his wet hair away from his eyes.

Face deathly pale and jaw tightly clenched, Connor nodded. "'Tis a feckin' dose," he managed to grind out.

Kevin got in and untied the rope that secured them to the rock. He tried the outboard just to be sure it wouldn't start, and when it didn't he sat down next to Connor.

"Can you row then?"

"To be sure," the lad answered, his voice a little firmer. "'Twill take my mind off the bugger."

And speaking of minds, Kevin reached for Amber's again. *Can you direct the seals from the bottom of the boat?*

She sent back a tentative yes.

He motioned to include Meriol as well as her. "I need you both to hunker down in the bow. If any shooting should start, I won't have you as targets."

Amber sent an immediate mental protest, which he steadfastly refuted. Meriol looked equally rebellious, but at his stern glare, they both grudgingly complied.

Shoving the curragh away from the rocky shelf, he twisted the oar into place and dipped it into the sea. Beside him, Connor did the same with the other oar.

"Carefully now," he instructed, and gave the teen an encouraging pat on the shoulder.

Behind them, he heard the seals launch themselves into the water.

At least the rain had decreased to a drizzle, but visibility remained poor because of the full-out darkness. Negotiating the maze of rocks might prove as dangerous as the smugglers searching for them.

A cadre of three seals quickly positioned themselves ahead of the curragh, while two others swam alongside just beyond the reach of the oars. Were they following Amber's orders? Or were they acting on their own? Kevin needed to believe the former, but he couldn't be sure because Amber wasn't fully engaged with his mind.

He glanced down to where she and Meriol huddled in the bow, but couldn't tell in the darkness if her eyes were opened or closed. Nevertheless, since she'd located her brother he suspected she was communicating with him. Looking up toward the horizon, Kevin strained his eyes, but could see no sign of a sailboat.

Concentrating on the task at hand, he fell into rhythm with Connor's rowing. They'd almost reached the open sea when Kevin heard the unmistakable whine of an outboard.

The inflatable! The thought blazed between his mind and Amber's.

An instant later Connor obviously heard it too and sharply sucked in his breath. "Shite!"

"Steady now." Kevin tried to reassure everyone, himself included. "They'll spot us in another minute or two."

"B-but Kevin!" Connor sputtered above the growing sound. "We bloody well can't outrun 'em!"

"I know. We're going to make for that grouping of rocks." He pointed to several humped shapes edged in white foam not more than fifty meters away.

The boy followed his finger. "But if we hit 'em—"

"We won't." Kevin interrupted. "We're going 'round 'em. Now row!"

He and Connor had no sooner put their backs into it than the whine of the outboard increased several notches. They'd been spotted, right enough.

"They have a light!" Amber cried.

A quick glance over and behind confirmed her claim. The round beam of a torch bounced up and down with the movements of the vessel. The illuminated shaft drew closer by the second.

To Kevin's dismay, Amber pulled herself up enough so that she could see over the side of the curragh. Her hand reached out toward the seal still keeping pace beside them. Before he could yell at her to get down, a shot rang out.

"Shite!" Connor hollered this time.

Amber jerked her hand back, but remained crouched next to the side. The seals on either side of them had vanished. Only one remained in front, swimming as if he were pulling the curragh after him.

The group of rocks suddenly loomed large directly in front of them. The inflatable was coming up fast behind, bathing them in torch light. The seal in front swerved to the left.

"Left!" Kevin shouted and heaved on his oar.

Connor scrambled to compensate, tilting the curragh to one side. Thrown off balance, Meriol rolled into Amber. The two of them thrashed under Kevin's feet in a tangle of limbs. He kept hold of the oar and continued rowing.

Another shot rang out, but passed harmlessly through the spot where they'd just been. The curragh righted and glided neatly around the rocks. But not before Kevin saw two seals leap into the air just in front of the inflatable.

A man yelled, and the boat jerked abruptly to the right. Not far enough to clear the rocks, however. The front of the craft smacked down hard and hit a glancing blow on the tallest of the jutting boulders.

More yelling came from at least two distinctly human voices, several seals barked, and the humming outboard screeched. With the grinding sounds of rock on metal and plastic assaulting his ears, Kevin slowed enough to look over his shoulder. The inflatable tipped completely on one side, dumping its passengers and dousing the motor to a gurgling halt.

She's going over.

Kevin had time for no more than that brief thought as the boat's wake hit them and nearly spun them in a circle. Icy spray washed over him and Connor, as if they weren't wet enough from the infernal rain. While the two of them struggled to get back on course, Meriol crawled across the wet bottom of the curragh to the backseat. The girl flung her arms across the wooden plank and stared toward the rocks receding behind them.

"Holy Mary, Mother of God!" she cried out in a strangled voice that made both Kevin and Connor stop rowing.

A seal popped its head above the water scant centimeters from Connor's oar, but that was not the reason for Meriol's consternation. Kevin's gaze followed the direction of her shaky hand, and he too could hardly believe his eyes.

The inflatable, listing badly, moved steadily toward them. Sideways.

"How…" Before he could form the question, he saw the answer. Two seals pushed the boat with noses, heads, and shoulders.

"Jaysus, Mary, and Joseph!" Connor swore as Amber pulled herself up next to him so that she could see over the side. "You really are a selkie princess!"

Chapter 15

WHEN THE TWO SEALS PUSHED THE EMPTY BOAT CLOSE enough, Kevin secured it to the side of the curragh with the rope. While Connor and Meriol continued to gape goggle-eyed, Amber stared for long moments into one of the creature's dark eyes.

"The two men who were in the boat won't be swimming this way," she said at last, and sent Kevin an image of several seals circling and shoving the hapless smugglers away from their capsized vehicle and toward the distant shore.

Nodding his understanding, Kevin finished with the rope and surveyed the damage. One of the front pontoons appeared to have lost about half its air, which was why the boat listed. That and the sea water covering the bottom at least a quarter of a meter deep. If he could bail out the water and get the motor to restart, the thing would be seaworthy enough, he judged.

Digging about beside the curragh's outboard, he found a bait bucket.

"Everybody to the other side," he ordered, and leaned over the edge to start bailing.

When the curragh dipped drunkenly, his three companions clearly were not pleased, and the whole thing was a decidedly inefficient method anyway. So after tossing out a few buckets full of water, Kevin decided he would get into the inflatable. He pitched the bait bucket in and threw one leg over the side.

"What are you doing?" Amber cried, clutching at his sleeve. "Kevin, what if that thing sinks?"

"'Twill not go far lashed to the curragh," he replied, pulling his other leg over.

The moment the icy sea water filled his shoes and sloshed halfway up his shins, he regretted his decision. But there was no help for it in any case, so gritting his teeth, he began bailing with a vengeance.

Once Amber realized that he was right about the thing not sinking, she moved to join him, sending a mental warning. *No arguments!*

As much as he didn't like the idea, Kevin knew that to have any hope of finding and rescuing her brother, Amber had to come with him. Sending her his own mental thread of reluctance, he reached out a hand to steady her.

She splashed into the smaller boat and caused all the water to shift in their direction. Sucking her breath in sharply when it washed up her pants legs, she grabbed the bucket out of his hand.

"I'll do this. You work on the motor." And she began flinging out water at a furious rate.

"What are we supposed to do?" Connor demanded, his voice wavering on a high-pitched squeak.

"You are going to row that curragh for all you're worth." His deadly serious tone made Connor snap his mouth closed on whatever objection he was about to raise. "Make for Malin Head, and don't stop for anything until you get there. If you get tired, let Meriol help you. But don't stop. You hear me, boyo?"

"I hear ya," Connor replied softly and reached for both oars.

"But what about Prince Par-Ker?" Meriol protested, sounding ready to weep again.

"We're going after him," Amber said, pausing long enough to meet the girl's gaze.

Whatever mental image or command she sent along with her words, Meriol silently tucked her chin down to her chest and turned away.

The smaller speedboat bobbed lower in the water than its wood and canvas counterpart, even without the extra water in the bottom, and it had no seats for the passengers. Not that he would consider endangering the two young ones by bringing them along. Seeing that they were in no danger of sinking, Kevin unknotted the rope from the curragh and secured it to one of the plastic handles on the side of the inflatable, freeing the two vessels from one another.

"God speed to you, Connor Magee," he said.

"And to you, Kevin Hennessey." The youth dipped the oars into the water and began a brisk, steady rhythm of rowing.

As the curragh pulled away, a yip sounded from one of the seals. A pair of sleek brown bodies skimmed over the water, one moving ahead of the boat, the other following behind. A third animal circled the inflatable once, then disappeared below the surface of the sea. Within a few moments, the black and brown curragh was swallowed by the night.

While Amber continued to bail, Kevin moved to the outboard and pried open the outside casing. He squinted in an attempt to discern anything in the dark.

"So help me God," he muttered. "If those two wee eejits go back to that cave, I'll kill them myself with my bare hands."

"They won't stop," Amber huffed out, stopping to push tangled wet locks out of her eyes. "They don't need to. Meriol has the money wrapped in her hat and stuffed inside her shirt."

The unexpected pronouncement gobsmacked him. "She what?"

"I felt it when we rolled into each other a little while ago, so I probed her memory."

With a hearty guffaw, Kevin slapped his thigh with his own sopping wet headgear. "Well, send me to the devil with the hounds of hell on my heels! I didn't see that one coming."

Amber gave a snort that was almost a chuckle. "Neither did I."

Suddenly, a seal surfaced not more than two meters from them. The creature seemed to have something in its mouth. She paused again and extended her hand.

"Careful," Kevin cautioned, not that she paid him any mind.

The critter spat something in Amber's direction. Reaching low into the water, she scooped it up and shook it. Suddenly, a bright beam of light shot out.

The seal had fetched the smugglers' torch!

"Now I've truly seen it all," he said, as Amber offered him the plastic contraption that had neither a crack nor a dent on it. A warm thread of amusement wound from her mind to his.

The seal disappeared again, and Amber went back to bailing the much lower water level. Kevin shined the torch into the outboard, drying out parts as best he could with the end of his shirttail.

He tried to start the thing, and it coughed and sputtered but didn't quite catch. With a curse, he cast the torch beam down the side of the boat and saw the single paddle still secured to one pontoon, his last resort. One he wasn't quite ready to accept.

Using the other side of his shirttail, he dried and fiddled a bit more before he tried the outboard again. Much to his surprise, the thing started. Perhaps their miserable luck had turned at last.

—•—

The sudden noise of the motor made Amber jerk her head around and stare.

Kevin banged the metal casing back into place and grabbed the handle that steered the inflatable. "Hang on tight!"

She crouched beside him as the boat leaped forward. The two inches of water still on the bottom rushed back to gather at their feet as the front of the craft rose. As she dipped the bait bucket to fill it one more time, she saw more water spilling over the damaged pontoon.

"Not so fast!" she cried.

Kevin saw it too and eased back on the throttle. Going slower seemed to cure up most of the problem, though a little water splashed in every so often. The farther they ventured from the shoreline, the choppier the sea grew.

Definitely not a fun ride.

They needed to find Parker and soon. Amber dropped the bucket and put her fingertips against her temples.

But a hoarse cry from Kevin stopped her. She gazed into the darkness in the direction he indicated.

In the distance she could faintly distinguish a pale smudge of another boat. Her heartbeat accelerated to triple time, while Kevin made a slow, wide turn.

Parker must be all right.

He had to be!

Since she had a point on which to focus, she didn't need to cast a wide search. She angled a mental probe in the direction of the other boat and scant seconds later found her brother's answering thoughts.

Amber! It's working. I feel the boat moving!

Yes! We can see you. Hang on! She sent him the image of what she could see, and then the impression of Kevin and her in the inflatable.

Careful! Parker sent the image of a hand gripping a pistol.

Can you walk?

No, he has me on the floor tied to a bench. He sent a jumbled image of all he could see from his low vantage point.

She also knew without him directly telling her that his wrists were bloody from trying to get loose.

We'll get you out. I swear we will! She sent as much optimism as she could muster. But she was scared, same as he was.

"They're coming up fast," Kevin said, drawing her attention back to the smudge on the horizon, which had grown considerably larger. "If their wake hits us, it'll probably swamp us."

Even in the dark, Amber could plainly see the white vessel. They weren't using a sail.

Can you slow him down a little? she sent to Parker.

I'll give it a shot.

Leave it to her brother, even at a time like this, to try to be a wise-ass.

"Parker's trying to slow them down," she told Kevin, who never took his eyes off the other boat.

"I'll maneuver behind them. Probably better if they don't see us until the last moment."

If only they could somehow turn invisible. Then again, in the darkness, with the boat so close to the surface of the water, their chances of being seen were slim. The sound of the motor might give them away, but she doubted Parker's captor could hear it over the sounds of his own vessel's engine.

Hope sprouted and grew alongside her fear. Watching Kevin strengthened her confidence. His expression looked grimly determined, not the least bit fearful.

Time and place seemed to stop. Amber forgot about being wet, cold, and miserable and put all her concentration into Kevin. She kept her eyes firmly affixed to his face, and her anxiety shoved into the distant back corner of her mind.

When she finally moved her gaze from him, the sailboat loomed large in her field of vision, making her recoil with shock.

"Whatever he's doing, 'tis working," Kevin reassured, and Amber saw he was right.

The sailboat moved much slower than before. Slow enough for them to keep pace, she noticed, even though it was a much larger craft. Also, Kevin had managed to position them on the seaward side of the other boat, running parallel.

"Can your brother get loose?" Kevin asked. Amber shook her head. "Then he'll have to get it to stop so I can board."

"We," she automatically corrected, as she reached for Parker's mind.

He responded slowly. What he was doing obviously required all his concentration. She showed him that they were only a few dozen yards away, and he answered with a thin thread of relief.

Get him to stop, she sent, along with a picture of her and Kevin crawling over the side of the sailboat.

Don't! Panic laced Parker's thought. *Too dangerous. There may be two of them. Not sure. Can't isolate.*

Abruptly, he broke their connection. Her fear roared back, freezing the blood in her veins.

"H-he thinks there may be two guys on the sailboat after all."

"Bloody hell!" Kevin swore, his eyes never leaving their objective.

Fighting her fear, she reached back into her brother's mind. *Show me your captor's thoughts. I'll try to link with him too.*

Another thing they'd never considered, much less done before, but she was willing to try anything at this point. She transmitted all this to Parker in a couple of quick bursts.

Her brother shared the pathway he'd opened into the other man's mind. *Use images.* Parker warned. *He doesn't think in English.*

Well, neither did the seals, and that hadn't stopped her from communicating with them. She sorted through the rapid succession of pictures flying through the man's memory.

The submerged rocks and ragged escarpment worried him. He feared the sailboat's deep centerboard might hit one of them. Amber decided to play up that fear and sent impressions of the things she'd just seen, boulders and rock shelves shallowly covered. She sensed more hesitation from the man, and at the same time Parker sent a mental thumbs up.

She felt her brother cautiously withdraw from the man's thoughts and take his mental search through the rest of the boat. Left alone in the stranger's mind, Amber kept the images flowing and slowly increased her efforts. As a matter of fact, she did everything but shriek, "You know you want to stop!" into his mind.

Blood pounded in her temples.

Suddenly Parker gave a mental shout, abruptly severing her connection to the stranger.

Amber! They know something's wrong!

She got a fast, fleeting impression of the two men who'd been in the inflatable before her brother's mind went unexpectedly blank.

"Parker!" Her scream of anguish was both mental and physical.

At the same moment, Kevin gave a loud yell and swerved their little craft hard to the left. The much larger sailboat narrowly missed sideswiping them. Chilly seawater swept over the side, drenching their feet.

Oh my God, Parker!

Amber reached frantically for her brother's thoughts while Kevin sent them careening through the other boat's wake. More water flew at them.

"What's happening?" Kevin demanded.

"When the men from this boat didn't contact the

sailboat, their buddies got suspicious. They might even know we're here." Amber gasped as the cold spray washed over her. "I think they've knocked Parker out."

"'Tis now or never, then," Kevin declared. "Hang on."

And he opened up the throttle and aimed them directly at the back of the sailboat.

Holding her breath, Amber gripped the hard plastic handle on the side of the pontoon as the inflatable bucked and leaped across the short space of water separating it from the larger vessel. In the seemingly endless moment before the inflatable slammed into it, she glimpsed an L-shaped notch molded into the stern of the sailboat right next to the outboard motor. Undoubtedly how they got on and off the inflatable, the ledge dipped down to mere inches above the water level.

Air exploded from her lungs and seawater rushed into her mouth as their impact sent her sprawling. Somehow she kept hold of the side with one hand, or she'd have been facedown in the water beneath and around her. Pain streaked from her shoulder to her wrist as she hung on and gagged.

Kevin jumped over her, yellow nylon rope in hand, and grabbed the bottom rung of a small metal ladder.

"You all right?" he shouted over the sputtering of the outboard and her own choking coughs.

She managed to nod while he secured them to the ladder with a couple of deft twists of the rope. The sailboat banked to one side and sent the inflatable sharply up too. All the water rushed to the back, nearly taking her with it. One last wheeze brought the outboard to a final, shuddering halt.

Feeling Kevin's arm around her waist, Amber let go

of her death grip on the pontoon's handle and grabbed him instead. He pulled her tight against his body and used their combined weight to bring the inflatable back to a more upright position.

Muffled clanking and rattling sounds sent Kevin down into a defensive crouch, taking her with him. He eased her arm from around his neck, and an instant later, Amber felt him press something heavy into her palm.

She gasped in horror as she recognized his pistol.

"Hold it with both hands, but keep your finger outside the trigger guard until you're ready to fire," he instructed. Then he took her free hand and pressed her fingers into place. "You only have to squeeze the trigger. 'Twill keep firing as long as you keep squeezing. You have sixteen shots. Just don't point at anything you don't intend to kill."

"N-no! I've never… I can't!" She tried to shove it away, but he wouldn't let her. "But… but you told Connor—"

"You're not Connor, and this threat is real. Aim for the body, 'tis a bigger target. Now stay down."

Thrusting himself away, he turned and bolted up the ladder. Before she could protest further.

Before she could tell him she loved him.

Kevin! She sent a mental call after him, but he didn't answer that either.

Biting her lip to keep silent, Amber lifted her head enough to see over the edge of the inflatable. With a flying tackle, Kevin hit a man standing at the wheel and sent them both to the floor of the sailboat.

The boat veered sharply, causing her to almost lose her balance as the inflatable shifted. She heard the loud thud of the men's bodies banging on the wooden floor.

Curses, grunts, and the unmistakable whack of flesh against flesh quickly followed.

Clutching the gun in her right hand, she inched her way upward so that she could peek up at the deck. Flinching at what she saw, she couldn't look away.

The man, who was wearing a yellow slicker, elbowed Kevin in the midsection and shoved him backward. As Kevin staggered against the rail only a few feet from her, she watched frozen in horror as the other man pulled a pistol.

But Kevin was fast, amazingly fast for his size. He lashed out with his foot and hit his assailant directly in the groin. The gun flew from the man's hand and bounced on the deck. Kevin dove for it. But just as his fingers closed over the barrel, the other man's foot came down on Kevin's wrist.

Though it trembled badly, Amber raised her right hand to eye level. She heard Kevin give a groaning growl, and before she could raise her left hand to brace her right, he punched his enemy in the back of the knee.

The man went down with a howl while Kevin leaped up with the pistol in a two-handed grip, poised and ready.

A shout brought everyone to motionless silence.

The cabin door burst open, and a second man in yellow tugged a shambling figure up onto the deck.

Amber's heart threatened to pound out of her chest at the sight of the second man holding a pistol to her semiconscious brother's head.

Parker! But her mental scream of agony elicited only a flicker of response.

The man with the gun shouted something and

motioned with his head. His intent was unmistakable. Amber watched the adversary who faced Kevin hold out his hand, a nasty smirk etching his features.

Kevin let go with one hand and held the gun out to his side, dangling loosely in his fingers.

Shoot now! Kevin's sudden mental command startled her.

Now, Amber! Save Parker!

But she knew if she shot the goon holding her brother, the other one would shoot Kevin. And, God forbid, if she should miss! They were both dead men.

She couldn't save them both.

Sucking in her breath, she gripped the cold, hard handle just the way Kevin had, with both hands. Then she rested her finger against the trigger, while Kevin's words echoed inside her brain, "Don't point at anything you don't intend to kill."

Gloating in triumph, the goon snagged the gun from Kevin's hand.

Bracing herself for the recoil, Amber took aim over Kevin's shoulder and squeezed the trigger.

Time slowed to a standstill as the deafening crack rang in her ears. She watched the man's torso jerk backward, his triumphant expression melting into soundless shock as the gun slid from his fingers. A red spot blossomed and spread across his yellow slicker a few inches below his shoulder. His partner's jaw went slack with surprise, his pistol wavering.

But before anyone could move, the very image that Amber had painted in their enemy's mind came suddenly to life. A loud grinding, grating noise echoed up from below, and the sailboat shuddered violently

266   LOUCINDA McGARY

as the deep keel scraped against a shelf of shallowly submerged rock.

The unexpected movement made all five occupants stagger as the sailboat bucked and shook. While the pistol slipped from her trembling fingers, Amber glimpsed Kevin diving for the wheel as the boat started to tip.

Another loud shot rang out, and in the split second before she lost her balance, she saw her brother grasp his abdomen. Intense pain lanced into her body as chaos erupted all around her.

———

What had Amber done?

Kevin's fingers grasped the hard plastic of the wheel, and he yanked it down as he himself landed on the floor. Another shot rang out, and the shaking boat wrenched sharply to the left, heaving up onto its side, almost vertical.

From the corner of his eye, Kevin saw Parker double over, clutch his gut, and then slide past the rail into the sea. The knacker who'd shot Parker dropped his gun and scrambled wildly for the side of the open cabin door to stop his own fall. Amid horrible groaning and crashing, everything in the boat shifted.

The other goon fell and tumbled across the tilted floor, leaving a bright red trail of blood. *Amber had shot him, not the man holding the gun on her brother.*

The thought finally registered in his stunned brain, and Kevin gave a mental as well as physical shout. "Amber!"

Then his feet slipped and slid on the slanted floor. He grabbed the plastic seat bolted behind the wheel and fought to regain his balance.

"Amber!" he shouted again, as he watched the mast dipping at a dangerously low angle while every part of the boat seemed to screech in protest.

They were going to capsize.

Shite! He and Amber couldn't be caught underneath when it happened, which looked to be in the next moment. Shoving himself upright, he leapt for the stern and the nose of the inflatable barely visible below and behind him.

The fecking boat was twisted almost completely on one side too. He caught sight of Amber in the far corner next to the outboard. Slumped over, her hair trailed into the water rising round her.

Shite! Shite! Shite!

Kevin clawed at the rope he'd knotted to the ladder, miraculously working it loose in a heartbeat. Gripping the front of the boat with both hands, he pushed with all his strength to shove it away from the sailboat.

Unfortunately, Amber's weight in the back flipped the inflatable upside down, dumping her into the icy, black waves.

He followed without a moment's hesitation.

In spite of the darkness, he saw her flailing, a foot hung up on one of the inflatable's handholds. In three strokes, he reached her, freed her foot, and hauled her to the surface.

Their heads had no sooner broken the water than the sailboat stood poised perpendicular for one astounding moment before it tipped back and righted itself with a mighty crash. While Kevin treaded water with Amber coughing beside him, the enormous backwash hurtled over them, pounding them toward the bottom of the sea.

Chapter 16

FOR ONE TERRIFYING MOMENT, KEVIN COULDN'T distinguish up from down. Then he saw a sleek brown shape circle them and streak away. A seal, undoubtedly headed for the surface. Kevin tightened his grip on Amber and followed.

As soon as their heads broke through, she coughed and struggled in his arms. Both good signs. And so was the sight of the inflatable floating less than a dozen meters from them, even though it was upside down.

With Amber still under one arm, he reached the little boat in the space of two breaths. He couldn't see any way on God's green earth he could flip the thing upright and keep his hold on her. But as long as the vessel was afloat, they'd be out of the cold water, so he paddled round to the half-deflated front pontoon and wrestled her and himself up onto the smooth plastic floor. Behind them, he heard the sound of the sailboat's motor growing fainter with distance.

Amber continued to cough, and when the cold wind hit her, she shivered violently. He pulled her into his arms and tried to warm her as best he could. She stopped coughing, and finally after several long moments, her trembling abated a little.

But when he looked into her beautiful golden eyes, they stared back in blank emptiness, like earlier when she'd gone too far in her mental search for Connor.

Like Caitlin when her broken mind couldn't accept the tragedy happening around her...

"No! Amber, no!" He smacked her icy cheeks with both his palms, but she didn't respond, so he grabbed both her shoulders and shook.

"Parker," she moaned, her head lolling from side to side. "Oh God, Parker..."

If her brother was dead, did that mean she was dead too? At least the part of her that shared her brother's thoughts and feelings?

No! Kevin couldn't—*wouldn't* accept that.

"Come back to me!" he demanded and shook her again, all the while calling out to her in his mind. "I bloody well can't live without you. You hear me?"

Then he crushed her against his chest, hoping and praying that if he just held her close enough and long enough...

A tiny whisper feathered next to his breastbone. "I hear you."

He glanced down and saw comprehension once again registering in her eyes. Whooping loud enough to be heard in Scotland, he clasped her even more tightly.

The air whooshed out of her lungs, and she squirmed against his overzealous embrace. Reluctantly, he loosened his hold.

"Parker's alive," she rasped out, drawing in a deep breath. "I felt him."

The man had taken a bullet to the midsection. If he were still alive, he wouldn't be for long. But Kevin wouldn't acknowledge, much less voice, such a thought.

"We'll find him, then," he said, and looked about for some way to move the inflatable, short of swimming behind and pushing like the seals had done.

Then he remembered the paddle, secured to the inside of one of the pontoons, and he tried to reach into the water to locate it. Unfortunately, his arms weren't long enough, and he wound up having to go back into the water over Amber's protests.

The wooden oar was still there, but he didn't have enough breath to pry the bugger loose. He surfaced, shouted "I've got it!" to Amber, and ducked back under to give it another go.

The second time, he pulled it loose and resurfaced with the slender piece of plastic firmly in his grasp. He tossed the paddle to Amber before crawling back onto the overturned boat, which bobbed little more than a hand's breadth above the sea. The shaft and propeller of the outboard stabbed upward like a bizarre kind of mast.

Since the back of the inflatable seemed more stable than the front, Kevin positioned himself near the outboard with Amber next to him. But before he could stick the paddle in the water, a seal popped up a couple of meters away with the same plastic torch in its mouth.

Amber reached to retrieve the light, but it had not fared so well this time. The front glass had a jagged crack with sea water inside, and no matter how hard Kevin shook the bugger, he couldn't get it to illuminate.

Meanwhile, Amber crouched down and exchanged intent stares with the animal. No doubt connecting mentally with it. After several long moments, she drew back, and the seal dove under and disappeared.

"I ordered him to find Parker," she explained, her expression tense in spite of her declaration that her brother was still alive.

"Then we'll head for shore, at least for the moment,"

Kevin responded, though he had no bloody clue how far away land—any land—might be.

Even if they were warmer out of the water, being exposed to the breeze as they were felt deucedly cold. Staying out here all night guaranteed them both a case of hypothermia.

Frustrated by the darkness, he strained his eyes in all directions, searching for signs of the headlands. Finally, he discerned what could only be cliffs on the horizon, but they seemed an impossibly long distance away. Doggedly, he began to paddle.

The single oar, coupled with the weight of the outboard directly in front of them, made progress painfully slow. Amber slumped beside him, her head in her hands. He hoped to high heaven that dry land wasn't as far away as he feared.

After ten long minutes of paddling, a bobbing light on the edge of his vision captured Kevin's attention. It grew bigger and brighter by the heartbeat, so it had to be another boat.

He nudged Amber and nodded in the general direction of the approaching light. "We're about to have company rather soon."

She jerked upright and looked over his shoulder. "Who do you think it is?"

"No way to tell." But whether friend or foe, the boat would be upon them within a few minutes no matter what they did.

Pulling up the plastic paddle, he placed it under his knees and grasped the shaft of the outboard to brace himself. "Hang onto me in case we get swamped."

Amber scooted close and hugged him around the waist, resting her cheek between his shoulder blades.

Her breathing felt shallow and rapid with fear, probably in part because she wasn't much of a swimmer. If the worst happened, and they ended up back in the water, he wasn't sure how long he could swim towing her.

Within moments, the beam of light cut through the darkness, illuminating a wide swath of water in front of the oncoming craft. This obviously wasn't the sailboat returning. Nor was it any other boat with an outboard motor, for Kevin could feel the rumble of the large engine all the way to his bones.

Another moment and the light swept over them, blinding him with its intensity. Immediately, the engine cut back to a low growl. He couldn't shield his eyes because their capsized inflatable bobbed wildly as the wake washed around them.

At the same moment, a tinny voice called out through a bullhorn, "This is PSNI. Throw down any weapons."

Police Service of Northern Ireland? Kevin could hardly believe his ears.

He wanted to whoop for joy, but instead he shouted, "We have no weapons!"

"Hennessey?" a somewhat familiar voice yelled back, sans bullhorn.

"Yes!" Kevin struggled to stand, no easy feat with Amber still clinging to him and the inflatable continuing to rock. "'Tis all right, luv, the cavalry's come at last," he reassured her.

<hr />

The much larger boat seemed like a leviathan as it idled closer. The blinding light moved slightly to one side. Amber loosed her stranglehold on Kevin and watched a figure leaning toward them from the tall height of the vessel's flying bridge.

"Great God in Heaven, 'tis you," the man cried.

"Walsh?" Kevin seemed to recognize the speaker. "Brian Walsh from the academy?"

"The same! Can you climb?"

The two must have been in police training together, Amber surmised. She reached for the metal shaft of the outboard motor to steady herself, but without Kevin's body heat close to her, she shivered with the cold.

A moment later, a ladder made of rope and plastic pitched over the substantial boat's side. Kevin caught the end with one hand, teetering to keep his balance.

Silhouetted in the glare of light, he untwisted the long, sinuous length, standing on a plastic rung to pull the entire thing taut. Then using sheer brute strength she couldn't help but admire, he dragged them closer to the side of the other boat by hauling on the ladder and standing on each successive rung.

When their wobbly vessel was about six feet from the police boat, he motioned to her with a nod of his head. "C'mon, up you go then."

Still trembling, Amber gazed up the skinny, unstable ladder with dismay. Would this nightmare never end? Her mind balked at the impossible-looking climb.

Drawing in a trembling breath, she sent a tendril of uncertainty into Kevin's mind.

Help me.

He let go with one hand and held it out to her, sending her a warm flurry of conviction at the same time.

You can do it. Climb as fast as you can. Don't stop and don't look down.

Still feeling like she was in a bad dream, she clutched his hand and shuffled across the two steps that separated them. He clamped their joined hands on the rung just over her head and slowly slid his hand away.

Go! He ordered, and she obeyed without stopping to think.

Hand, foot.

Hand, foot.

Kevin called out to her in her mind, and Amber forced herself into the rhythm. She knew he was holding the ladder steady below her, but she couldn't think about that. Above her, she could see two men's faces staring down. She focused on them and kept moving.

Their faces grew closer and closer with every rung. Then their hands were grasping her forearms, and they heaved her up the last few feet and over the side, breaking her mental connection with Kevin. A third man caught her as her rubbery legs gave way. He enveloped her in a warm, dry blanket that felt a teeny, tiny half-step from paradise.

But she wasn't about to relax until Kevin was beside her. When the man tried to steer her into the boat's cabin, she pulled away and leaned back over the side.

If she'd thought her climb horrendous, Kevin's was worse because without anything to anchor it, the ladder swung free. He made it halfway up before the thing twisted and he wound up knocking against the side of the boat.

"Hang tight!" one of their rescuers called down to Kevin. "We'll haul you the rest of the way."

Amber pressed one hand against her mouth to keep from crying out as she watched the three of them pull

Kevin and the ladder up the side of the boat. When they finally hoisted him over the side, she flew at him, the blanket billowing behind her.

"Didja think we'd drop him?" One of the men chastised her, and she noticed he wore a wet suit.

"You gotta admit, he's nearly as heavy as a bleedin' whale," a second one joked.

"More like a walrus," said the third, who then turned and disappeared inside the cabin.

"Very funny," Kevin muttered, but he brushed his lips across hers before he asked their rescuers, "How in the name of all that's holy did you get here?"

"'Twas yourself, or at least that call you made yesterday morning."

She recognized the voice of the man Kevin had called Walsh. He snagged another blanket off the bench seat and handed it to Kevin before he continued. "We've been tracking these Albanians for weeks. After your call, we doubled our efforts, and the moment they slipped over the line into our jurisdiction, we were waiting."

"So we're in Northern Ireland now?" Amber asked, while Kevin unfolded and wrapped himself in his blanket.

"By at least fifty meters," Walsh replied with a wink.

"And you caught the sailboat?" Kevin persisted, moving closer to her.

The red-haired man nodded, completely serious once more. "Our other boat did, but 'twas just the one knacker on board along with quite a cache of weapons and explosives. Surely there was more than just him and the two of you?"

"My brother..." Her throat clogged up, and she

couldn't continue. The terrible choice she had made threatened to engulf her.

Kevin's arm encircled her shoulders, and he pulled her close. "And one other Albanian. They've both been shot. Plus there's two other smugglers clinging to a rock somewhere over on the Donegal side."

Walsh's sandy-colored eyebrow quirked, but before he could say anything, a seal barked. Breaking away from Kevin's embrace, Amber rushed to the side opposite the one they'd scaled. Clutching her blanket with one hand and grasping the metal rail that ran the length of the boat with her other, she leaned over to search the dark water below.

As Kevin scooted next to her, the seal barked again, and she saw his sleek, dark head bobbing about six feet away from them. Quickly, she reached for the animal's mind and was rewarded with an image of Parker's body lying on wet sand and ringed with seals.

Lead us! She ordered the animal, then turned to Kevin, her excitement almost preventing her from forming words. "He's found Parker!"

The seal yipped and swam for the front of the boat. Amber clung to the thin mental thread connecting her to the creature, praying with every unoccupied part of her mind.

"Is that thing your pet?" asked Walsh, who stood on her other side.

"Not exactly," Kevin answered for her. "But he's going to lead us to her brother."

Walsh wore a skeptical expression but headed for the ladder connected to the high bridge. "In that case, I'd better get up top and let McAdams know."

The man who had disappeared minutes earlier opened the door to the cabin and called out to them, "I've fixed you both a cuppa."

Her connection to the seal momentarily severed, Amber pulled herself together enough to follow Kevin down the half dozen steep steps into the boat's cabin. She noticed this officer also wore a wet suit, the hood pushed off his head, leaving his short brown hair rumpled.

"Morrison, Danny Morrison," he said with a nod. "Do you take milk or sugar in your tea?"

"Neither, thank you, and I'm Amber O'Neill." The sudden rumble of the engine almost drowned out her voice.

She sat on a bench at a table, all affixed to the cabin wall. Kevin sat next to her. She could see a tiny fridge, sink, and two-burner stove on the other wall. Cabinets lined the wall above them. A couple of bunks filled the small space behind the stairs.

"Good to meet you," Danny Morrison said, deftly handing them both heavy plastic mugs of steaming tea. "You too, Hennessey. Walsh has mentioned you."

The boat moved forward, but slowly. Apparently the movement and the engine noise had no effect on Morrison, who opened a cupboard and offered them a package of shortbread cookies. Kevin grabbed a handful, but she shook her head. Her stomach was already balking after just two sips of hot tea. She couldn't just sit here having tea and cookies while Parker bled to death.

"I'm sorry," she apologized to Morrison. "But I need to be up top when they spot my brother."

"There's nothing you can do now, luv," Kevin murmured, his blue eyes filled with sympathy and concern. "Stay down here for a bit and warm up."

"At least finish your tea," the other man urged. "And I'll find you some dry duds."

He ducked under the stairs, sat on the bottom bunk, and rummaged through the narrow closet built into the wall.

While Kevin shoved two cookies into his mouth, Amber took another gulp of tea and felt the warmth trickle all the way down to her knotted stomach. She clasped and unclasped her hands, thinking sea slugs must move faster than they were.

Morrison came back with two hooded sweatshirts bearing PSNI insignias on each right sleeve. Kevin wasted no time peeling off his soaked shirt and T-shirt.

"Head's over there," Morrison indicated with a nod.

Sweatshirt in hand, Amber rose and crossed to what she had assumed was a pantry. In fact, the tiny bathroom was much smaller than the walk-in closet in her bedroom at home. Turning on the light, she shimmied out of her dripping windbreaker and T-shirt, but left on her wet bra. No point in giving the crew a free jiggle show.

The sweatshirt was too big for her to put the windbreaker over it, so she zipped the dry garment up to her chin and hurried back out without daring to look in the mirror.

She emerged to find Kevin and Danny engaged in a low conversation. They went silent at her approach.

Suddenly, so did the engine.

Before Amber could form a question, the other man in the wet suit threw open the cabin door.

"Get up here, Morrison!" he cried. "You won't believe this."

She practically trod on Morrison's heels rushing up the stairs and out onto the deck. Kevin grasped her wrist and tried to pull her back, but she jerked away and charged for the front railing where the other man in the wet suit stood.

A chorus of harsh barking filled the night air. She squeezed between Morrison and his buddy and stared at the illuminated space in front of the boat. On a soggy arc of sand, twenty or more seals reared up in a fierce wall of trumpeting cries and snapping teeth. Even though Amber couldn't see him, she knew Parker lay somewhere behind them.

Oh please, God, let him be alive!

She pressed her fingertips against her temples and sent out an urgent mental call.

Nothing.

Desperation and frustration clogged her throat as she dropped her hands to her sides. The terrible possibility that they were too late hovered on the edges of her mind. She felt Kevin's hands on her shoulders and leaned back against his solid warmth, awash in weariness and self-reproach.

"Is Parker down there?"

Because of her, he was alive and breathing and whispering in her ear. Because she had saved him instead of her brother.

Numbly she nodded and replied with her mind. *He must be, but he's not answering.*

"This is gonna be dicey," Morrison muttered.

From above her on the bridge, Walsh yelled over the din, "More friends of yours?"

"Not exactly," Kevin shouted back. Then he spoke into her ear again, "You need to call them off, Amber, like you did the other night in the cave. Otherwise Morrison and Feeney can't go after Parker."

What if we're already... too late? She could barely bring herself to form the thought, much less speak it.

We're not! Kevin sent back emphatically. *Those buggers wouldn't be so loud if he were dead.*

He was right!

Breathing deeply, she shook off the feelings of recrimination and doom, grasped the metal railing in front of her, and pulled herself against it. Kevin's arms encircled her, and he dropped his hands on top of hers.

"Get the basket," she heard him order Morrison.

Then she leaned over the railing at the same time she reached mentally for the first seal in her line of vision. She felt the animal's single-minded determination and raw brute strength. He would defend his own at the risk of his life.

She sent gentle waves of calm, soothing reassurances. Searching the creature's mind, she found the image of Parker lying on the sand, a dark stain widening under him. She fought to remain composed.

We've come to help him. Heal him. He needs us now.

Amber felt the seal respond, grow quiet. She moved on to the next one.

Behind her, she could vaguely hear and feel movement. Not Kevin, whose hands still gripped hers, but the two men in wet suits. She heard them scuffling about the deck, but couldn't break her concentration to see what they were doing.

Instead, she reached for the mind of the third seal.

The two she'd already pacified must be spreading her message to others, for the cacophony had noticeably lessened. She squeezed her eyes closed and cast her mental net over all the creatures, broadcasting her message of calmness.

"That's the ticket," Kevin murmured in her ear. "Whatever you're doing, keep it up."

Through the perceptions of the seals, she watched the scene unfold. An odd-looking figure she recognized as Morrison rappelled down the side of the boat and into the sea. A strange contraption, which must have been the "basket" Kevin had mentioned, lowered into the water after him. Then his partner, Feeney, rappelled down to join him.

All around her, Amber felt the minds of the animals, curious now, no longer on guard in defense of their wounded charge. But vigilant nevertheless.

The two men reached the sandbar in a matter of moments, pulling the oversized basket between them. She felt the animals shifting aside, some with remaining traces of reluctance, to let the men pass. Another part of her mind heard startled exclamations from the bridge as Morrison and Feeney drew the long, narrow basket over the sand between the now placid seals.

She almost lost control when she glimpsed her brother's crumpled, bleeding form. Only Kevin's closeness and his whispered, "Steady," kept her from crying out in anguish.

Unable to watch as the two men performed a quick examination and applied some field dressings, Amber blended her thoughts back into the instinctual minds of the sleek creatures. They shuffled and grunted into a ring of wary spectators, and she sensed their collective mood teetered between trust and hostility.

Your work is done, she sent on a wave of gratefulness. *You've saved him.*

I didn't.

Two or three of them broke from the circle and slid off the sandbar into the lapping waves. However, the rest seemed to sense her worry and continued to watch as Morrison and Feeney carefully lifted the unconscious Parker into the stretcher-like basket and strapped him down. Her overarching link began to unravel, and Amber was forced to narrow her focus to the mind of only one animal. She continued to observe through its lone perspective.

Four of the largest seals followed Morrison and Feeney into the water, swimming around the two men as they guided the basket to the side of the waiting boat. She opened her eyes in time to see Walsh and McAdams rushing down the ladder from the bridge.

"Will you be all right for a bit?" Kevin asked, lifting his hands from atop hers.

Fighting to maintain her connection to the single seal, she nodded. Kevin dashed after the other two men, leaving her cold and utterly bereft.

Parker's still alive! she reminded herself as she shivered and continued to observe the scene through her shared mental link.

A link she might never again share with her brother.

Under the continued observation of the four large seals, the two men hooked the basket to two lines. It rose smoothly out of the water and up the side of the ship. As soon as it bumped over the railing and disappeared, the plastic and wooden ladder tumbled down. Morrison and Feeney easily scrambled up, and with her heart aching over the way she'd failed her brother, Amber severed the mental connection between herself and the seal.

When she turned to rush after Kevin, her legs buckled, and she stumbled, catching the rail just in time to prevent herself from sprawling across the deck. Large hands grasped her shoulders and steadied her.

"You all right then, luv?" asked Walsh, his brows raised with concern. Amber managed a half-nod, and he gave her a rough pat. "'Twill be all right. He's in a bad way, but I've seen worse."

Then he turned and scrambled up the ladder to the bridge. She scuttled sideways and crumpled at the foot of the basket, where the four men all crouched around Parker's pale, still body. An open bag of medical supplies sat on the deck near his right shoulder.

Kevin twitched the blanket over her brother's torso, but not before she saw the thick pad of gauze the man, who must be McAdams, pressed against Parker's side. Next to him, Morrison shoved a wet, bloody bandage into a plastic bag with his gloved hands.

Walsh might have said he'd seen worse, but Amber honestly couldn't see how. She would have thought her brother dead except for the rattling wheeze escaping his nose and mouth. She covered her own mouth with both hands to stifle a shriek.

"One of his lungs is partially collapsed," Kevin explained, no doubt guessing the cause of her reaction.

"Probably caused by a busted rib," added Feeney, shoving back the hood of his wet suit with his forearm. "And there's no exit wound so the bullet's still—"

The loud rumble of the engine drowned out the rest of his words. The boat leapt forward and threw her off balance. Kevin knelt and tugged her back to a sitting position, but she fell against him like a rag doll. Purposely she huddled next to his chest for a moment, gathering strength. She refused to let herself cry no matter how scared she was.

"I've already called the bird," she heard McAdams shout over the engine's roar. "We'll rendezvous in five, six minutes tops."

She straightened and searched Kevin's face, sending a hesitant mental query. *What? Where?*

The touch of his thoughts comforted her far more than a physical caress.

Chopper to hospital. Derry. He sent the image of a helicopter settling on the roof of a building, and she understood. They were airlifting Parker to a trauma center.

She refused to let him die before they got there. If she had to breathe for him, open a vein for him…

Whatever it took.

Not your fault, luv. Kevin's gentle admonishment was meant to soothe her guilt. But she knew it wasn't true. She'd made a deliberate choice, and Parker had suffered the consequences.

Pulling away from Kevin both mentally and physically, she crawled to Parker's head. His face had the waxy look of a corpse and felt ice-cold when she cupped her hands around his cheeks.

Don't leave me! she silently ordered, and probed deep into his psyche, trying desperately to find some sliver of his mind.

Stay with me, Parker!

Please don't leave.

Over and over, she called out to him, searched with her mind, pried at the mental barriers separating them. She knew he was still there somewhere, if only she could find him…

"Amber, luv!" Kevin's voice was soft but insistent.

She felt his fingers gripping her shoulder, shaking her away from her quest. Raising her head, she realized her forehead had been touching her brother's. Kevin's worried blue eyes locked with hers, and then she noticed the boat had stopped moving except for a gentle rocking motion.

A strange whirling noise had replaced the rumble of the engine. Before she could open her mouth to speak, it grew much louder and seemed to be coming from overhead.

"The chopper's coming," Kevin said, and looked up and over one shoulder.

Following his gaze, Amber saw the approaching beam of light shining down. The air from the whirling blades ruffled the otherwise smooth surface of the water. They intended to take Parker away, somewhere she might never reach him again. Unreasoning fear seized her and shook far more violently than Kevin's fingers.

"No!" she cried, flinging herself across her brother's motionless form. "I have to stay with him. Please! I have to be there when he wakes up."

Chapter 17

"CAN THIS CONTRAPTION SUPPORT THE PAIR OF THEM?" Kevin raised his voice so that he could be heard over the noise of the approaching helicopter.

Morrison nodded. "To be sure, if we could fit 'em both in. But 'twouldn't be wise to move him, and I expect 'twould be one damn scary ride if she weren't strapped in."

Not half so bad as her not being there if the worst should happen. Kevin knew all about the pain of living with that, and he didn't intend to have it happen to Amber.

"I'll get her strapped in then. Go and tell Walsh to radio the bird to expect two instead of one."

The other man's eyes flicked briefly over Amber clinging to her brother's body, then back to Kevin.

Kevin didn't need telepathy to know that all four of the PSNI crew had witnessed things tonight that stretched the limits of their beliefs. He could scarcely believe some of it himself, and he'd been living with it for days. In truth, he was glad he wouldn't be the one to figure out how to file it all in a report.

Luckily, Morrison didn't argue. He stood and trotted off toward the bridge while Kevin turned his attention back to Amber.

"C'mon, luv," he coaxed, prying her away from Parker. "You're going with him, but you need to move down a little."

Her golden eyes filled with hope. "I can stay with him?"

He nodded, barely able to hear her over the pulsing of the chopper blades overhead. Undoing the straps across Parker's legs, he cautiously moved them to one side. Precious little space resulted, but Amber knew what to do. She crawled close to her brother's feet and hunkered down into a tight ball. Kevin secured the strap across her and Parker, anchoring it as strongly as he could.

Meanwhile, the light from the chopper illuminated the deck as the aircraft hovered directly over them. Morrison returned and helped Feeney fasten a harness of ropes and chains on both sides of the basket.

Kevin gave the canvas strap one final tug, his fingers trailing across Amber's cheek. "Hold tight, and don't look down!"

The wind from the blades whipped his words away as Feeney shouldered him aside to secure the last piece of the harness.

While Kevin wondered if she had heard him at all, Morrison waved both hands to signal the pilot. As a length of heavy rope snaked its way down toward the deck, Kevin felt the familiar brush of Amber's mind.

An image of her face with eyes squeezed shut flashed through his head.

Not looking, she sent.

She'd heard him after all.

Nothing to see at any rate, he sent back.

Then he had to jump aside as the rope, bristling with loops, nearly smacked into him. Morrison wrestled it into position and laced the harness into the loops while Feeney kept the slack portion untangled.

You're something to see, Amber sent on a wave of tenderness.

Abruptly, Morrison jerked Kevin backward and waved his arms again.

His link to Amber severed, Kevin reached frantically with his mind as he watched the rope go taut and the basket lift off the deck. He clasped both hands over his ears in an attempt to mute the chopper's noise and reconnect to her thoughts.

For a moment, the basket dangled just above his head. One gossamer strand drifted into his mind, and he grasped at it, silently calling her name.

I love you, Kevin.

The slender thread connecting her mentally to him unraveled while the basket lifted skyward like a shooting star in reverse. He watched it wind its way back into heaven where it belonged. And when he could no longer see the tiny speck, the only light in his life disappeared too.

———— ∿ ————

A hand patting her arm roused Amber from a fitful sleep. Slowly she opened her heavy lids and stared into the pale gray eyes of a nurse wearing a surgical cap and gown. A white mask obscured the bottom of her chin.

"Miss O'Neill? Your brother's surgery is done. They'll be moving him into recovery directly."

Amber jerked upright on the plastic chair, instantly alert. "Can I see him?"

"Only for a few moments," the nurse said, giving her a final pat. "He's not conscious yet, but the doctor will give you an update."

Scrambling to her feet, Amber followed the nurse, the soft soles of her borrowed slippers making no sound on the tile floor. After the trauma team had stabilized Parker, prepped him, and taken him off to surgery, one of the nurses took charge of her. Fortyish Meghan O'Malley had noticed Amber's wet and bedraggled shoes and clothes and found her a few temporary replacements.

"They'll need to work on your brother for several hours," the dark-haired woman had said. "You'll feel much better with a shower and clean clothes."

The soap and hot water had felt heavenly, and when Amber emerged, Meghan had left a set of green scrubs, clean underwear, socks, and a pair of open-back slippers. Everything seemed about one size too large, but such a vast improvement that Amber didn't care. Shortly after she'd returned to the waiting room, Meghan came back with a plastic container of soup and threatened to force-feed her if she didn't eat it. Amber had grudgingly complied even though she hardly tasted anything.

Soon, time ceased to have any meaning. Meghan's shift ended, and she bid her a reluctant farewell. The tiny surgical waiting room remained empty of other people with hospital staff bustling about their duties in the corridor. Amber alternated between pacing and staring into space, with an occasional short bout of disturbing sleep. The events of the previous hours spiraled over and over through her exhausted brain.

Now the surgical nurse led her through the swinging doors at the end of the hallway. She easily spotted Parker, for he was the only patient in recovery at this late hour, and several staff members crowded around his tube-, wire-, and monitor-festooned bed.

Her breath jammed in her throat when she looked at his starkly pale face, nearly the same shade as the bandage on his forehead. Almost every visible part of him seemed to have some sort of bandage, and an oxygen mask rested over his mouth and nose. At least he wasn't making that horrible wheezing sound that would be forever imprinted in her brain.

She stepped to the foot of his raised bed and mentally reached for his mind.

Still nothing.

Amber bit her lip to stifle the urge to scream.

"Miss O'Neill?" The trauma surgeon, whose name she could not remember, looked up from scribbling notes on a clipboard. "All things considered, he's doing rather well. The lung reinflated without incident, but we couldn't save the spleen. A portion of the right kidney was damaged, and as I told you before, two ribs were shattered. The bullet was still imbedded in one of them."

Her knees wobbled at his last statement, and he carefully guided her backward to a swiveling stool.

"S-sorry," she apologized, sitting with an ungraceful plop.

The doctor's expression and tone never changed as he continued jotting notes. "He lost a great deal of blood. We gave him three units but may need to give him more. Our chief concern now is the repeated head trauma. If he doesn't regain consciousness in the next few hours, we'll need to re-evaluate."

Taking a deep breath, she rose to her feet. "Can I talk to him? Do you think he can hear me?"

"Couldn't hurt to try."

The nurse standing closest to Parker's head stepped aside so that Amber could take her place.

She rubbed her knuckles across his cold, bristly cheek. "Come back to me, Parker. Please don't leave me." While she spoke, she probed the recesses of his mind, but he remained beyond her reach.

The nurse who'd brought her from the waiting room grasped her elbow. "Time to go. You can come back when he's settled in intensive care."

Reluctantly, Amber gave up her mental search and let the nurse lead her away. Her footsteps dragged down the hallway.

"There's a chapel on the first floor," the nurse said. "Shall I show you where 'tis?"

Amber nodded numbly.

She was still sitting there alone, staring at the single pane of stained glass above the small altar, when the nurse returned.

At first, Amber didn't recognize her without her surgical garb, but when she spoke Amber realized who she was. "You can see your brother now, Miss O'Neill."

"Is he conscious?" Amber asked as she pushed herself to her feet.

The nurse shook her head without comment and led the way to the elevators. When they walked by a bank of windows, Amber saw it was finally light outside. The long night had ended, but her waking nightmare continued. She followed the nurse out of the elevator, past another waiting area, and through yet another set of double doors.

The intensive care unit had a central nurses' station, several patients, and a score of beeping, bleating, and blinking machines. Hospital staff moved briskly between the glass-partitioned rooms.

She immediately spotted Parker in the room directly across from the nurses' station and hurried to his side. The oxygen mask had been replaced by a plastic tube under his nose, and his chest rose and fell in a slow rhythm. He still had an IV and numerous tubes and wires running over and under the blankets covering him, along with a couple of glowing monitors tracking his internal functions.

Tracing his cheek with her fingertips, Amber searched again inside his mind, but met only hollow emptiness. After mentally calling for him at least a dozen times, she pulled a plastic and metal chair near the foot of his bed and sat down to keep her physical and telepathic vigil.

Once again, she wasn't aware of how much time passed, but she was aroused from a mental stupor by an unexpected spark stirring inside her mind.

As she struggled to shake off the drowsy haze, a faint but familiar voice echoed inside her head. *Move over. You're breaking my legs.*

Her eyes popped open, and she saw she was slumped half out of her chair and lying across her brother's shins. She jerked upright.

Parker? Oh God, Parker! Are you awake?

She grasped his hand, not realizing it was heavily bandaged.

Ow! No! Leave me alone. Feel like shit.

Tenderly, she cradled his hand against her cheek.

No wonder. You were shot.

A wisp of memory leaked out before she could stop it.

The report of the pistol and the fleeting image of Parker doubling over… She felt him recoil at the sight.

Good thing you saved me.

Guilt and sorrow washed through her as she admitted, *I didn't.* Then she sent him the picture of himself on the sandbar ringed by seals.

Amber felt his confusion and doubt. He hesitated a long moment before he sent again. *Suppose Hennessey saved you.*

Him and the Police Service of Northern Ireland. She briefly showed him the boat, the four officers, the helicopter. But she sensed his weary mind fading, and she couldn't let him slip back into oblivion.

Stay with me, Parker! She gave him the equivalent of a mental shake.

Tired. Hurt everywhere, he protested weakly.

Too bad! You have to open your eyes now. Show them you don't have brain damage. She mentally shook him again.

All right, already! Stand back. It's gonna get busy around here.

Carefully, she laid his hand back down on the blanket. But she couldn't quite bring herself to completely sever their mental connection and held onto a single strand.

A low groan rumbled up from Parker's chest. One of his monitors beeped, while another screen began to blink furiously. A nurse rushed into the room as his eyelids fluttered.

"Mr. O'Neill?" she cried, poking at the noisy monitor. "Can you hear me, Mr. O'Neill?" She turned to Amber. "Sorry, you need to step outside for a moment."

With her brother's presence resting comfortably in her mind, Amber complied. She slipped down the corridor to the waiting area and curled up on an industrial vinyl sofa before Parker sent to her again.

Here comes the brain guy. And he broke their link, just in case.

A half-hour later, the neurologist had pronounced Parker in possession of his full mental capacity. Once he'd left, Amber telepathically filled in details of the long night's events for her brother.

No wonder I'm so tired. And hungry! Parker sent. He insisted talking took too much effort and hurt his throat.

Amber wasn't about to argue.

Go have some breakfast for me, and see what you can find out about Hennessey and the kids.

She refused to let herself consider that Meriol and Connor might not be all right. If she let her imagination wander where they were concerned, she'd be in crazyville in a matter of minutes.

Kevin was an entirely different story. She didn't know where he'd ended up after the helicopter had taken her and Parker away. But he knew where she was. Her memory replayed the mental caress of his mind.

Chopper to hospital. Derry.

He'd tried to comfort her, and she'd pulled away.

With no way to contact him, she had no choice but to wait and see if he came to find her. She couldn't let herself hope for more, could she?

Then she remembered the looks on the faces of the other men when she'd mentally calmed the seals. Their fear and suspicion had been easy to read. They didn't need to shout "Freak!" at her for her to know what they'd

thought. They were Kevin's colleagues and friends. If
he didn't show up, perhaps in the cold light of day, he
had decided they were right.

As Amber stood dejectedly at the entrance to
the waiting area, a grandmotherly woman pushed a
rattling cart loaded with trays of half-eaten food down
the corridor. Amber scooted aside, but the woman
paused anyway.

"I expect you been here all night, ain't ya?"

Amber nodded without speaking, and the woman
bent and pulled a tray with two covered dishes from the
bottom of the cart and shoved it into her hands. "Here's
an extra. Looks like you can use it."

Before Amber could stutter out her thanks, the woman
rolled her cart into the nearby elevator and disappeared.
Amber carried the tray into the waiting area and demol-
ished every last morsel of hot cereal, scrambled eggs
and toast. She even finished off the tepid cup of tea.
With her stomach comfortably full, she curled up on the
sofa and drifted into sleep.

Heels tapping on the tile floor and a soft voice
querying, "Miss O'Neill?" awakened her. She opened
her eyes into the mossy green gaze of Cara Mulrooney.

"So sorry to wake you." The petite woman anxiously
clasped and unclasped her hands. "They told me on the
phone that your brother was in serious but stable condition. I just had to see for myself that he was all right, to
thank him…"

"You drove all the way here?" Amber hesitated. She
didn't exactly know where here was, but she didn't think
it was very close to Malin Head.

Cara Mulrooney nodded, her expression anxious.

Amber noticed her dark hair appeared to be freshly braided, but her pantsuit and blouse were badly wrinkled.

She stretched her arms and ran her fingers through her own tangled mop of hair. "What about the children? Are Meriol and Connor…"

"Fine," the other woman reassured in a rush. "Well, Connor's foot is broken, but he rowed them all the way to the breakwater last night before someone spotted them. Meriol and Ronan are at Mrs. Fitzpatrick's, probably still sleeping, but under strict orders to stay put. Not that they could go anywhere with so many Garda all over the village, questioning everyone." Her voice trailed away as if she'd run out of fuel.

"So Malin Head's smuggling days are finally over," Amber mused with a relieved sigh.

"I doubt it," countered Cara Mulrooney. Her voice dropped to a conspiratorial whisper. "Meriol had over forty thousand Euros and several thousand British pounds on her last night. Whatever her father and Coyle were doing—"

"Cost more than one life," Amber interrupted, and the other woman quickly crossed herself. "Thank God it's over."

"Yes, the Garda caught two of those awful men, and the PSNI got the other two. And thank the good Lord your brother is all right," Cara Mulrooney added. "Do you think I could see him now?"

Amber nodded and rose to her feet. At least a hundred questions bubbled through her brain, but she could see that Cara Mulrooney was obviously "on a mission." Her questions would have to wait for a while longer.

She launched a questing mental thread to her brother as she led the other woman down the corridor. Parker responded groggily.

Wake up. You're about to have company. She sent an image of Cara Mulrooney with her words and received an answering burst of anxiety.

The kids?

Fine. Then Amber couldn't resist teasing him just a bit. *But you might not wanna bring up her stolen car.*

With her brother's favorite expletive echoing inside her head, Amber pushed open the door to the ICU. Cara Mulrooney beat her to Parker's bedside.

"Oh, Mr. O'Neill!" Tears clogged her voice as she touched his shoulder and then his cheek. "Thank all the saints in heaven you're all right! I'm so, so sorry this happened to you, Mr. O'Neill."

"Par-her," he corrected, stumbling over the hard "K" sound and looking abashed. "Don' be sorry…"

"Parker," she repeated, her fingers caressing his cheek again. "How can I ever thank you for saving my niece and that boy, Connor?"

Amber felt a sudden wisp of lust drifting from her brother's mind. She rolled her eyes and sent, *You are unbelievable!*

"Jaysus, you almost died!" Cara Mulrooney sniffled.

At least she's not mad about the car, Parker sent back as he laid his bandaged hand on Cara's arm.

"Don' worry, I'm fine. T-ell me what happened with Meriol." He glanced at Amber over Cara's head. *Don't you have someplace to go?*

Don't forget, everyone is watching you, she reminded him with a mental jab.

"I'll be back in a few minutes," she said aloud, and sidled out of the room.

Leave it to her brother! He wasn't even eight hours post-op from a potentially fatal gunshot wound, and he was already flirting.

Shaking her head, Amber pushed through the double doors of the ICU and shuffled into the corridor. As she paused outside the waiting area, the elevator opened, and Kevin stepped out.

Chapter 18

AMBER'S STOMACH DID AN UNEXPECTED LOOP-DE-LOOP, and she mightily regretted how she'd scarfed down breakfast. As Kevin strode toward her with a maddeningly unreadable expression, she clutched the doorframe for support and couldn't help but notice how the dark blue henley shirt he wore made his eyes look indigo. His jeans looked new and presented a marked contrast to her baggy scrub suit and hopelessly tangled bed hair.

Story of my life, she thought with an inward sigh. And perfectly consistent with the first time she'd seen him. She'd been a bedraggled mess then, too. How appropriate to end the same way she'd started.

He stopped half an arm's length from her. "Are you all right?"

"Fine," she answered automatically, dying to peek inside his mind and at the same time scared spitless to do it. "Parker's going to be fine, too. He's down the hall in ICU, and right now Cara Mulrooney's with him."

"Cara Mul…" He blinked twice in confusion, then shook his head as if to clear his thoughts. "I know your brother's all right. I rang, and they told me 'serious but stable.' He's doing better than the knacker you shot. Thanks to Parker's guardian seals, no doubt."

"I'm sure you're right," Amber agreed, trying not to do something stupid, like kiss him or swoon at his feet. "I know Parker will appreciate you coming here to see him.

Looking nonplussed, Kevin cleared his throat. "I'm happy he's recovering. But that's not why I'm here."

"Then why—?" she began, but before she could finish, Kevin's hands closed over her shoulders.

She forgot to breathe as he pulled her against him and slanted his mouth over hers. Then a wave of heat laced with longing and desire inundated her mind as his tongue plunged between her lips.

This is why, he sent. *Surely you knew I'd come for you.*

I wanted you to. Oh God, how I wanted you to! She poured her own yearning and need into his mind as she kissed him back, exploring the luscious recesses within his mouth.

Joyous thoughts and lustful feelings flashed and burned between their eager minds as they pressed and clung to each other. Amber lost herself in the wonderful shared intensity until a passing hospital staff member coughed loudly. Self-consciously she turned aside, breaking the kiss.

"I think that's a not-too-subtle hint for us to get a room," she murmured as Kevin continued to nuzzle the side of her neck.

When he finally stopped long enough to look at her, a hint of mischief sparkled in his dark blue eyes. "No worries, I already have one. There's a hotel on the next street over, and when I explained about your brother being shot and in hospital, they let me have an early check-in."

She couldn't suppress a giggle. "Are you riding to my rescue yet again?"

Kevin took a step back, his expression all seriousness. "I told you before I'm no knight in shining armor. Truth is, Amber luv, you're the one who rescued me.

You stormed into my life and broke down the prison I'd built for myself. You forced me into the light, and now I want to stay. With you..."

His voice trailed away as the elevator dinged open and a man pushed a cart piled with sheets and blankets past them. Suddenly aware that her mouth was hanging open, Amber closed it with a snap. A wave of anticipation made her knees wobble.

"I'd rather talk in private," Kevin continued. "But I'll announce it over the PA system if I have to."

"No! I mean, private is better," she quickly agreed. "Let me say bye to Parker first."

Kevin clasped her hand at the same time she reached for her brother's mind.

You better be decent! she sent, pushing open the doors of the ICU.

"Hennessey," Parker greeted with a lift of his chin.

Cara Mulrooney backed away, looking flustered. "I-I was just leaving."

Parker gave her a pathetic puppy-dog expression. "See you soon?"

Red spots glowed on Cara's cheeks and several strands of loose hair framed her face. "Yes, in two days, then." She must have realized how breathy her voice sounded for she gave a little cough. "I... uh, I'll bring Ronan and Meriol."

Parker's favorite expletive bounced into Amber's brain while Cara expressed a quick thanks to Kevin.

Guess that wasn't in your plans, she sent to her brother.

Like you didn't just lock lips with Hennessey out in the hall.

She arrowed a bolt of outrage between his eyes. *So help me, Parker…*

I didn't eavesdrop! he protested. *Your lips are red as chili peppers.*

While Parker smirked, and then exchanged greetings with Kevin, she covered her mouth with her hand.

"I guess I owe you for saving my ass again," her brother told Kevin.

"'Twas nothing," Kevin replied, shifting his weight from foot to foot and looking uncomfortable.

"Not to me, but I'm too pooped to argue. Being shot twice in one week really knocks a guy out."

"Then we'll get out of here for a while and let you rest," Amber quickly intervened.

"Sounds good," Parker agreed while he sent, *Please do, Miss Hot Tamale! Find an empty bed somewhere so at least one of us can get lucky.*

No eavesdropping! she warned narrowing her eyes.

"I really am tired," her brother said aloud, and what felt like a genuine wave of exhaustion washed through her mind.

Kevin flicked a glance between the two of them, no doubt guessing there was a lot more not being said aloud. His arm encircled her waist, and he eased toward the door. "See you in a few hours, then."

Poor sap's got it bad.

He's not the only one, Amber sent, and then severed their link.

Bright sunlight streamed through the lace curtains at the window as Amber stepped over the threshold into the hotel room. A room that looked rather small, but only because the bed in the middle of it looked so very large. She supposed shoving Kevin onto it and jumping his bones wouldn't be exactly proper, no matter how much she wanted to do just that.

Kevin closed the door and flipped the security lock before he turned to face her. "Your brother can't…" He tapped his index finger against his temple. "You know."

"No, and he's under strict orders not to try."

He blew out a small sigh of relief. "Good. Performing for an audience, even of one, wasn't precisely what I had in mind."

"So what did you have in mind?" She gave him what she hoped was a salacious smile and moved so that they were standing almost toe-to-toe. "Please tell me it involves that lovely big bed."

"It might," he said, but remained unsmiling. Then he scrubbed his palm across his face and blew out his breath. "God knows, I love you, Amber. And I wish to high heaven I could give you some kind of guarantee about the future, but I can't."

Her heart pounding loud in her ears, she put her arms around him and laid her head against his chest. She could hear his heart beating out the same fast rhythm. "Nobody can guarantee the future. That's not what I want. I want us to be together."

His heart gave a decidedly loud thump, and she felt some of the tension drain out of him. "I want that too. More than I want my next breath." He pushed her out at arm's length and probed her face with his dark blue eyes. "Walsh wants me to join their task force, be a real policeman again."

She pictured the look on the red-haired Walsh's face, heard his tone of voice when he asked, "Is that thing your pet?"

"Walsh and his buddies think I'm a freak."

"No, they don't. They think you're special, and that I'm the luckiest bastard in Ireland." He pulled her close again, rubbed his cheek over the top of her head. "Soon as your brother's out of ICU, will you come with me to Armagh? Spend the rest of your holiday there? Maybe if you like it, I can convince you to stay on longer than your holiday?"

No guarantees, she reminded herself. There would always be things neither of them could control.

Misinterpreting her silence, Kevin said, "But if you don't want to stay, I'm willing to give America a go."

"I thought America didn't need another bloody, fecking Irishman," she murmured, running her hands under the edge of his henley and across the smooth skin of his back.

Amber could feel his suppressed laughter. "I don't give a bloody tinker's damn what America needs. Nor the bleedin' PSNI neither. I need you."

"That's good, because I happen to need you too." Standing on tiptoe, she spread a line of kisses across his neck, then murmured. "And I think I'm going to like Armagh. A lot. You might convince me to never leave."

Raising one dark eyebrow, he vowed, "I'll try my best to do just that."

Deciding they'd talked enough for the moment, she caught the edge of his shirt and pulled it up to his chin. "Remember, actions speak louder than words."

"Still the impatient Yank," Kevin admonished,

jerking the shirt over his head before tossing it onto the floor.

Not stopping to admire the sculpted muscles of his chest, she grabbed for the waistband of his jeans. But he already had a grip on her baggy top, so she lifted her arms and let him return the favor.

When her bare breasts sprang free, he groaned. "If I'd only known you'd nothing else on under there, we'd have been here a bloody hour ago."

"Now who's impatient?"

He didn't answer, just dove for the bed, dragging her with him. Connecting to his mind, she sent a hot shower of lust and urgency, and got an equally powerful dose back from him. The rest of their clothes and the coverlet fell away in a frenzied haze, except for a long streamer of condoms Kevin pulled from his pocket an instant before his jeans hit the floor.

The shared intensity of their perceptions and feelings nearly overwhelmed her as Kevin's lips and hands wandered everywhere.

Her throat.

Her breasts.

Her stomach.

And Amber touched him in the same places, mentally and physically, eliciting the same exquisite pleasures, heightening the anticipation. His panting groans became hers as the boundaries between their minds and bodies blurred. She didn't know how much more she could take, but knew she would die if they stopped.

Every nerve in her body felt electrified, especially the ones at her hot, liquid core. The ones Kevin's fingers massaged inside and out.

Amber didn't know she'd opened the wrapper, but she realized a condom was in her hand. She smoothed it down the hard length of him and begged without words for him to fill her with more than his fingers.

When he did, the explosion carried her higher than she'd ever dreamed possible. And best of all, he was with her. They rode the shock waves of orgasm for what might have been forever, shattering and tumbling back together as one.

Coherent thoughts were beyond her grasp for what felt like a very long time. But when she finally managed to form one, she sent it to him.

I love you now. Always. Forever.

And Kevin sent the same thought back to her. Then he rolled to one side and pulled her close against him.

"I hope those actions spoke loud enough," he said, sprinkling kisses under her jaw.

"Loud and clear." Amber squeezed his forearm before rolling over to face him. "In fact, one more round like that, and you can probably convince me to live in the stinky cave with the seals."

"Would you now?" He quirked a dark brow at her once more. "Wonder what you'll do after two more?"

And he kissed her again.

THE END

About This Book

For centuries, the rugged Donegal coast has been home to fishermen, smugglers, and a vast array of marine life. At least two of these three probably exist today, but this author would not presume to guess.

Malin Head really is the northernmost point in Ireland. The villages of Carndonagh, Ballyliffin, and Buncrana all exist, though not exactly as presented by this author.

Grianan Ailgh or Grianan Fort is an Iron Age fortress dating back to at least the second century AD. It was the seat of the O'Neill chieftains for over a thousand years.

Celtic folklore and mythology is full of tales, many of them with tragic endings, about seals and selkies. One of the common threads in these stories is that selkies are magical beings who shed their seal skins and pass for humans.

Acknowledgments

For me, each of my books is unique and comes with its own set of joys and challenges, and this one was no exception. To properly thank the many people who aided and abetted me in this story's creation would undoubtedly take more pages than the book itself. However, I would like to single out a few people for specific acknowledgment:

First and always, for Dave, my favorite Irish-American and infinitely patient "better half." Thank you for giving up numerous excursions both foreign and domestic while I remained chained to my keyboard writing this tome.

My editor, Deb Werksman, who gave this book the green light based on the absolute worst synopsis in the world. Thank you for loving my Irish hunks, and for trusting me when I asked you to.

My FRE (First Reader Extraordinaire) Terri S. Thank you for being a neverending source of encouragement, even if you weren't too sure at first about those seals, but you were ever enthusiastic about Kevin (and his parts).

My terrific critique partner, Jo Lewis-Robertson. I can't thank you enough for all the time and effort you put into critiquing my chapters (the good, bad, and ugly) with incredible insight.

Special thanks to my grand-nephews Christian and Zachary, who may not know it, but they gave me a

whole new perspective on twins. And a special shout
out to their father, my nephew-in-law Silas, who will
probably never again ask to be included in one of Aunt
Cindy's books!

I never thought I'd admit to this, but thank you to my
brothers Ed and Wes because your constant wisecracks
inspired me to create Parker.

Special thanks to Gary D. for the info on Glocks and
for the wonderful line about not pointing at something
you don't intend to kill.

Thank you to my BFFs Shirl and Whit, and all my
many wonderful friends (especially Cathy, Aimee, and
Guy), for telling me to get back to work!

And finally, to the writing sisters of my heart who
are a constant source of inspiration and support (in
reverse alphabetical order this time): Suz, Christine,
Tawny, V. Anna, Susan, Kirsten, Nancy, Cassondra,
Trish, Donna, Jo (again!), Christie, Joanie, KJ, Kate,
Caren, FoAnna, Beth, and Jeanne, aka The Romance
Bandits. Banditas Rock!

About the Author

Blessed with the gift of "Irish Blarney" Loucinda McGary (everyone calls her Cindy) became a storyteller shortly after she learned to read. If she didn't like the way a story ended, she made up her own ending. In high school Cindy wrote stories featuring herself, her friends, and their favorite movie and rock stars. After college, she published a couple dozen poems in magazines and even wrote a couple of novels. Then life intervened. Family and career became her top priorities, though she could never quite stop dabbling in writing. She also developed an almost legendary love of travel that took her all over the United States and abroad.

A longtime reader of romances, Cindy discovered and joined Romance Writers of America in 2001. At the end of 2003 she decided to leave her management career to pursue her twin passions of travel and writing. She is the author of *The Wild Sight* and *The Treasures of Venice*. Cindy likes to set her novels of romance and suspense in some of the fascinating places she has visited.

Cindy loves to hear from readers, writers, and just about everybody! Please drop her an email: cindy@loucindamcgary.com

Or send her a postcard for her ever-increasing collection:
P.O. Box 15492
Sacramento, CA 95813